Parallel Lives

((A Novel of the 1960s))

Martha Alderson

PARALLEL LIVES ((A NOVEL)) by Martha Alderson

Copyright @2016 by Martha Alderson

Parallel Lives ((A Novel)) is a work of fiction. All of the organizations, incidents, and events portrayed in this novel are either products of the author's imagination or are used fictitiously. Any references to historical events, real people or real places are used fictitiously, although the author has tried to keep as historically accurate as possible. All dialogue and all characters with the exception of some well-known historical figures are products of the author's imagination and not to be construed as real. Where real-life historical figures appear, the situations, incidents, and dialogues concerning those persons are entirely fictional and not intended to depict actual events or to change the entirely fictional nature of the work. In all other respects, any resemblance to persons living or dead is entirely coincidental.

Illusion Press
Santa Cruz, CA 95062

Cover and interior designed by Kit Foster

ISBN 978-0-9790596-3-6
eBook ISBN 978-0-9790596-4-3
LCCN 2016913240

First printing
August 2016

Dedicated to
My Husband, with love

PART ONE

AFTER

1971 – MAJ

The city sleeps while rumbling blue newspaper trucks scuttle the avenues, filling stands with stories of the latest overdose, the number of dead in Vietnam, and the ratification of the 26th Amendment giving eighteen-year-olds the right to vote.

Headlines fade to filmy patterns of frowning reprimands stamped on the sidewalk along Lincoln Way, slick with heavy fog.

Forget him, he's not even real.

You should to be preparing for the ground-breaking, not chasing a dream.

Grow up, Maj!

You'll be arrested and thrown in jail.

Think of the kids depending on you.

I ignore all the "*shoulds*" calling my name and turn back to my task. For one year, three months, and two weeks—though in truth, my entire life—I've been readying myself for fate to intervene, again. Now impatient and done with waiting, I head where all clues point, directly into the Native American takeover of straight-jacketed bars and chains on the deserted rock prison in the middle of the San Francisco Bay.

Veils of dew drip from overhead streetcar cables that shiver and moan. Smoke from the chimney of a shabby

Victorian mixes with the scent of the sea. On the sidewalk in front of me, a pile of battered, cardboard boxes against a dry-cleaner's storefront collapses as a straggly hippie emerges without a sound.

I step off the sidewalk and slip into Golden Gate Park through a break in the crumbling rock wall. Full moon shadows cut through a protective stand of trees blocking the unsteady stream of sleepwalking cars. A breeze promises warmth.

Ignoring my stomach's plea for a hash-brown sandwich on-the-go from Lou's Place, I keep hidden and stick to the shortcut instead. I touch the tiny wolf carving at my neck for luck that I'm in time to catch the last supply skiff to Alcatraz before President Nixon's National Guard storms the island. Hunger turns anxious as I hurry toward Geary for Market and Pier 18.

PART TWO

BEFORE

1955 - JULY

i.

Grandma sank beside eleven-year-old Billy Wayman Wolf on a fallen laurel tree. On the off chance she brought him some food, Billy stoked up the measly fire he'd barely been keeping alive for the past four days. Ginger crept from the shade of a rosemary bush and stretched. With her tail wagging every which way, she greeted Grandma with licks across her face, making her laugh. She caught a whiff of something and buried her nose in Grandma's apron. Laughing and pushing Ginger away, Grandma snatched a slab of bacon wrapped in green corn husks from her pocket and held it high over her head.

Try as he might, even with Grandma finally showing up—and with food—Billy couldn't rein-in his foul-temper. After spending another sweltering and hungry night alone, he was ready to hear he could come back home now. He stabbed the meat with a pointed stick he'd carved. With the slab over the heat, his mouth got to watering like a hound dog.

"Fall's coming," Grandma said, watching early leaves fall and scatter across a dry land.

For a time, the two of them were silent, but for the racket his stomach made every time a drop of fat sizzled on the fire. The smell tormented him crazy enough to eat the bacon raw.

A dove passed over their heads.

"CooooOOOO-woo-woo-woo," Grandma called.

Billy listened and heard cooing.

"Dove's rain song," said Grandma.

"New waters," he said, turning the meat, careful not to burn it.

She nodded.

"So what's about to change?" he demanded, in no mood for her double-talk. "School's starting? You're going make me go this year? They'll just hold me back. You want that?"

"That's not true. Why do you say that? Anyway, this isn't about school."

"If I don't pick cotton, we have no money. Without money, we have no food."

"Your ma's coming," she said, straightening her apron.

Layers of dirt and ash and smudges of red and black ceremonial stripes tightened across Billy's cheeks. His heart dropped to darkness.

"Could be the dove was just announcing it's going to rain tomorrow," he mumbled.

Grandma stroked his back, cooing softly. He watched the pork catch fire and burn.

"She's found herself a new man. They're coming to take you back with them."

Wincing like he'd been stabbed, Billy swallowed wrong and ended up coughing like a barking dog. Crouching with his head low to his chest, he rocked back and forth. Ginger came to his side. Billy buried his face in her neck.

ii.

At the same time some miles to the south, seven-year old Maj Hawthorne kneeled next to her grandmother in the corner of the limousine. She whispered garble meaningless to anyone else and nonetheless comforting to the young girl. Fussing since they drove away from Disneyland on their way home to the San Francisco Bay Area, Maj still didn't have a plan how delay their arrival home—preferably long enough to miss all of first grade next month. She shuddered, having kept away from school for an entire year, and well aware she was heading toward a snarl even MorMor may not be able to untangle. She slung an arm across her grandmother's shoulder.

"Once upon a time," MorMor started, patting Maj's cheek as if reading her mind, and then picking up her knitting.

Straightening the Mickey Mouse hat Daddy had crowned Maj with at the opening ceremonies of Mister Disney's theme park, she watched MorMor's mouth carefully as she spoke. A buzzing masked another sound, like a song or a chant from far away. Maj flicked off the distraction, determined to learn how to make the sounds come out right, so people understood her. MorMor said Maj didn't speak correctly because Mother stood under an elder tree when she was pregnant. Mother said the reason she spoiled her sounds was from listening to too many Swedish fairytales.

"A little princess lived in a faraway country." MorMor's accent turned the story into a dancing rhyme. Her voice lifted at the end of each phrase, helping Maj follow the story.

"Olle-the-Loyal watched over the princess, for she

was delicate and pale as a lily."

Imitating MorMor's lips as she told the story, Maj quickly turned dizzy from the kaleidoscope of speeding movements. Her lips fell out of beat, and her tongue knotted in on itself—her breathing troubled and hot. MorMor knew the answer to every puzzle, like where to dig for the firmest and tastiest wild mushrooms and how to steer clear of troll forests. Whispering to herself, Maj skimmed a hand across white flakes littering MorMor's shoulder. She was annoyed that her grandmother didn't just invent a magic spell and fix her.

MorMor unraveled a row of her knitting. "It was not her beauty people spoke of. The princess was most renowned for her wondrous blue eyes, which spoke of things without words." Her story kept time with the click-clacking of her knitting needles.

"Don't tell her that story," snapped Mother, raising an eyebrow.

The tongue of the fire-spitting dragon singed Maj's make-believe wings, and she crumpled in the seat of the limousine.

"Fem, sex, sju, atta, nio, tio." MorMor muttered tightly, counting her stitches in Swedish.

Barely swiveling her head, Maj sneaked a look from the corner of her eye. Mother's fierce scowl spun Maj's attention straight ahead. Silent and still, she willed herself invisible.

"Maj must learn to use her words," said Mother. "She could be in the movies someday. Like Greta Garbo. I still think it was unfair of you, Richard, not to let me look up Greta."

Mother's voice floated faraway and wispy. She pulled a lace handkerchief from the cuff of her glove and dabbed behind Maj's ears. A field of lilies spread across the car.

"Disneyland is right next door to Hollywood. You have eyes just like Greta. I told you that. Remember?"

Nodding, Maj was distracted by a chant hurled from bush to bush streaking past the car.

Soon, he is coming.

For he is coming.

The words sent a party of popping bubbles through her bones, just as an odd trilling flickered in her throat. She immediately opened her mouth for her pure and clear speech to magically emerge.

"Maj! You're gaping," shrieked Mother. "Shut your mouth."

Ripped from the sound of the chant and all possibility of speech, she writhed against Mother's impatience. This time, however, Mother's harsh words didn't shrivel her in anticipation of being stomped out like a sow bug. And this time, the sequins in her eyes weren't tears. They were burning embers of light, like tiny spinning fireworks. A thread of longing dangled just out of her reach, as the chant vanished like a dream upon waking.

iii.

"When is Ma coming?" Billy asked, straining to get past the rock in his throat.

"Soon," answered Grandma.

"You coming, too?"

"This is my home."

He dropped the stick in the coals and rose to his feet. "Then, I'm not going."

"Now Billy—"

"You can't stay out here all by yourself." Glaring, he jabbed a finger at her as she fished out the bacon and cut it into squares with her pocketknife. "Who's going to see you got food to eat? And who's going make you eat it before you give everything away to the next tramp at the back door?"

Grandma urged him to take a chunk of bacon. He ignored her, concentrating instead on kicking dirt in the fire and smothering the flames. Smoke billowed up, and he considered the old ones' way of signaling for help. Only Grandma could rescue him now.

"I'll be better," he pleaded. "Let me stay, and I promise you won't have to worry about me anymore. I'll keep my mouth shut and do everything I'm told. Go to school. Pick cotton. Lots more, too. I promise."

"You got little brothers you never even met."

"They aren't my brothers."

His voice was as flat as an old bicycle tire as he gouged a hole in the ground, bloodying his big toe. Cuffing a tear from his cheek, he tried to picture Ma, but he couldn't anymore. He did remember the day she left. He was barely five. She had only just come back, and he sensed she was planning on leaving without him again. All day he planted himself as near to her as he could get. He wanted to be real close by in case. . . what? He couldn't remember anymore what he'd been waiting around for, what had been so important to him back then. Whatever it was never happened.

He circled the sacred enclosure of rocks and logs Grandma and him marched to at each changing of the seasons. This time, Grandma had hauled him to the fire pit and left him there for a ceremonial attempt to tame him. He snorted, as if a secret door to power and protection would ever open for the likes of him.

"I used to wait for her every day when I was a kid." He slapped himself upside the head, loosening an avalanche of feelings. "Now I don't care anymore."

"Don't get to fussin'." Her eyes sagged at the corners. "I worried about you out here on your own." Grandma talked as she rolled up the blanket and retrieved the drum to call in their ancestors he'd ignored. "You're a mite young at eleven for a *Mkede'ke'wen*."

Billy shouted over his shoulder, as he stomped away.

"Having nothing to eat and no water for four days ain't much different than all the other times we gone without food."

"Had you a vision?" she asked, catching up to him. She leaned forward and studied his face.

"Nah." He took her things to lighten her load. "Anyway, I don't see how me getting one of your visions is going to help Old Jim feel any better. If that bus driver pulls that again, acting like he's waiting for him and then driving off as soon as Old Jim is at the door, limping and wheezing and ready to board. Ain't right. Picking cotton is hard enough without a prick like that bus driver starting out our day bad."

"Now, Billy, I do admire you for taking care of others, but it's that kind of talk I sent you out here to do some thinking on."

"He only picks on the parolees. Next time, he ain't going to like none what—"

A knowing weaseled its way into Billy's mind. He wouldn't be around for a next time. Miserable, he took in details left and right of him as if for the last time, and ended up staring into Grandma's face.

She looked away. "I had me a vision."

"Ah, Grandma," he protested.

"You listen to me, and listen real good, Running Wolf." She grasped his arm. Her grip was too tight.

"This is your calling. You're *Bodewadmi gdaw*."

"Speak English," he growled.

"You're Potawatomi, the true people of great leaders," she said, unbuttoning his frayed shirt and buttoning him up right, so a tail wasn't hanging down long on one side of him with half his chest exposed. She went on speaking, smiling in the aggravating way she had when she'd stopped listening, like she stepped into a dream.

"Your spirit is too big for this place. One day you'll find the woman of your other half, and you'll become a *wkamek*—a chief of big medicine. I've been expecting this. They got good schools up in the city. We'll put down tobacco for your journey. Whenever anything bothers you, you'll have that tobacco to depend on just like our ancestors did. Offer your *sema* to the fire, pray, and you'll be safe. I saw it in a vision. *Iwkshiye'tuk*."

Billy suddenly wondered if other half-breeds like him were where Ma lived, and immediately convinced himself that no one there walked like Grandma did, toe-heel, to lessen the noise of her step. Down to the wrinkles across her face, she was all Potowatomi.

"I don't need me no damn Indian ghost to tell me what's going to happen," he yelled, leaving her behind. "I can tell you myself right here and now. Me going with Ma is gonna end up a disaster."

Billy took off running. Ginger sped alongside him. Racing together down the path he'd bushwhacked, tromping back and forth to hitch Grandma rides to town, he stubbed his toe. His heart jerked. Cringing, he refused to cry.

Ginger surged ahead, as Billy followed the sound of thundering hooves from a herd of wild ponies. Ponies turned to tires slapping against asphalt and gear changes from Route 99, the highway he'd always believed led to escape and would one day reconnect the lost sections of his life that had been washed away.

Screeching tires snapped him from his pain.

"Ginger!" he yelled.

He ran to stop her from crossing the highway, when his eyes started acting peculiar. His vision turned jerky.

"Ginger! Come, girl," he called, rubbing his eyes to clear the blurry landmarks.

A thud reached him, like through an underground tunnel.

"Ginger," he whispered, suddenly unable to see or talk.

He stuck his hands out into empty space as a real peaceful full feeling came over him, and he crossed over into a hallway smack in the middle of a cold, blue shadow from a moonless night—even with him being outside during the day. Goose-bumps raised up. His scalp tingled, and he wondered if he was having one of Grandma's visions. Not much used to touching scared, Billy rubbed his arms, hoping to chase the willies away. Instead, a yellow-haired girl stood in the hallway mumbling something and shaking so hard, fingers of fear started creeping up his spine, too. They both knew something bad was going to happen. Before he saw what it was, his eyes cleared to a car smashed against a tree on the side of the highway with its horn blaring.

iv.

Meanwhile, Maj shifted uncomfortably in the limousine to avoid getting scorched, as Mother rearranged the ruffles of her white ankle socks just so. Mother said Maj must learn to pay attention, but words crowded into everything. They droned on and on, shouted and whispered, hollow and confused. Without words, she could hear other sounds, like chanting and a car horn from up ahead. She wondered where the horn came from and how mournful the sound felt.

As the car horn blared louder, Mother crossed her legs. She smoothed a hand down the back seam of her silk stockings and sank against the cushions with a sigh.

The driver slowed the limousine behind a car pulling off the road. Wearisome cotton fields snapped into a stand of trees. Like following a pointing finger, Maj craned her neck for a better view. A car smashed against a tree on the side of the highway flew into flames. Startled, but strangely unafraid of the explosion, she threw her hands over her ears. A man leaned over a woman with blood on her forehead. Two other men held something long and furry between them, the color of dusted brick. A dog.

Maj rolled down the window and poked out her head, slapped with a rush of summer heat. Smoke burned her eyes. A nasty odor crinkled her nose. Beneath the sound of the car horn, trees whispered and bushes sighed.

He is coming.

For he is here.

"Knock on the driver's window, Maj," nagged Mother. "I don't want him stopping."

Daddy cleared his throat.

"Now, now, Birgit," he said in a low voice, with a smile on his face and his jaw twitching.

As Mother complained and Daddy pointed, a boy stumbled from the flames of the burning car. Confused about what was happening in real life and what was the chant, Maj grabbed hold of the window frame so as not to topple out of the car.

The men dropped the dog in an open trench. Running to the ditch, the boy's jaw set, and his lips pressed into a do-not-cross-the-line-to-my-heart. Her heart slumped. The dog was his. He raised his chin, pooling the tears in his eyes to keep them from running down his face. Even with both of Maj's hands stuck out like a shield, loneliness crushed hard. The doggie was dead.

"For heaven's sake, Richard, the driver is stopping. Maj, stop mumbling and roll up your window."

Mother yanked her foot and spoke so loudly that even if Maj were deaf, which she wasn't in the least, she'd still be able to hear.

"Your father will take care of this."

Emboldened by a dare to disobey, Maj thrust her head out the window, holding tight to her hat. The boy was tall and skinny and proud. Even with layers of dirt and a thick ribbon of hair hiding most of his face, he appeared strangely familiar to her. He also looked like he could shout his name out in school and make himself understood. If they took him home with them, he could teach her how, too.

An old woman with a long braid and sad eyes held him against her to stop him from running to his beloved dog. Somehow also known to Maj, the woman was like a tap from the other side of a covered window.

The driver stopped the car on the side of the road. The boy turned his head, and Maj's heart leapt like a bunny over the moon. In his eyes, lines of trees and the shapes of bushes softened. His face glowed like a crown of peacock feathers on a sunny day.

Whispering, Maj yanked open the door lever, tumbled out of the car, and ran to the boy who controlled the seasons and the wind. Just short of him, she tripped over trampled weeds. He reached out. At his touch, Maj couldn't remember if she'd come to comfort him or hoping he'd comfort her. Warmed to her toes and suddenly shy, she bowed her head. Through her eyelashes, she stared up at shiny wet tears gushing down his cheeks like a rainstorm.

Hugging his hand in both of hers, she dragged him with her to the limousine. Unlike Daddy's smooth and soft skin, his hands were scratchy and rough.

The boy looked over her head. His eyes flashed. With a miserable smile, he squeezed her hand and let her go.

Swept up high in Daddy's arms, Maj eyed the boy over Daddy's shoulder and peered at her hands tingling like chimes in the wind. Branded by hope burned from his touch, she pressed the palms of her hands against her lips.

NOVEMBER

i.

Due to the uncommonly hot fall days they'd been having, Billy kept waking up with sweat in his ears. Even after two months of wringing out his earlobes and rubbing reality into gritty eyes, he still found himself smack dab in the middle of a hellhole. Damn, if only he hadn't been proved dead right. Living in Oakland with Ma was a disaster.

He stretched, and then remembering what today was, leapt off the couch that also served as his bed in the middle of Ma's front room. Time he got started.

Unlike back home in the central valley with Grandma, the air in Oakland with Ma hung like a cloud of sticky blue exhaust. The front room, his bedroom, stank like an overheated car engine even with all the windows open. Her two-bedroom flat sat above The Drop-In Club, a neighborhood bar that also served as the Pentecostal church on Sundays—and where daring, devil-may-care older girls with soft curves and sleepy eyes kissed him out back. Not that he minded, not by a lick.

Howls coming at the same time, from both his little brothers, slowed his getaway. He yanked open the icebox. Punching the hood of it, he swore. As usual, Ma had forgotten to buy food. With the howling intensifying, he snatched a scrawny orange he'd grabbed from a street vendor and hid under the couch for help when hunger scrapped his gut. He peeled it, the aroma teasing his nose. Fighting his own need, he gave half to each boy, tousled their hair, and dried their eyes.

Just as he was at the screen door, Ma stumbled from her bedroom wearing her ratty pink robe. Damn. He froze, while Patti Page wailed from the jukebox downstairs.

Ma sang along with the song, one side of her face swelled nearly twice its normal size. He swore under his breath. He didn't need her. Never had. Never would. He turned to sneak out of the apartment, nearly knocking over the rifle leaning up against the doorframe that Ma used to scare off the repo man. He steadied the gun, about ready to bust a gut, and eased shut the door behind him.

Soon as he took off down the stairwell, she yelled after him.

"Billy Wayman Wolfe! You get back here!"

He flew over the railing and hit the ground.

"Goddammit, Billy. I need your help."

She might say that, but Ma didn't need him—not now that Ray was gone. Only good thing about Billy's birthday so far was his stepfather driving off in his moving van to pick up a full load for the Phoenix-Tucson run. Lucky for Ray that he'd snuck out before Billy had a chance to see what he'd done to Ma. She was safe for now. Trouble was, Ray would come back, and she'd let him in. Billy shook his head and clenched his jaw.

Sopping sweat off his face, he stopped at the cracked and broken sidewalk and spit, wishing he could spew Ray out of their lives for good. Billy's balled-up knuckles throbbed, but he resisted the urge to unknot them, sure that his rigid spine and ready fists held him up.

"Tell me, Ma. Why does Ray beat you right before he leaves, anyways? So you don't forget him?"

"Billy Wayman, you best get up here. D'you hear me? I'll take the strap to you. This time, I will. Truly, I will."

She shouted from the stair railing, the pointy silver sunglasses he bought her after the last time Ray left at least sitting right. Time before her nose was too broke. He could take Ray's shoving and bashing him around, but to bully the little boys—his own sons—and beat up Ma got Billy imagining aiming the rifle at Ray and pulling the trigger. Now that he understood Ray's pattern, he planned on being around to guarantee there wasn't never going to be a next time.

With the hair out of his eyes, he shouted back, not caring he was standing in front of the club with all the doors and windows open.

"Or make you so ugly no one bothers looking at you."

Mister Sanchez stuck his head out of the bar. Billy took off running.

She screeched.

"Least take your little brothers with you."

He pushed out his chest and pumped his arms. The air lifted the hair off his forehead, cooling his agitation. He ran through the block happy to break free of the knot she'd made of his life, of all of their lives. The pavement burned his feet, but not so bad he needed shoes. Didn't matter anyways. Never owned him a pair of shoes that fit. Today he was going to change all that.

ii.

A few blocks away, a police siren pierced all the way inside the doctor's 10th Street, Oakland office, giving Maj the shivers. Mother and Daddy and MorMor and her best friend and neighbor Clay huddled around her in the doctor's examining room. Like watching a tennis match, their heads bobbed back and forth between the doctor sawing through the plaster cast on her arm and watching for her reaction. She sat stoic on the examining table, knowing, always knowing just like her name Maj meant—She-Knows—and just like everyone else in the room would too, if they'd quit pretending, the cast hadn't worked. Troubled that she still couldn't talk right tightened anger around her throat, nearly choking her.

She wished the doctor would hurry up and cut off the cast, so they could go to the candy store like Daddy promised. Imagining the soft gooey marshmallows in her favorite Rocky Road fudge kept her from whispering.

"Six months is a long time to wear a cast," droned Dr. Blemmer as he sawed through Mother's paintings of butterflies and flowers on Maj's cast. He spoke slowly as if Maj were dumb as well as unable to talk right.

He raised his eyes to her.

"No, no, please don't apologize," said Mother, reaching out and touching Dr. Blemmer's shoulder. "Whatever she needs for success."

"School should be easier for her now that she's firmly right-handed like everyone else," he said.

Maj bit the inside of her cheek. She may be firmly right-handed. She also still talked funny, and kids at school still teased her for the way she wrote her letters backward on the blackboard, and they still laughed at her when she blushed.

Her failure was all Mother's fault. She'd concocted the idea of a cast from reading an article in Good Housekeeping just days after they'd returned from Disneyland. Mother said she talked funny because sometimes she did things with her left hand and sometimes with her right hand. All that switching back and forth confused the part of her brain for talking. Before Mother even had a chance to finish explaining, Maj had run to the linen closet for a cloth for a sling. The idea reignited the mysterious connection Maj had made with the flame boy and his loss and noble heart that demanded no words, and calmed her fears about never talking right. But it wasn't true. Forcing power into one hand was not her magic elixir.

Now, whenever she thought back to the certainty she felt when MorMor helped sling her arm against her body with a dinner linen, she heaved a great sigh.

The doctor returned the saw to the table and picked up a pair of scissors.

"Your speech therapist reports you've been practicing hard."

Feeling everyone's eyes on her, Maj nodded without any pride or satisfaction. Mother had acted so hopeful when she started speech therapy. She'd even begun talking about Maj in the movies again, going so far as to ask Daddy for modeling lessons to get her comfortable in front of the camera. Though Daddy refused, Maj knew Mother wouldn't quit at a simple no. More than anything, she wanted to please Mother. And so she had practiced and practiced and practiced, for no reason.

At each snip of the scissors, cold metal pressed into

her skin. With the chills, her lips tightened and her forehead knotted.

The cast split open. Nodding at her, Dr. Blemmer eased her arm out of the cast. Finally able to scratch her skin, she chewed her lip instead, refusing to give in to the pleasure in front of the mountain trolls, surrounding her with their judging eyes. She cradled her limp and scrawny arm against her body, and wished everyone would quit staring at her.

"So, how do you like first grade?" the doctor tested, holding both halves of the cast in his hands between them.

Her family held their breath. Clay gave her a buck-up with a lift of his chin. She squirmed and took a nervous breath, unable to look at Mother.

"I hate school," she growled, speaking with her very best pronunciation between clenched teeth.

There was a dreadful silence as Mother raised her eyebrows at Daddy as if to say: *what did I tell you?*

Dr. Blemmer stuck out his neck and tilted his chin, giving her the same stupid expression nearly every single person gave nearly every single time she opened her mouth. Defiantly, she held his gaze.

He frowned and cleared his throat.

Not giving him the opportunity to nag her to try it again, only slower this time, she slammed both halves of the cast to the floor and stomped out of the clinic into the sunshine and busy shoppers and fussy baby carriages.

Pushing through the crowd and whispering questions about what Mother would say when they got home, Maj wandered down the sidewalk, passing tall, stone buildings with no idea where she was going. If she couldn't be in the movies, what use would she be to

Mother? She wouldn't say anything to Maj right away, maybe not for days. Waiting would be awful because eventually, in her own time, Mother would say something sure to tear Maj wide open.

iii.

Billy jerked his bicycle out of hiding, jumped aboard, and mad-pedaled down the sidewalk. Old Miss Jenkins and her ma out on their morning stroll, aimed dead center in his path. He steered hard to the right, pulled up on the handlebars, and rushed onto 10th Street, tires squealing behind him. Darting through two lanes of traffic, he ducked into an alleyway and shot into a blast of sunlight, smack in the middle of the bustling world of commerce.

All along Broadway, everything blazed shiny and new, making his clothes look all the rattier and the bicycle he stole rustier. Grim, he considered the fancy jewelry, made-to-order threads, and the latest cars— glistening new cars—that were everywhere. Snubbing a call to feel sorry for himself, especially not today, he daydreamed about the keenest car, hands down, he'd ever seen. He'd looked up the yellow-haired girl's car on Route 99 in the library—a Cadillac Fleetwood, Seventy-Five series. That limousine with the flushed little face had melded together in his mind to be nearly one single dream of getting for himself a little of the life she had. Today marked his first step in that direction and, he hoped, the first step toward helping out Grandma and making life with Ma more livable for all of them.

He sped past Vern's Market, where his little brother Joe liked nothing better than ripping open cookie packages. If Joe weren't bad enough, Mikie, the baby, was apt to barf if he smelled anything with the least little stink to it.

Everywhere he looked, there were little bitty kids, skipping and laughing with their parents. He dodged in and out of ladies pushing baby strollers every which-way. There were so many children when he got to Ma's neighborhood, he figured Eisenhower was running a special on babies.

He'd already decided one thing for certain—he wouldn't never have him no kids, no matter how much the government paid him, and that was the damned truth. He spat on the sidewalk, sealing the promise in stone.

At 10th and Franklin, Hanes Department Store loomed into view. Grinning at the burst of excitement in his chest, he pulled to a stop next to a newspaper stand where his buddy Webb waited on his bicycle. Though he'd picked the meeting place, now he regretted not taking into account the nearness to the Open Market.

Webb stood in front of Toccoli's Delicatessen, with hanging deep-fried pigs gaunt with dried up eyes still in their heads; turkeys and hams for Thanksgiving; wine barrels overflowing with briny, sour pickles; and what must be the most mouthwatering baked bread he ever had the honor of smelling.

He breathed deep, just about keeling over with hunger. He made a mental note to swing by on their get-away and steal himself a sausage and one for his brothers, too—none of them high-priced ones behind the long glass counter, but the tastiest ones hanging from the awning nearly above his head like a tease. His stomach bellowed.

"You missed school yesterday," said Webb.

"Had me some business to attend to."

"What sort of business?"

Billy took a minute to consider how best to word his answer. Seeing as they both were part Native American, he was tempted to tell Webb that side of his plan. But Webb had made him promise to keep quiet about being an Indian. Webb was a Negro from Georgia. After the war when he was just a baby, he and his folks came to California on a troop train filled with returning soldiers. Grandma and Billy had traveled the same way when he was two years old, and she moved the two of them out of Oklahoma to the San Joaquin Valley. Webb said being poor and colored was bad enough. Billy actually liked being Indian, but he assured Webb that being poor and Okie wasn't so great neither.

"I aim to steal me the alligator wallet in Hanes," Billy said, spilling it right out. He kept his voice low.

Webb scowled and turned a mite peaked around the gills. "You don't need you a wallet."

Billy didn't bother filling Webb in on how the wallet was for all the money he planned on making from his very first store job, sweeping up and doing odd jobs for the jeweler. He'd sent Grandma every quarter he made weeding and hauling trash since he got to Oakland that Ma didn't steal from him first. He worried about Grandma all by herself, and he was done with being poor. Work hard, fill the wallet, and he'd have him plenty to buy a house for Grandma with an inside bathroom and a yard with a fence, so a dog could be safe. He was even thinking about letting his little brothers come live with them. Ma, too—provided she didn't bring Ray along.

Billy's hands slipped from the handlebars. He knew

full well if he didn't steal the wallet soon, he never would. Not that he planned on squawking out. He was just about ready to blast off with nervousness was all.

"No sweat," said Billy. "Hold my bike in the ready. When you see me split from Hanes, I'll be hauling ass straight for you."

His heartbeat swelled to a fevered pitch as he left a dubious-looking Webb holding their bikes at the newspaper stand. He crossed the street, dodging traffic and just about getting run over by the police, and arrived in front of the giant double glass doors of the department store taking up the entire block.

His legs started shaking so hard that to get over the threshold, he had to march locked-kneed. Even with all the practice he'd had stealing food in the valley for him and Grandma, he knew full-well that Oakland was no one-sheriff, backwater town. Poor Okie boy at the counter with the most expensive items in the store, he was bound to stick out like a lightening bolt. He had to get in, grab the wallets—one for him and surprise Webb with one—and get out without the weekend security guard spotting him.

Then he remembered. He was twelve years old today, a man. Couldn't very well go out and kill him a buffalo to mark the day, not that he ever could. By way of celebrating his birthday and his newfound resolve to work his way to success, Billy stuck out his chest and marched inside. The display case with the most expensive items stood dead center in the store.

He pictured himself bare-chested with red and black stripes across both cheeks, a spear in his left hand. Rather than put down tobacco for the rite, last night behind the Drop-In Club at precisely midnight, he'd coughed his way through his first cigarette. Grandma believed in symbols and ceremonies, and he felt like he was doing this for her, not that she'd approve. Just the opposite, she'd have her a full-on hissy-fit and come at him with the broom, not that she could ever catch him. He doubted anyone would understand, but to him, stealing the wallet was his ceremonial declaration out of poverty.

Under the cover of customers milling around, Billy turned his back on his childhood and walked into becoming a man.

iv.

Maj found herself in front of a store window with a grand curved and hollowed-out horn, like what was sitting in the middle of the dining room table at home at Great Oaks. Instead of pomegranates, little orange pumpkins, yellow squashes, and red grape leaves tumbling from the horn, instead there were glowing bracelets, necklaces, brooches, and rings.

Clay caught up to her. Maj turned away from him.

"Don't give up," he said, quick and wiry, an elbow to her ribs. He copied the face the doctor made, sticking out his neck and tilting his chin just so, and laughed, always the kidder.

"Come on, Maj. You're not confusing your letters as much."

In the middle of talking, Clay's voice squeaked to a high note and then dropped back to normal. Maj had been warned more than once by Mother not to laugh when Clay's voice went funny—that he was growing up and soon his voice would always be deep. This time, his high-low notes didn't make Maj feel like laughing.

"You're getting better. You know it's true," his said, his voice breaking and cracking like a duck. "Now give me a smile."

She shook her head no.

"Maaajjj," he said, dragging out the letters of her name.

Brooding, she pressed her lips upward, when really what she wanted was to cry.

Daddy and Mother and MorMor emerged from the doctor's office. Daddy clapped his hands and hustled them to the candy store. Maj stood still, so Mother could tie a scarf around her neck. With her face tense and distracted, Mother wouldn't look at Maj. Having lost her only chance, Maj clasped her pale arm nearer to her body, hating everyone but mostly hating herself.

Distractedly, she scratched her arm. Until Mother slapped her hand away, Maj hadn't known she'd drawn blood. Her body turned rigid. Instead of a scolding, Mother dabbed Maj's arm with Daddy's handkerchief. Mother smiled like a warm hug, as if completely forgetting all about Maj's miserable performance only minutes earlier in the doctor's office. Mother's touch was so gentle and unexpected that the second she stopped and stuck the bloodied handkerchief up the cuff of her glove Maj thought she had imagined it. A double quiver of happiness and confusion shot through her heart.

After choosing their favorite candies, sunlight glanced off the tree-lined sidewalk of the wide boulevard. A shout sounded, and the sky turned brighter. A warm feeling rushed into Maj's weak arm.

In a fit of unexpected confidence, she practiced first in her head what she wanted to say instead of just blurting it out. She formed the sounds exactly like Miss Sally taught her.

"Did you hear that?" Maj watched for a sign that her

parents understood her.

Daddy pushed back his felt hat with its wide brim, grinning like the first time she dived off the deep end of the country club swimming pool. He squatted beside her and offered her a piece of candy from a crumpled, white sack. Mother looked away without saying anything.

"Gee, Maj. Hear what?" asked Clay with a screech, coming to her rescue as usual.

Feeling better now, she did her best to keep a grin off her face at Clay's disobedient voice.

Clay was her nearest neighbor in the east foothills and her only friend outside of the family. Their two families shared deep roots in the area and a friendship that spanned generations. He spent loads of time at Great Oaks because his parents were rarely home, and he liked playing tennis with Daddy. Maj idolized Clay like an older brother and felt special when he didn't mind helping with her speech practice. No one besides MorMor understood her when she spoke, and he always knew what she was trying to say. Mother often looked for him when she couldn't understand her and turned frustrated when he wasn't there to help.

"I don't hear anything. Where?" he probed, his voice back to regular.

"Those people. There," Maj said.

Daddy absently ran his fingers across his skinny mustache. He winked as they waited for a tight group of shoppers to pass and the view to clear.

"Could it be any hotter?" complained Mother, looking wilted and a bit bedraggled. She had a preoccupied expression on her face as she twisted open the little metal latch on her woven, willow-basket purse.

Vibrating with excitement without knowing why,

Maj craned to watch people scatter on the sidewalk.

Daddy pointed, shaking Maj's arm like rattling her awake.

"There," he said.

A boy with wild hair darted from a crowd parted in two. With her mouth open, Maj turned to share her parent's surprise. If they recognized him, they didn't show it. Even so great a distance from where they'd first met, the coincidence of the boy who'd emerged out of flames on the side of a forgotten highway, now standing on her very same sidewalk, didn't seem odd. She'd wished for him daily, and there he was.

The boy had both hands stuck out, as if suddenly blind. A dark-skinned boy rushed forward and helped him mount his bicycle. The two boys leaned across their handlebars, pedaling like a blur.

Maj imagined ripping off her yellow belt and double-collared little jacket, with long, narrow cuffs that matched Mother's outfit down to the polka-dot dress. Mother went to a lot of trouble sewing their clothes, so they would look alike. She said it would attract attention. When Mother was Maj's age, she'd wanted to be a model, and MorMor refused to help her. More interested in turning invisible than showing off clothes in front of strangers, instead Maj imagined zooming on the back of the boy's bike, holding tight to his waist. She'd much rather travel the universe with the two boys than do what Mother told her she must.

Then the boys disappeared altogether. Not wanting to lose the swell feeling they stirred in her, she felt they were still near.

"Those are bad boys," said Daddy.

Maj started to stick up for them, and then didn't bother when Mother laughed and kissed Daddy on the lips. Together with MorMor, her parents strolled to the car.

Clay came up behind her and pushed her forward.

"I've got a secret," he said, his voice lower than usual.

"Me, too," crowed Maj, thinking of the boy and wishing Clay would just tell instead of always having to tease her first.

He snickered.

"What is it, Clay?" she asked.

"I said go on," he answered innocently enough.

"Tell me your secret and I'll tell you mine," she teased back, not hesitating about which words to use or whether her tongue tripped on itself.

Distracted and unusually quiet, Clay acted like he didn't hear her, so she said it again.

"Tell me yours and I'll tell—"

"Not now. Tonight, after your parents leave for the opera."

Unlike his kidding self, Clay sounded serious. His eyes were glassy and unfocused.

"Please," she, using her very best manners and deciding that his grown-up voice must be making him act so strangely.

"You'll like it," he said, more to himself than to her.

He stared up at the old clock tower at the end of the block. Peering into his face and then following his gaze, she thought he appeared not to be looking at anything at all. Heat flowed from him like something inside was about to boil over.

Maj trembled, suddenly frightened that an evil twin had replaced Clay. She searched up and down the sidewalk for the real him.

Breathing heavily, his voice rose. "Let's go, silly

goose." He pushed her toward the car, sliding his hot and clammy hand down the small of her back.

v.

Confident on his bicycle that the store security guard didn't stand a chance of catching him, Billy pulled to a stop several blocks away from Hanes department store. Successful and safely in the clear, he clapped Webb on the back just as his sprawling gaze came to rest on a yellow-haired girl. Startled at first, several seconds passed before he registered that she was the same girl from the side of the road after Ginger died. His world dropped away on all sides of him. Lonely without Ginger and Grandma, and overcome by the shocker of seeing her again, Billy gripped the handlebars to keep from stumbling.

"You alright?" asked Webb, peering into his face. "What happened back there? Seemed like you all of a sudden went blind."

Billy shook his head, knowing the vision would be impossible to explain and distracted by a boy around his age talking to the yellow-haired girl. He recognized the look the boy gave her and immediately didn't like it, or him.

"I'm fine," Billy said, and peeled away one of the wallets he stole, offering it to Webb.

Together, they smelled the genuine leather and grinned. Out of the corner of his eye, Billy saw the girl slap the boy's hand away and reel backward, her face blazing. The boy slinked toward a woman wind-milling her arm like a crossing guard. The girl stayed.

Billy raised a hand. "Thanks for your help, Daddy-O!"

"Where you going?" asked Webb.

"Crazy," Billy shouted over his shoulder and sped toward the girl.

The odds of seeing the yellow-haired girl here on the sidewalk in Oakland were ten thousand to one, and worth investigating.

Next thing he knew, Billy was standing motionless with his bicycle only steps away from her. She must have sensing him staring at her because she stopped whispering and glanced his way.

Her face rose up and, in burning recognition, glowed like the fourth of July.

As her eyes traveled from his wild hair to his torn shirt and bare feet, he studied her, this time noticing her pale white skin and wide-apart blue-gray eyes, her one good arm, and he ended up scrutinizing the scrawny one. Their eyes snapped back at the same time.

On an impulse, she waved. He pushed from his eyes hair in need of a good pruning and returned the greeting. He cleared his throat to say something that would protect her.

Timid herself, she stepped toward him and pointed. A block away, the guard—now with a purple face like a dried up plum—emerged from a parted crowd. Spittle bubbled from the guard's mouth as he staggered to a stop with both hands on his knees.

Still, Billy didn't move. Finally, he hopped on his bicycle. She sucked in her breath as if not wanting him to leave.

Instead of speeding away, he pedaled straight to her and laid the bicycle on its side. Ignoring the danger he was in, he took her bad arm, and she let him lead her away from the main thoroughfare. That she was so trusting of him at this moment, in the shadow of a great stone building, felt a curiosity to him. Like the last time they met, as if spellbound, she wouldn't let go of his hands.

"Hey there!" shouted a man with a candy sack. "What do you think you're doing!"

Chocolates scattered on the sidewalk. The nasty boy raced toward them.

Worried, Billy hesitated and then squeezed her hands, sending a swell of friendship.

"Did he hurt you?" he asked, ready for a fight.

She shook her head, though he spotted her hesitation.

"Keep away from him." Billy growled the warning, his voice deep and barely in control.

As the boy passed the wheezing policeman, Billy rooted his hands on his hips. With his elbows cocked and chest pushed out, he staring rigidly at the boy surging toward them, low and hunched and glaring. Billy's dagger eyes seemed to slow his forward progress. Billy felt their shared vision of colliding, as if hurting the other wasn't everything—it was the only thing.

"Go," said the girl with a shake of his arm.

Lingering, he rubbed his hands together and looked down at her. She nodded. He bent for his bike, and his shiny new soft leather wallet fell out of his back pocket. She snatched it up and motioned for him to go, as if truly afraid if he stayed he'd hurt the boy or get hurt himself.

"Quick," she urged.

Startled, he wondered quickly if she was a foreigner. He gave the bad kid one last warning glare. Then, with his eyes flashing, he smiled an invisible cloak around her shoulders. She grinned and cupped her hands together like holding a butterfly.

Billy sped away.

THAT SAME EVENING

Soon after Maj's parents' car disappeared from Great Oaks over the rumbling wooden bridge on their way to the opera, the doorbell rang. Maj's skin jumped. Having spent the afternoon with good feelings from the boy's touch and the protective sound of his voice, she'd practiced her speech and let herself forget all about Clay. Now she worried who was going to show up. Clay, the kidder? Or his evil twin? Maj hoped it was her friend.

"That will be Clay," said MorMor.

Clay lurched into the living room, hunched-over and hairy. Could be *Loki*, the handsome fire-giant of mischief, crouched beyond the big black windows that sent his face in shadow. A movement in the giant oak tree out front made Maj flinch. She rubbed her fingers together, searching her imagination for a spell to change Clay back to normal, and quick. Instead of making the night disappear, his looks brought on mad and wicked fears of things she couldn't see. Whatever his secret was and why he had wrongly touched her, she didn't care anymore. She wanted back her friend and protector of the dark.

Settling into her favorite chair in the family room off the kitchen, MorMor pulled out her knitting. "Maj, you're shivering. Go get a sweater," she ordered.

Alarmed, Maj nodded absently, unwilling to travel alone down the long dark hallway for some silly old sweater. Without meeting MorMor's eyes, and even though the boy had warned her to stay away, Maj retreated to the kitchen to help Clay prepare dinner—this being Carmen and Ramon's night off. He'd turned on the oven and taken three TV dinners from the freezer, a special treat saved for her parents' nights out.

Maj sat down at the table, waiting for him to turn around, and fearful who she'd see. Suddenly dreading that he'd say something nasty about the boy and wreck everything for her, she rose to her feet, set on keeping the boy her secret. Before she could escape, he spun around.

"What has a neck and no head?" he asked, his voice back to normal and kidding around as usual.

She let out a relieved sigh.

"I don't know," she answered lightly and in the way they'd practiced a thousand times together. "What has a neck and no head?"

"A bottle, stupid!"

He laughed, looking through her, and turned back to pulling the foil away from the potatoes.

As slow as Maj was with her speech and backwards with her writing, no one had ever called her stupid. The word shrank to the size of a thimble and shoved her into a tiny little box. She didn't know what she had done wrong and couldn't think of anything to say.

In the other room, MorMor's knitting needles fell silent.

Clay copied MorMor's snoring and end up snorting like a pig. Laughing at himself, instead of big and broad, his smile twisted like he hurt inside from eating too much candy. *Loki* truly did put a curse on him.

Even with tears stinging and unsure how to help, concern for her friend tugged Maj toward him. Acting like he didn't see her reach out, he turned his back and arranged the trays.

"You can at least do the silverware and napkins, can't you?" he said over his shoulder, ending in his high voice—irritated or cross, she couldn't tell which.

Feeling miserable, Maj hurried to help.

*　*　*　*　*　*

In the living room, Maj arranged three tray tables. MorMor sputtered and pulled herself up in her chair. Clay turned on the television and sat down beside Maj on the sofa. Together, they watched *The Ed Sullivan Show*, the only television program deemed suitable for Maj.

"You're shivering and not eating," warned MorMor.

Startled, Maj scooped a forkful of mashed potatoes and forced herself to swallow.

MorMor moved her tray table to the side. Using her cane, she got to her feet and turned up the volume of the television. When MorMor's back was turned, Clay speared the piece of ham on Maj's tray and dropped the meat on his. His knee jiggled with his foot tapping the floor about a thousand miles a second. Maj smiled at him. His grin was normal this time. Relieved, she mushed her food into a little wad on her plate. Even before the television program ended, MorMor insisted Maj go for her sweater.

"I'm not telling you again," she said, her eyebrows knitted together.

"I'll dump this in the garbage," Clay said in an

important voice and gathered up their empty dinner trays.

Maj froze, wondering if his evil twin had taken over again. Not giving Clay time to come back, she tiptoed to the hallway. If she asked him, Clay would go after her sweater but she couldn't risk having him switch places again.

Whispering Tomete, the name of the good-luck gnome MorMor said looked after the house, Maj peered around the archway to the hall. Tomete was nowhere in sight. She wasn't surprised. The only actual sighting she'd had of his gray smock and red tasseled cap was late one night, when her bedroom was the darkest. He'd danced a jig in the middle of her bed. After he disappeared, the night wasn't as scary, and she'd been able to sleep.

Laughter broke from the television behind her.

"Go," commanded MorMor.

The highboy towered on one side of the hallway, next to Mother's newest oil painting, dark and murky and smelling of fresh paint. On the opposite side of the hall, French doors—uncovered against the twilight hour—revealed the in-between time when the regular world thinned to the invisible world of trolls and giants and magic. Soon it would be pitch-black outside. Fear stabbed the back of her neck.

Careful not to awaken an imp or sprite, Maj stepped into the hallway and kept to the middle of the hall. She looked neither left nor right nor even where she was going, staring only down—self-conscious of her heart cringing and shrinking, how much noise she was making, and how big her feet were. The heavy stillness made her wish she hadn't started.

At the end of the hall, she peeked inside her

bedroom. Hunched where her bureau should be swayed an evil old troll with craggy eyebrows, a nose as thick as a turnip, and massive hairy hands. She wrenched her eyes away and flung herself up against the hallway wall. Breathless, her legs went weak.

When her heart slowed enough for steady breathing and nothing bad happened, she poked her head back inside her bedroom. Her familiar chest of drawers stood like a watchman in a puddle of icy blue mist. Her relief at finding the troll gone and her bedroom safe sent her giggling. The sound came out a squeak.

Whispering assurances that her sweater was on the hook just inside her closet, Maj slid open the door. A hand slapped over her mouth. Unable to breath, she squirmed to free herself.

"Don't say a word," Clay whispered.

1960 - MARCH

i.

Maj turned thirteen tall for her age, slender, and quiet. High on a ladder, she reached for an orange. A breath of air trembled, blowing the sunrise away. Leaves on the trees shuddered.

"The elves have arrived," announced MorMor, about the nature sign from where she sat in the shade of the citrus grove behind Great Oaks.

Pine trees framed orange trees near and silent on three sides. MorMor's fairies pulled at Maj like a lullaby, but she was grown up now—too old for such nonsense. She'd stopped asking for MorMor's tales the same day she let go of thoughts of the mysterious boy, gave away all things make-believe, and turned her vengeance on Clay. More sad than mad, she pressed her lips together.

"You're not invisible," said MorMor, knitting as usual.

"Why did you say that?" Maj asked, defensive that MorMor could read her mind. "I know I'm not."

"There!"

Maj started at the sudden shout and grabbed the sides of the ladder to keep from listing backwards, her heart erratic. MorMor dropped her knitting needles and pointed to a bird squawking like a scrub jay in a nearby pine tree. In almost the same breath, the bird trilled like a songbird.

Its tweets mingled with MorMor's voice. "The great communicator."

The excitement in MorMor's voice made Maj look down.

"The white of the mockingbird wing is your sign to talk," exclaimed MorMor.

"I talk." Maj defended herself and then withered under the receiving end of MorMor's deliberate stare.

"I do," Maj insisted.

With more important things on her mind than birds and words, Maj quickly filled the basket with oranges, careful not to offend bees buzzing around her head. Mother was due home any minute. Even with an anxious taste in her mouth, Maj planned to be ready for their trip together to San Francisco. Nothing MorMor said was going to stop her.

Maj snapped a plump orange from the tree's interior.

"Ouch!" she cried, pricked by a thorn. A spot of blood mushroomed on the meaty part of her finger.

"All things beautiful have thorns to protect them," recited MorMor and, like every other sign and omen and message from nature, they required no letters or reading or spelling. "Orange trees. Rose bushes."

People would like beautiful things better if they didn't have thorns, Maj thought to herself and stuck her finger in her mouth. The blood tasted foreign and forbidden.

"Learn to speak up, or you'll be destined to live by your looks alone," MorMor pressed. "Your words will protect you, but you must use them. Your teacher wants you to speak in class. You must promise you'll try."

Maj rolled her eyes and started down the ladder, not bothering to explain that she wasn't the least bit interested in taking part in class. She was still in speech therapy, and though she finally spoke so most people could understand her, that didn't stop kids from laughing at her. All she'd ever gotten out of talking in school was teasing, and junior high school was proving to be more of the same. Humiliation belonged hidden away, not pointed out, explained, and reorganized.

"You mustn't let this idea of your mother's interfere with your school work," MorMor cautioned.

"I won't," Maj said, but the truth was that school was still difficult for her. Having her picture taken sounded easy.

She'd thrown herself into Mother's plan of modeling like Mother's idol Greta Garbo had started out, believing she'd found the entry to worm her way into Mother's good graces, finally.

"You have a lot to learn," said MorMor. "When the time comes for you to meet the one true wild and precious someone, destined for you and you alone, threshold guardians will demand a demonstration of your readiness. You are far from ready now. You must practice. When the time comes, you'll be asked to speak up to your mother."

Maj shook her head, remembering when she believed the mysterious boy was her one wild and precious someone, destined for her and her alone. She would have done anything for him.

At nearly the bottom of the ladder, Maj missed a rung and took a giant step backwards, landing hard with oranges scattering everywhere. Her jaw hammered together, and she bit her tongue. As determined as she was about Mother's idea, an edge of fear about today's photography session seemed fixed on pricking and cutting and tripping her up. Maj closed her eyes and cleared her mind of thinking and breathing and feeling, in the exact numbing way she'd closed herself off during the terrifying times Clay caught her off-guard.

"Stop daydreaming and listen to me!"

Maj jerked at the harshness in MorMor's voice and peered into milky white eyes that glowed like opals.

"You're a woman now. It's time you know. Your words are your thorns. You must use them," said MorMor.

"We should go," Maj said, ignoring MorMor as she gathered the oranges and picked up MorMor's cane from the lawn beside her chair.

The smell of smoke, from a fire Ramon tended behind the line of garages, mixed with the scent of oranges.

Maj collected MorMor's knitting and helped her to her feet, anxiety pulsing at Maj's temples at how slowly MorMor unfolded her body. Finally, she straightened into a standing position. Cane in hand, MorMor slipped an arm through Maj's and leaned on her.

Tires crunched on the long gravel driveway. Soon after, Mother's green station wagon with wooden side panels appeared from around the entrance of Great Oaks. Maj panted, not yet dressed for the city.

"If you're nervous about going, tell her," said MorMor firmly.

"I'm not nervous," Maj answered, watching the cloud of dust catch and sink over the car.

Mother emerged, looking radiant in her flared white tennis dress. Maj's stomach flip-flopped at the thought of what lay ahead, scared and hopeful at the same time.

"Then why are you whispering?" asked MorMor.

Maj glanced at MorMor's certain face, surprised and frightened. She'd practiced hard to stop whispering to herself, not wanting to give away her hiding places to Clay.

"Cover your shoulders, and put on a hat, Maj," called Mother. "Mustn't have a sunburn for today's shoot."

Maj sucked in her breath and answered quickly.

"Yes, Mother," she called, eager to please even as MorMor tsked beside her.

The little white straw hat Mother wore and her oversized dark sunglasses made her look secretive, like Greta Garbo. Tennis racket in hand, Mother entered the house with a spring in her step. Greta Garbo had begun her famous career by modeling, and the chance that Maj could turn out like her filled Mother with more joy than Maj had ever seen. No longer judging from afar what Maj couldn't do and what Maj should do and what Maj should say, Mother pulled her near. What had started out a secret from Daddy a year ago was now a reality with a photographer and her very own agent. Mother won her argument by predicting to Daddy that Maj was always going to talk funny.

"Now, now, Birgit," Maj overheard Daddy say, and imagined his jaw twitching.

"She's never going to find a husband."

"She's not even thirteen years old," he said at the time.

"Modeling will help her get what she wants with her looks."

For the past month, with eyes turned to the future, Mother demonstrated along the length of the main hallway how to pivot and turn.

Warmed in the glow of her enthusiasm and the time they spent together, Maj imitated the tilt of Mother's head, swing of her hips, and the daring pout of her lips all in preparation for today. Now with the photo shoot nearly upon her, Maj's fledgling excitement sank. She clenched her fists, refusing to peek over the edge of the sink-hole, filled with all the ways she was sure to disappoint Mother now when success counted the most.

*　*　*　*　*　*

Double-parked at the photographer's studio, Mother opened the backdoor for Maj's clothes, as Maj dragged her feet like slogging through molasses. At home she had liked the clothes Mother picked out for today and imitating the poses in her Swedish fashion magazines. Now Maj felt dizzy and had to concentrate not to trip over her own feet.

"Hold this for me," said Mother, producing a hand mirror from an unfamiliar bag in the back seat.

Maj positioned the mirror, following Mother's instructions up, down, over, and tilted ever so much.

"Hold still," Mother complained, lifting the mirror to the right height.

"I'm sorry, Mother."

Watching Mother carefully reapply her lipstick, Maj didn't remember Mother's eyes ever burning so brightly. Unlike her characteristically cool manner, Mother seemed nervous or excited. Maj couldn't tell which one.

"I expect you to do your best today," Mother said, rubbing a finger across her teeth.

Though Mother's words weren't a scolding, Maj

nonetheless felt like she was in trouble.

"Yes, Mother," she said cautiously.

Mother leaned in for a closer view, peeled back her lips, and checked for lipstick smudges.

"Grace and poise will go a long way in helping you snag a great husband when you're older. Every man loves a pretty girl on his arm."

Maj shrugged. "Yes, Mother."

"Do I look alright?" Mother asked, straining to see her side-view.

Nodding vehemently, Maj answered quickly. "Like a movie star." Worried she'd been abrupt, Maj added, her voice trembling, "You look very pretty, Mother."

An unmarked door swung open, and a dog trotted out as big as a pony and sniffed her. Maj immediately recognized the man who followed as Jimmy, her agent. He was dressed in the same red jacket, red plaid tie, and red oxfords as the first time she met him. His oversized glasses with big, red frames made him look like a gaudy librarian. He held open the door with his cigarette hand and greeted Mother with a peek on each cheek. He took a puff from his cigarette, in a long red lacquered cigarette holder, and wagged his fingers at Maj.

"Come along inside, darling. I want you to meet my friend, Ned."

As she puzzled how to pass the dog to get to the door, a man joined Jimmy at the doorway and said something to the dog.

"Birgit, this is Ned the photographer. Ned, Maj's mother," Jimmy introduced.

Mother stuck out a gloved hand to Ned. Usually stately and formal when meeting new people, Mother's eyelids fluttered as fast as bumblebee wings, and she sighed like she was breathless.

"Maj, meet Ned," said Jimmy, throwing his cigarette on the sidewalk and squashing it under his heel.

Puzzled, Maj did a double-take for a clue why Mother was acting so strangely, and then she turned to meet the man who would take her pictures.

"Do you like dogs?" asked Ned, ruffling the dog behind its ears. "Charlie won't hurt you."

Maj hesitated, believing she did like dogs, but having never encountered one before she wasn't exactly sure. Zooming through her mind for the right words, she struggled to form an answer when Mother took Ned's arm and pointed out the clothes to take into his studio. Then, she pinched Maj.

Sinking her voice to a hoarse and furious whisper, Mother insisted, "Stop mumbling."

Maj snapped shut her mouth.

Mother disappeared inside with Jimmy.

The light in the studio was so dim that Maj couldn't tell where the ceiling ended and the walls began. Jimmy and Ned and Mother walked together to a piece of white fabric hanging in the middle of an open room. A solitary light bulb hung from overhead and illuminated a stool sitting in the middle of the backdrop.

Ned smoked a cigarette, and his hair hung over the collar of a yellowing long sleeved shirt, opened at the top.

"Ned is going to take lots of pictures today," explained Jimmy, as Ned walked around Maj slowly, his eyes roaming over her the same way Daddy considered a new car—with Mother chattering along beside him.

Maj's cheeks burned. With her eyes on Ned, she stood very still and ready to kick back if, like Daddy tested car tires, he tried to kick her.

"That way when I hear about jobs I think are right

for you," continued Jimmy, "I'll have your composite to show the client, so they know what to expect."

Mother, still sighing and blinking, interrupted with a question about modeling jobs, her hands all a-flutter. Surprisingly, her flightiness made Maj feel calmer.

*   *   *   *   *   *

Maj watched as Ned positioned spotlights running along the length of two ceiling-to-floor poles on either side of the draped white cloth. Then he moved behind a black camera on stilts, a cigarette burning between his lips. His legs spread, one foot on either side of the long legs of a camera stand, and he bent over, as if taming a skinny, black flamingo. In her nervousness, Maj found comfort in the idea of a flamingo in the room with her. She named it Flame, which made her think of Flame boy, and thinking of Flame boy and his magic touch surged her confidence.

The door swung open suddenly, and Mother appeared on the threshold. She sprang into action—her cheeks pink, and clutching her purse—and flitted onto the white cloth where she threw out her chin just like she'd taught Maj in front of the long mirror in her bedroom. One right after another, Mother posed— hand on her hip, profile, coy, and ending with a full-face camera shot.

Maj clapped as Mother held the pose, in awe of her beauty and grace and poise. If only Maj could do as well. Her clapping sounded hollow as no one else moved. Suddenly confused whether Mother was posing for a photograph or reminding her how, Maj stared at the photographer helplessly. She wished Ned would snap a picture of Mother, knowing she'd swoon with joy.

Mother took a breath and slowly seemed to come out a trance. She looked confused, so Maj joined her on the little stage and took her hand. Mother slapped her away, scanned the room, and sauntered out with her head held high.

Barely breathing watching her go, Maj felt a sure fear creep to the surface that any success of hers was never going to be enough for Mother, when she'd once wanted to model so badly herself. Maj longed for Ned to hurry and this day to be over.

A skinny Asian man, carrying a huge suitcase, broke the tension.

"This is Tyrell," stammered Ned, looking uncertainly toward the door where Mother disappeared. "He'll do your make-up."

Tyrell applied the same make-up Mother used before a party: foundation, blush-on, mascara, eyeliner, and lipstick. Mother tried advising him with her back as straight as usual, her breathing back to normal, and her eyes calm. When Tyrell quietly went about his business, she left to discuss something with Jimmy.

Tyrell was gentle, and before long, his touch put Maj in a daze. She was nearly asleep when he positioned a mirror in front of her face. She didn't recognize herself, giggled, and felt safe in her disguise.

Ned stubbed out the cigarette in a rusty Folgers Coffee can. Spotlights snapped on. The air heated up. Music started.

Maj didn't understand the words, but the slow, sad melody felt like church—only from somewhere deeper.

*   *   *   *   *   *

After what seemed like all day, Maj heard silence. She shook her head and wondered how long she had been floating. Flame, the winking flamingo, was still there.

The overhead light came on, and the pole lighting clicked off. Ned returned. Flame turned back into a camera on stilts.

Maj looked to Mother for approval, and saw Ned grinning like a kid. Suddenly she worried she'd given him something she might wish she hadn't, something that should be hers alone, not in a photograph for others to see. Mother had taught Maj that she could communicate with a pose, like finding the right words to say. She worried the pictures revealed her shame strangers could judge.

"So, what do you think?" asked Mother, her voice tense as she pulled up her gloves and touched her hair.

"Enough here," answered Ned. "We'll take some shots in Golden Gate Park before we lose the light. You can't teach what your daughter has. She's raw and got something out of this world. The public is going to love her."

Shy on the outside, inside Maj glowed like a lantern. Mother frowned. The glow sniffed out. Maj hadn't measured up. Alone on the cloth, all she wanted to do was rub off the make-up, so they could go home. Dizzy, she couldn't remember the last time she'd eaten.

"Part your hair on the side and put on that tennis dress," instructed Ned. "Bring the racket and meet me at my van. There's no turning back now, baby. From here on out, it's straight to the top."

Ned tweaked Maj's cheek and smiled at her. She flinched and lurched into the dressing room, locking the door behind her.

ii.

Sixteen years old and driving his step-father's moving van, Billy kept his trap shut as he steered the van through the avenues. He'd like nothing better than to bark at Ray to can his harping on how Billy should brake and shift and keep both hands on the steering wheel and both eyes on the road—and oh, don't forget to check the side-view mirrors, over and over again. They'd half-loaded the van for a family of four and were headed to Seattle for two more families' belongings before heading east.

Billy flicked his cigarette out the window and downshifted. Trees in Golden Gate Park rose to greet him. The cold and the fog slinking in didn't stop a guy from pulling stuff from the back of a van across the street. He yawned, already tired and antsy and irritated at Ray, and they'd only just started a three-week trek across country.

iii.

The air turned cold as the winter sun moved lower in the sky. Wearing only a short tennis dress, waiting for Ned to set up—and with Jimmy and Mother huddled together—Maj gripped the tennis racket and shivered. Her head ached, and she tried relaxing her pinched eyebrows before Mother could nag her about lines on her face.

The setting sun reflected into the windshield of a giant moving van on the far side of a four-way stop. Rather than cast a glare, the sun combined with an amber traffic light to illuminate the inside of the cab to a glowy yellow.

Maj sucked in her breath, recognizing her mystery boy before he spotted her.

At the sight him—his hands on a steering wheel as big as a nightstand—Maj let out a long pent-up breath, relaxing for the first time since she'd last seen him. Three times, she counted. Three different times in three wholly different places meant something special.

The first two times she'd been too young to trust that the boy was not just an imaginary crowned prince to her lost soul. Now she decided he was about four or five years older than she was, and that he was indeed very real.

Turning dreamy, Maj looked him over with her heart bubbling. She imagined threading her fingers through his again and how hot his skin had been, rough as sandpaper. Blushing, she cringed at how she must have appeared to him when she drew his hands to her nose, inhaling the scent of sweaty handlebars and a tiny whiff of orange. His deep and defiant voice echoed in her head. That he was so bold and confident at her age, back then, Maj was encouraged to try for the same.

Now he had a teenage slouch and the serious look of a man. She didn't remember, when they were younger, him flicking his gaze every-which-way. She wondered if he was still a thief and if that explained why he was so skittish and on the lookout.

She started to wave her arms as the light turned red. Then she flinched and abruptly turned away. Her heart filled with tears. She used to draw strength from imagining what he would do to Clay. But when Clay caught her off-guard for a second time, and she realized she was on her own, for a long time nothing seemed to matter, and she stopped hoping the boy would save her.

Until she discovered what she'd done wrong to deserve Clay's meanness, she erected a thick wall around herself and hid in shame.

Now, through half-closed eyes and clutching her elbows to her sides to control her shaky arms, Maj watched the boy out of the corner of her eye. Ashamed and embarrassed and refusing to let him see her vulnerable and confused, she sighed and dropped a veil over her eyes.

Out of sight, she safely hid in the corner of her imagination.

iv.

Tucked in the greenery across the street from where Billy waited for the light to change, a skinny girl with windswept blonde hair shivered. Billy's eyes twitched. Rubbing them, he froze at the sudden contented and satisfied sensation in the pit of his stomach. Hands on the steering wheel and a foot on the brake, he barely breathed, afraid of scaring away one of Grandma's visions.

But an image didn't appear, just the same girl in the park across the street. She ran a hand across her forehead and caught her hair. Billy knew that hand and speed-cranked down his window. The wind from the bay tugged at his hair as he kept his eyes trained on the girl, coaxing her to turn.

"What're you doing?" growled Ray. "Get going."

Surprised to find the light had changed so quickly, Billy shifted and ground the gears. Without taking his eyes from her, he pressed on the gas slowly, only to find he'd shifted to third. The green light switched to yellow. Even stopped in the middle of the crosswalk with horns blasting behind him, Billy let the signal go to red, buying him time.

"What are hell are you doing?" shouted Ray. "At this rate, we won't get to Seattle until next year!"

Ignoring his stepfather's bitching and moaning, Billy concentrated on the girl. She looked about thirteen or fourteen years old, lining up with those first couple of times he'd seen her. Young as she'd been then, just an awkward pint-sized little kid and more than slightly goofy, he wouldn't have remembered her except for the visions that came just before she showed up. He struggled to believe in the oddity of seeing her in such different places and the novelty of such a thing happening to him.

Back then she wasn't even a real girl, all sharp angles. Still, her mysterious appearance and her connection to Grandma through the visions used to sometimes keep him awake at night, helping him through tough times when he first moved in with Ma. When he'd finally fall into an exhausted sleep, he'd jerk out of heart-skipping dreams of windswept moments, trunks of jewels like treasure chests, snowy white skin, and huge eyes that turned into an owl. Softhearted and brave, the way she ran to him; her concern made him feel special. The visions added to that feeling, not something he was much used to feeling.

Still wide-eyed innocent, with a longer neck and smooth skin, she pushed through a crowd of tourists. She appeared to be to be excusing herself for bumping into them or could be talking to herself. Then he remembered she'd been mumbling the other times he'd seen her, too.

Seconds ticked until the red light changed to green, when a guy with a camera pointed. Hands behind her back, the girl leaned up against a tree, with the full sun beaming against her face like a shiny gold coin.

Cross-traffic began to slow. The light was going to change any second to green. Now Billy knew for certain their meetings, and his visions, hadn't been accidental. As crazy as the notion sounded, even to him, he knew they were meant to meet. Here she was again. The girl in the park was the yellow-haired girl.

"Hurry," he whispered for her to look at him. Her head turned, as if she'd heard him.

A car horn blared from behind them.

Ray hit him upside the head.

"Get going!" His voice was raw and gravely.

Disgusted, and wishing for the ten-trillionth time he'd had him a real dad, Billy imagined slugging his stepfather, punching him in the face like Ray used to hit Ma. Instead, Billy pulled hard on the steering wheel, giving the girl one last look before the moving van swept onto 19th Avenue.

What had he expected? The sky would open, money pour down, and the girl come running to explain what the heck was going on?

In his side mirror, he saw her turn. With his heart surprising him at full throttle, Billy looked over his shoulder. She was gone.

BLIZZARD

Thanks to Billy's insistence, they kept driving, right into in the worst storm Billy had ever seen, by far. A couple of hours outside of Wolf Point, Montana—and with little more than fifty miles to make it to North Dakota—a blizzard blustered against the tandem axle of the cab-over tractor rig, muffling the usual roar of the 500-horsepower Cummins engine.

Billy's plan was to get east as quick as possible, unpack the van, and immediately start back. No stopping needlessly, no sightseeing, just get there and back. He had a girl waiting for him at home. But, at this rate they were never going to make it. Damn. He slammed a fist against the steering wheel.

Fantasizing about the homecoming Brenda had promised, he imagined all the ways she'd find to please him. The black-haired vixen turned especially spirited when he went on to her about his dreams of the future—a fancy car, him in a felt hat, her in gloves, hand-in-hand with their daughter on the way to the candy store. Speeding up, and passing the time dreaming about what Brenda would come up with if he threw in a kidney-shaped swimming pool had his heart pumping like an oil-rig.

His heart got to pumping even faster when he found

himself suddenly unable to make out anything beyond the snub nose of the cab except for billowing blackness.

"Slow down," nagged Ray.

Peering through the frosted windshield, Billy gave all his attention to driving just as the truck began to skate.

"Black ice!" shouted Ray.

The urgency in Ray's voice made Billy blink in a snowy stupor as the truck skimmed sideways. Clutching the steering wheel with both hands, he braced to turn against the slide. Ray grabbed the wheel from him and fixed their direction in a locked position.

Lifting his foot to shove down on the brakes, Ray yelled at Billy to stop.

"Tap 'em," Ray snapped. "Easy. Little touches. Now ease off," he instructed.

The cab hurled forward, whip-lashed by the trailer, and whacked up against a snow bank. Billy cursed. Both of them sucked in their breath, posed in a fragile balance between disaster and staying upright. Feeling responsible, Billy's heart squeezed in on him.

Just about ready to congratulate themselves that the van had come to a stop without a mishap, snowflakes shifted in the headlights. With the cab freefalling on its side, Billy flung his arms across his chest to stop from slamming into Ray. The cab crashed into the snow bank of a gully off the shoulder of the road. Billy fell against Ray with his full weight. Ray's head thumped against the frozen windowpane. The wind turned quiet.

"Damn," said Billy, stuck on his side, trapped by gravity up against Ray in a sideways-cab. "You okay?"

"Yeah, but we can't leave the motor running, not with the cab on its side. Least we're off to the side of the road and not in danger of getting hit."

Billy struggled to sit up, so he could see Ray's face

and determine why he was acting so cool and calm, for once. "You forgetting we're stuck smack in the middle of a blizzard?" he cried.

"You think I can't see that?" said Ray, his body burning against Billy. "Do as I say. Shut off the engine. We'll flag down the next car we see."

Ray stretched for his hat and coat on the hook behind his seat. Turning, he knocked Billy in the head and didn't bother excusing himself.

Billy took the abuse, knowing he deserved it. Besides, being pressed up against Ray, he could barely breathe, much less move. He shut off the engine. Quiet cold slipped around them like an icy lover.

"Crazy thinking anyone's out on a night like tonight," Billy mumbled.

Ray pressed his hands against Billy's side, giving Billy the leverage he needed to reach the door handle. Working against gravity and snow piling up on the door outside, he suddenly panicked. "I can't do it," he howled. "We'll be buried alive. We're going to freeze to death."

"Keep at it," said Ray, shoving him nearer to the door.

Leaning against the steering wheel and using his feet, Billy strained in a battle against the storm. Finally the door opened a crack, then more and a little more, until it stuck straight up in the air. He hauled himself out of the cab with Ray scrambling right behind him.

Pinpricks of ice stabbed Billy in the face. He kicked shut the door, even knowing they'd never get it open again in this storm. Damn. Not bothering to consider the impossibility of finding a rig big enough to haul them upright in this isolated place far from help and how slim his chances of ever getting out of here, he knew he best concentrate instead on staying alive.

Teetering on the side of the truck, Ray threw Billy his coat. Ray cupped both hands around his mouth and shouted. "Watch where you jump. Don't get buried in a snowdrift."

There was a beat of silence. Then Billy squatted and shimmied himself to the edge of the cab. With one arm wrapped around the doorstep, he tried his weight in the snow. Sinking to his ankles, he hit firm ground. He let go of the rig.

Fumbling to button his coat with frozen fingers and not wanting to imagine how much worse this could get, Billy waded through the snow to the middle of the road.

Forty miles per hour wind gusts scratched his face, and his nose started running. In less time than it took him to lift a hand, snot froze to his upper lip. Ray dragged himself through the snow with mincing little steps. Billy could only grab short, shallow breaths. The cold froze his temples the same way as eating ice cream real fast—with a much crueler pain.

"Dear, God," Ray breathed, as they studied the damage.

The cab was at a 45-degree angle to the side of the road. To Billy's relief, and their unbelievable great fortune, the 50,000-pound trailer carrying a full load stood. More than six days of loading furniture saved, for now. He groaned at the possibility of freezing to death and the impossibility of ever getting the cab hauled upright.

A gust of wind rocked the trailer. Billy's jaw slackened, and he stopped breathing. When it didn't tip over, he ran to the back of the van, but couldn't make out in the snow how near the tires were to where the highway dropped off into the ditch. With his dream of a quick trip dashed, and unwilling to witness all that work careen on its side, he decided his first course of action was not freezing to death. He pulled up his coat collar and yanked down the brim of his hat. He checked his watch. Only a fool would be on the road at 12:30 at night in a storm as fierce as this. The cold and the noise of the wind rattled him.

*   *   *   *   *   *

Miserable, slogging through ice and snow against a head wind, and fixed on stepping in the holes Ray's boots left, Billy peeled back the layers of clothes and checked the time. Only five minutes had passed, and they'd barely moved. His cheeks were frozen, and shakes rattled over him every other second. They weren't going to make it. He would never again feel Brenda's silky body up against his, and he wasn't ever going to have a chance to find out what the yellow-haired girl had to do with him. He wondered how death came in the freezing cold. Given his choice, he preferred real sudden.

He crashed into Ray's back. "What the—?"

"Someone's coming!" shouted Ray. He waved his arms over his head.

A car emerged out of the wind and snow and cold with one headlight burned out. Billy ripped his hands from his pockets and joined Ray jumping up and down in the middle of the road. Pain shot up his legs like frozen pins rammed in the soles of his feet, each landing pushing them deeper.

"Stop!" Billy cried, through his frozen lips sounding more like *sop*.

The car weaved, traveling at least fifty miles an hour. Wide-eyed, Billy stopped jumping, uneasy the speeding car wouldn't stop in time. The lone headlight blinded and confused him which way to jump. Six feet, five feet, three feet, a '47 four-door Ford sedan with bald tires and no snow chains slid to a stop less than a foot away from him.

Breathing heavy, he ran for the back door and hopped into the smell of wine and sweat. The door slammed shut behind him. Inside, heat stung his cheeks.

Two guys in the front seat had Indian hair. The driver, wearing two braids tied in fringe with a feather, turned around. "Shame about your truck," he said.

All four of them looked at the rig in the distance.

"Least the trailer's still standing," Billy noted with relief.

Ray's guffaw at the ridiculousness of their position pinned all the blame directly on Billy.

The other guy in the car had one braid hanging straight down his back. The two in front turned in unison. Billy outright grinned when he saw that they had the same flat, round face as Grandma. Her hair wasn't as black anymore, or as coarse as theirs, but the resemblance was there all right.

"Name's Longtree. This here's my brother."

"I'm Ray. This here's Billy. We'd be much obliged if you'd take us to that little motel just outside the next town."

Brother had a grin plastered across his face as wide as could be, like he'd just won himself a prize pony or passed the peace pipe. The fact that they could help appeared to please him to no end.

Longtree thrust the car in gear. Off they flew.

Brother held out a half-full gallon jug of red wine. From this angle, Billy saw that though his mouth was happy, Brother's eyes hung down sad-looking, like Billy's friend Webb.

"Won't find this at the Trading Post," said Brother, nudging the bottle toward them.

They all laughed at that.

Ray slid a finger into the ring at the top of the jug. "Thank you kindly," he said. "Don't mind if I do. Could have froze to death out there." Ray tipped the opening to his mouth and took himself a long swig. He handed the bottle to Billy and lighted himself a Lucky Strike.

"Won't find no arrows or bows or stone axes at the Trading Post neither," said Brother.

The car turned quiet. Grandma often went on about the old days before white men tarnished the land. Now that those days were dead and gone was no laughing matter. Wore out from shivering, Billy fell back in the seat, took in the heat, and felt his body burn.

Ray held the cigarette pack over the seat. Brother popped a cigarette in his mouth for Ray to light, and lit another one off the fire for his brother.

Billy took a swig of wine and decided right then and there that getting rip-roaring drunk was the sharpest remedy for being stuck in the middle of nowhere in a blizzard. Besides, getting drunk would numb him to the car's torn interior and cracked seats, the dangling and broken glove compartment lid that lurched and slammed into the dashboard with every slip and slide, and the worn clothes the brothers wore—all signs of the poverty Billy had been running from his entire life.

By the third or fourth time the bottle made it back to him, he was pretty well toasted. The drunker he got, the more he thought about Grandma. The more he thought about her, the more he worried about her. He'd make enough money on this run to spoil Brenda, help out Ma, and send the bulk of his share to Grandma. Grandma needed his help more than ever since State Aid somehow found out about the pennies Mexican women had paid her to watch their kids while they worked in the fields. The more he thought about State Aid cutting her off, the drier his throat got, the more he drank, and the drunker he got.

"*Bode'wadmi ndaw*," he said, making a real effort not to slur his words. Even knowing Longtree and his brother wouldn't understand his citizen band's language, Billy was happy he remembered the greeting.

"*Akainawa*." Longtree followed.

Billy didn't need to know what Longtree just said. The tone of his voice and the quality of his language clearly marked a return greeting.

Brother slung the bottle over the seatback again. Billy's head buzzing with questions about their lives, the Trading Post, bows and arrows, and axes, he took another swig of wine—this time to wet his whistle and seize the opportunity to do some talking. He had a hard time speaking. His tongue was alcohol thick.

"Never had me no tribe," Billy said. "Only Indian I spent time with was Grandma. She always said I was going to be a leader of men someday."

In the rear view mirror, Longtree's eyes stayed on him, his face soaked with the green glow of the instrument panel. Brother nodded. Even Ray was quiet, looking out his window at nothing but black and blizzard.

The fury outside calmed. Fishtailing all over the road straightened. Ray handed Billy the bottle. He passed with a wave of his hand and didn't even mind.

"All the good ponies are gone now. Warriors, too. I saw it in a dream," said Brother.

For some reason, they all got to laughing at that.

A couple of minutes later, Longtree pulled to a stop behind a darkened motel, nothing else in sight anywhere except for snow. Snowflakes covered the windshield in the time it took the wipers to start back in the opposite direction. Billy could barely keep his eyes open.

"Knock on the side door 'til someone comes," said Longtree.

"Watch out for the BIA," warned Brother.

"Bureau of Indian Affairs," explained Longtree. "It's all right, Brother, these guys don't have to worry about the BIA."

Ray pulled his wallet from his back pocket. Billy reached for his, too. The feel of the leather reminded him of the day he stole it and the yellow-haired girl standing as his witness. Even after all this time, there was nothing like the feel of that wallet bulging with cash.

Longtree took Ray's paper money and refused Billy's. Billy and Ray each opened their door and stumbled out of the car at the same time.

"When she comes, she'll be riding the white owl," Brother shouted out the window.

He pulled his braid and winked, and the brothers drove off, one lone headlight flickering against a black night. Too drunk to appreciate what the heck he was going on about or run after him about some owl, Billy followed Ray as he checked them into a room and passed out cold.

* * * * * *

Next morning, sunlight bounced off huge heaps of snow outside the motel room window, blinding Billy. Least the storm and all that noise were over, for now. The tricky thing about these parts, early spring weather in particular was unpredictable—one minute calm, and next a blizzard. Seeing both his cheeks blue black from the freeze, he wished something fierce that Longtree and his brother would show up with their bottle of wine. A good long drink would numb the feeling that they were going to find the van tipped over, and them stranded in this podunk town forever.

Billy perked up when he saw the trailer still standing. Pressing shut his eyes against a cold sunlight blasting off the snow, he squatted and put his head between his knees to stop the light from spinning in his head. Blood-red ponies, bows and arrows, and stone axes glowed on the backside of his eyelids. Brother raised up old freedom days that fed Billy's imagination and the wildness to believe he could succeed at becoming a man.

The sky was dark and misty with a chill by the time the oil company's six-wheel-drive Peterbilt truck, which had been converted into a tow truck with an huge wench in back, arrived from the next town over—the temperature down another 30 degrees. Pick-up trucks lined the highway. To keep warm and put a lid on his frustration, his agitation, and impatience, Billy paced back and forth in two orderly rows, like seeding cotton. They'd already lost one day. He hated to think how many more were in store for them if this guy couldn't haul up the cab.

A three-inch-diameter cable with a giant hook

unwound from an equally giant spool sticking in the air in the back of the truck parked against the road shoulder. Billy paced past crowds of men betting whether the cab would right without sending the trailer on its side. From what he could make out, the odds did not appear to be in their favor.

Because of accidents like this mess, he worried how he was going to earn his way to the kind of life the yellow-haired girl had. Staying gainfully employed was tougher than he'd anticipated, starting with getting fired from the jewelry store for pocketing a thin gold chain for Grandma, a chain of break-ins along his newspaper route, a multitude of similar mishaps at other jobs he'd found and lost, and explained why he drove for Ray.

Someone shouted, as a car swerved at top speed straight toward them. Longtree's car forced guys into the snow ditch, before skidding to a stop a few feet from the cable. Men charged the car and hauled out Longtree and his brother. Smiling and reeling barefooted and bare-chested in the snow, Brother held out a jug of wine.

Billy had wished for them to show up with their wine bottle. Now seeing their poverty in full view of everyone, he cringed with embarrassment. Out of the corner of his eye, he saw a guy grab Brother with a raised fist.

Without thinking, Billy ran through the crowd of fuming men. "This here's Longtree and his brother," he said, real quiet and polite-like. "They were kind enough to help us out last night. I'd prefer nothing happen to them. If you don't mind."

The guy stared at him for a long time without moving. Billy stuck out his chest to let him know he was not one to mess with, and positioned himself between Longtree and Brother and the group of men. Ray casually strolled over and stood by Billy's side, surprising him to no end. Knowing Ray had his back, Billy lifted his chin. Even so, he hoped with everything he had, it didn't come down to a fistfight.

"Dammed Indian pieces of shit."

Billy winced and squared his shoulders.

The guy let go of Brother and spit.

"Start up the van," called the man with the cable secured to the front axle of the cab.

At the sudden break of tension, the air rushed out of Billy's lungs, and standing his ground took real effort. Ray sauntered to his moving van, pulling most of the men along with him and leaving Billy with Longtree and Brother. Without the wind and the snow, Ray was able to fling open the door and scramble inside.

The rest of the red-faced men left to watch, muttering racial slurs under their breath. The guy ready to slug Longtree's brother stayed.

Nervous as hell that the trailer was going to keel over, Billy clenched his jaw as the driver pulled the wench handle in gear. The cable started rewinding on the spool and, damn, the rig moved. Immediately, arguments started over bets. Finally, the last of the hostile guys joined the others.

With everyone watching the two upright tires edging nearer to the road, Billy wriggled open Longtree's tricky front door. He spun the car around, heading back the way it came, just as the cab of the moving van landed on the road and bounced on all six tires. The trailer stayed standing. Everyone cheered.

Overjoyed they'd get in a few good hours of driving before they had to put up for the night, Billy paused to shake hands with Longtree and took a swig of wine from Brother.

Brother clasped his upper arm. "Fellow warrior."

Grinning as part of an elite club, Billy encircled his grip on his arm.

"Let's go, Billy," shouted Ray, having paid the man.

Billy ignored Ray, not ready to move.

Locked together, Brother cautioned Billy not to give up.

"The white owl brings you the girl of your other half," he finished.

Surprised, Billy suddenly remembered what Brother had said the night before about a girl riding a white owl.

"Which girl?" Billy asked.

Longtree revved the engine. Billy held onto Brother, anxious for the answer to his riddle. "What about the girl?" he asked again, with a rasp in his voice.

A twinkle in Brother's eye distracted Billy. The next thing he knew, his friends sped off down the road.

Billy ran after them, waving his arms and shouting.

"Is it Brenda?" His girlfriend with her thrilling tongue had been relentlessly sashaying back and forth across his mind since the beginning of the run. In her hands, he cared not a wit whether their connection was an accident, a fluke, destiny, or chance. Damn. Just thinking about her gave him a hard-on.

Giving up solving the mystery of who Brother was talking about, Billy raced back the way he'd come to finish the run with Ray. Brother may have meant Brenda, but he also could have been referring to the yellow-haired girl. In early dreams, she appeared as a white owl. Why she'd appeared in his life at all, and in the way she had in the first place and the second—and then only allowing a random flash vision here and there, and withdrawing all together—remained a puzzle to him. His recent sighting of her was another piece of evidence he had tucked away.

Today he'd tried hiding himself, ashamed of Longtree and his brother's poverty and drunkenness, and ashamed of himself for feeling ashamed. Could be the yellow-haired girl was ashamed of something, too. Maybe at the end of the long hallway in his first vision waited the nasty boy. Billy's lip curled, and he swore that if ever given the chance, he'd deliver the kid a punishing lesson.

Crossing the road, Billy looked over his shoulder. Longtree's car turned into two good ponies at a gallop. They took a corner with tires squealing, and then they were gone.

Billy was still there. He'd lived with prejudice against Indians in the valley, but the hatred and disgust he witnessed in the men's faces today shook him. Screw those guys. He wasn't denying his heritage for no one, and that was final. No one. He'd learned something else from Longtree and his brother. If he was ever to become a leader of men like Grandma said, he couldn't be drinking like them. And, driving a moving van with Ray wasn't going to deliver him his dream of fulfilling her prophecy either. He'd have to find him another job, one better suited to him. What that job might be eluded him at the moment. Alls he knew was, on that job and whatever else he did in life, he would never again turn away from who he was.

PART THREE

MEANWHILE

1962 - JUNE

The priest put Billy, Ma, and Grandma in a little side room at the back of the Catholic Church in downtown Oakland. A rack of faded blue choir robes faced Billy, but he wasn't there to sing in no choir. He was five months shy of turning eighteen years old. Today was his wedding day.

Heat overtook Billy, but the feeling of being suffocated had nothing to do with the weather. Only one thing would bring him relief, and that was keeping Ma from causing a ruckus. The last thing he needed was for her to pull Brenda's mother into a catfight, like the one Ma had started with a neighbor woman a couple of months back. Not that Brenda's mother was the type to scratch and scream and pull someone's hair out, not by a long shot. But with Ma, you just never knew. She brought out the worst in people.

"Brenda got pregnant on purpose," Ma said, rising from the bench next to Grandma and wandering to a stack of velvet green chairs stuck off in a dark corner.

"She wants to tie you down," Ma said, running a hand over the fabric without looking at him. "D'you know that, son? Likely ain't even yours."

At her mention of what was growing in Brenda's belly, Billy's breath stalled out.

Grandma hobbled to Ma on silent moccasins, favoring her right hip. She'd gotten older since he'd last seen her in the valley. Hairdressers at the neighborhood beauty parlor curled her hair this morning, but couldn't bring back her shiny black hair.

"Jessie Mae, keep your voice down." She put a hand on Ma's arm. "People are bound to hear you."

The thought of Brenda's family sitting in the pews, waiting for him to step out and the ceremony to begin, caused his breath to rattle. If her three older sisters overheard any of this, their tormenting of him would only intensify. He rubbed his hands against his slacks and was immediately offended when the pant leg turned shiny.

"I don't give a damn who hears me. All them people ought to know just how I feel about this goddamn wedding." Ma raised her voice at the swearing part loud enough that even people still in the parking lot ought to be able to hear just fine.

"I had something to do with it, too," Billy said, deadly quiet. "You oughta know all about that. That's what you tried. Getting pregnant thinking you could tie down my pa, whoever he was. We both know that trick doesn't work, now don't we?"

By the end of speaking all them words, Billy was wheezing and wondering what the hell was wrong with his breathing. Ma raised a hand but instead of slapping him upside the head, she turned her back and crossed her arms. Buttons running down the back of her one good dress gaped open. Doughy skin showed on either side of the thick fastening of a dingy brassiere.

"You ain't going to find what you need with her, baby," said Ma. "You ain't even found it in yourself yet. I can't talk any sense to him," she said to Grandma.

Billy rolled his eyes. The room's one light flickered overhead as Grandma smoothed a hand over the top of his hand. At her touch, he stood real still. She smelled of the outdoors and burning wood.

Grandma didn't look so Indian anymore, with her braid gone and all her hair turned white. If he squinted, even her long turquoise skirt and bright red, hand-woven belt fit in with what some of the fashionable women were wearing nowadays, sort of anyway. Still, she walked and moved like a Potowatomi.

"You decide to leave," started Ma, opening the door. "I'll be at your side."

She strolled into the hallway, even darker than the room, and shut the door behind her. Footsteps sounded in the hallway. Then nothing. The release of tension made Billy slump.

"You sure you want to do this?" Grandma cooed softly.

Surprised by the question, Billy thought about his answer. He nodded yes, though being sure wasn't really at all how he was feeling.

"You doing this because your ma don't want you to?"

He said nothing to that.

"Do you love Brenda?"

"Everything I know about love comes from you, Grandma."

"Does Brenda love you?"

"All along I been so sure I was doing right by marrying Brenda. Now with Ma spouting off, my thinking's all messed up."

"You always longed for a settled down family." Grandma dug into a pocket of her dress. "When you were just a little boy, I told you about the trail of tears.

Back in the days before our people had the slightest notion of such sadness, when my mother's mother still lived in the North, she was given this on her wedding day."

Deep in her own world, she placed a tiny wooden carving in the palm of his hand. Billy held up to the light a wolf no larger than a dime. The carving smelled of high mountains and tears.

"It's a timber wolf," she said. "Your great-grandfather carved it for my mother's mother."

"Little guy sure has lasted a long time." He whistled at the accomplishment.

"Wolves steer clear of trouble of any kind. My grandmother never caused any fights and never started any arguments."

Grandma wet her fingers with spit and tried slicking back Billy's hair.

"What happened to her?" he asked, nearly purring. He wanted to keep her talking, anything to keep her near him.

"She lived more than one hundred years. Outlived her husband by sixty of them. She gave this carving to my mother on her wedding day. My mother gave it to me. Your ma never got around to marrying any of you kids' daddies. I want you to have it."

Her eyes sagged at the corners.

"Don't be sad, Grandma."

"I ain't sad. Just you remember, as much as family is important, so is the wild spirit in you. Like your great-grandfather who carved this, you're destined as the leader of men."

Billy slipped the carving in his suit jacket pocket, counting back how many years she'd been telling him that. If he believed it once, doubt dogged him now. The responsibility he felt from this tiny bit of wood gave him a glimpse into what marriage and becoming a father was going to demand of him. His arms turned weak. He didn't know the first thing about being a husband, even less about being a father.

"I'll always love you, Running Wolf. Now, huckleebuck. It's your wedding day."

*   *   *   *   *   *

Come Monday morning, Jack waited outside in his Olds Delta just like every other weekday. Only today, instead of walking out of Ma's basement, Billy strutted from his rental apartment—a man of work and action, married with a baby on the way. Jack took a swig of Everclear from his flask.

John Law drove up beside them in a black and white. Jack hid the flask. The copper passed them and kept going.

"You can't tell me he's five ten," Jack snorted, still stinging from the police department's rejection for not being tall enough.

Sensitive about his height, Jack had been wearing lifters in his cowboy boots and jacking up the seat of his car with bricks to make him sit taller for nearly as long as Billy had known him.

"Ready for your first day?" Jack asked.

More anxious than he'd ever admit to Jack or anyone else, Billy nodded. "I'm ready."

Knowing Billy wouldn't touch the flask of illegal, 100 percent straight alcohol and 180 proof liquor, Jack swallowed another swig and stashed the flask in his jacket pocket for later at the foundry. He didn't mention the wedding, though he'd been there, plastered as usual. When Jack had been married, he used to telephone his wife drunk at the bar—yelling about where the hell was she and accusing her of all sorts of nasty things, and her being home all along. After he'd sober up, he'd say it wasn't his fault—that women could just about drive a man crazy if you let them.

"I read in the newspaper this morning there's a pill that can stop a woman from getting pregnant," said Jack, one arm stretched across the length of the bench seat, the other resting in the open window with his index finger hooked in a spoke of the steering wheel.

"That so?" Billy said, thinking to himself: *medical miracle.*

"Yup. A doctor gives them to you. Pretty expensive, I hear."

Rather than drive straight to the foundry as usual, today Jack drove to 71st Avenue and MacArthur Boulevard. A blown furnace at the steel foundry had convinced Billy that his time for working with molten iron was over. Guys torched a lot worse than him had been taken to the burn unit at Saint Mary's Hospital. Burns seared across the small of Billy's back and gouged into the middle of his calves took a couple of months to heal, and now scabs were waiting to fall off.

None of the guys from the foundry had been invited to the wedding. Brenda's mother didn't think any of them qualified as family or friends. Billy did stand up about Webb from his old neighborhood. Against all her objections about inviting a Negro to the wedding, he insisted Webb was his best man and had to be there. Then Webb went and lied about his age, joined the Marines, and didn't come after all. A week ago, he'd shipped off to Vietnam.

Jack stopped at the cyclone gate to General Motor's

Fisher Body automobile factory, the same plant Billy had driven past all his adult life. Light-headed in anticipation of what was coming, he did his best to slick back his hair and got out of the car.

"Ain't going to make the kind of money you're used to making at the foundry," cautioned Jack.

"I plan to do double shifts at first. Two-forty an hour ain't much, I agree. But the pay is a whole lot better than the office jobs I looked into. The guy who hired me said my hourly goes up in ninety days. Then I'll be doing better," explained Billy.

Jack raised his eyebrows and cocked his head, showing he believed Billy was crazy to leave the foundry and fooling himself about the benefits of working on the line.

Just another example of no one thinking Billy could do it, give the best to his wife and child, and succeed. He found himself wondering, too, lately, quickly learning how much money it was taking to have a baby.

Factory noise slapped against the supervisor's words, as Billy did his best to follow him, squeezing past moving cars, dodging welding sparks, and ducking under automated machinery. Cars never stopped moving on the assembly line. Every sixty seconds, another car was built.

Some jobs appeared a lot harder than others. They passed a heavy-set guy hustling to pick up parts, set down tools, climb on and off the car, and then start all over again. He had the sorriest look on his face and was sweating heavy.

The supervisor left Billy at his station with a cold look and a warning.

"Doing your job at the right pace without making any mistakes?" he said, like asking a question. "Not going to be easy."

Six thousand men worked two separate shifts. Three o'clock in the afternoon to midnight suited Billy just fine. With those hours, he should be able to spend some time with Brenda, too, though he wasn't holding his breath. She'd taken real good care of him the first few days after the explosion at the foundry, tending to his wounds. Then, before long, she was happier when he wasn't at the apartment. The bigger the baby grew inside her, the more she pushed him away. Seemed she preferred discussing baby clothes with her sisters than to be with him.

Two-thirty the next morning, he stumbled home and into the bathroom. Not wanting to wake her, he closed the door before turning on the light. Glare off the white walls blinded him, and he fell against the toilet seat. Brenda moaned in her sleep as Billy untied his shoelaces and, taking his time and trying to be gentle, struggled to yank off his socks.

A guy on the line next to Billy had advised him to buy himself rubber-soled shoes. He figured that out on his own after the first few rotations of squatting and jumping in Corvairs and Chevy IIs—what with all the twisting and turning needed to install carpet and screw in the trim around the headliners, and then jump out again.

White socks at the ankles were stained black from popped blood blisters. He filled the bottom of the bathtub with warm water and groaned at the sting, easing his feet in, socks and all. As he watched the water turn pink, Billy decided Jack was right. First thing in the morning, he'd see about getting his job back at the foundry.

When he woke up, Billy felt differently and

reconsidered. The guys were all right, their storytelling and jokes made the monotony bearable, and there was room for advancement. He'd give it another try. By two o'clock, he started dreading the thought of work. At four o'clock he was back on the line, only today he wore rubber-soled canvas shoes with a little give. He'd had to borrow money from Jack to pay for the new shoes.

The auto parts for the assembly plant were made in Detroit, shipped to San Pablo, and assembled at the factory into finished General Motor's cars. A conveyer belt pulled a line of partially built automobiles through a long tunnel, bringing the work to him rather than him having to cross back and forth like work at the foundry. The factory was stifling, but compared to working next to roaring furnaces, the temperature was downright balmy. Even so, all day long, with his feet throbbing and his back aching, he imagined walking out. Only thing stopping him was not wanting to mess things up for the guys he worked with on the line. Somehow, he made it to quitting time.

The next morning, Billy was back at it again. It was for the money. If he could last ninety days and keep his eyes open, he'd earn an hourly rate higher than at the foundry and better provide for his family. The earplugs he'd bought blocked most of the shrillness of the drill and the machine gun racket from air-pressured wrenches. While he was planning his life, he became aware of his stomach grumbling. The lunch break whistle sounded.

Malakaton, a giant of a man who worked beside Billy installing the package tray in the back window, lumbered up beside him, humming one of the Hawaiian songs he was all the time singing. Up close,

Malakaton—or Mal as the guys called him—was even bigger than he first appeared. Not that he was much taller than Billy, maybe six feet, two inches, but Mal had to weigh in at least 300 pounds. How he got in and out of the cars to do his job was a mystery.

"Find a way to turn the routine into a song," Mal said. "Hypnotize yourself to it. Work as hard and as fast as you can, and keep your mouth shut. Survive for ninety days and Local 1550 will take you. With the union behind you, you protest this job of yours."

"Protest," Billy repeated, trying to keep up.

"You're doing the work of two men. You know that, don't you?" asked Mal.

Billy shook his head no.

"Work standards are a contractual area," Mal continued, rooting around in his breast pocket. "It's between you and your committeeman. He'll take care of you, but you're going to have to ride him to get anything done. Union reps aren't what they used to be."

To Billy's surprise, Mal flipped him a tiny white pill.

"What's this?" Billy asked, catching it. As he looked from the pile growing in his hand to Mal, Billy paused to nod at the fellas gathering around them.

"They'll give you energy and make you feel good," said Mal. "You better get yourself a load of Benzedrine because if you want to be taken seriously by the men in here, you're going to have to work twice as hard."

"Why's that?"

"Because you're white, and you're young, and you got you a good-looking face."

* * * * * *

"Hey, kid. You want to work a double?" Shouting over the noise of the factory, the supervisor kicked Billy in the sole of his shoe.

On his knees, Billy nodded without stopping installing carpet.

After that, he worked every bit of double time he could get, filling in for guys who failed to show up the day after payday. Seven in the morning to three-thirty, and then double back from four in the afternoon to one in the morning earned him more than twice his regular salary.

While he was keeping his mouth shut and working his tail off, life outside the factory speeded up. Brenda gave birth to a tiny baby girl they named Lisa May Wolf. Right after, he convinced Brenda to take the Pill, pleading for time to practice this father business with one. She wanted more kids real bad, so watching her swallow that first pill made him feel like she finally understood their money situation, and they were working together. He started carrying Grandma's carving in his pocket for good luck. His breathing even got a little better.

On the other side of the country, Joan Baez and Bob Dylan sang *Only A Pawn In Their Game* at the foot of the Lincoln Memorial, during Martin Luther King's march on Washington. Eighteen days later, a bomb went off at a Sunday school in Birmingham, Alabama. Four little Negro girls were killed.

*　　*　　*　　*　　*　　*

On November 22, 1963, Billy crammed a bent piece of trim around the headliner of a Chevy II. The more frustrated he grew, the more fiercely he prayed for a break.

Words boomed across the loudspeaker system.

"President John Fitzgerald Kennedy is dead."

Shouts ricocheted across the factory.

"I repeat. President Kennedy has been shot and killed."

They walked off the line in a show of respect.

* * * * * *

Four months passed, and still Brenda wasn't over Kennedy dying. Even with his assassination, she hadn't stopped believing in life like *Leave It To Beaver*. For Billy, the vision he'd been following faded a little more everyday, but he hadn't lost hold of how things were supposed to look. If the days Brenda longed for actually ever did exist, they just might be over now forever. And not just because Kennedy was dead, but because of how he died.

Johnson took office, giving speeches about "building a great society, a place where the meaning of man's life matched the marvels of man's labor," whatever the hell that meant. The factory moved to a new plant out in the Fremont sticks. They bought a little two-bedroom house that nightly, when Billy walked through the door to his wife and daughter, softened his cynical heart. The bills kept piling, as Brenda bought plates and sheets and things she said were necessary. He worked every bit of overtime and all the double shifts he could get.

At least the job was getting a little better. He joined the United Automobile Workers union and, just like Mal told him to, Billy complained to his committeeman about his job. With only the vaguest idea how things ran, he made a point every day to go to the glassed-in office, where guys in the factory saw him harass his committeeman to stand up for his contractual rights. The last time he stalked by, his reflection in the windows looked like an Indian staring back at him. The next day, Billy got a crew cut.

Finally, management hired another guy to install carpet. Now all Billy had to do was screw in headliners morning, noon, and night. This was the first union he'd ever known. Thanks to them, his pay didn't go down. That, and the protective gloves and goggles, medical benefits, and bathroom breaks—all thanks to the union—and still the grind was grueling.

DECISION

Like most days, Billy didn't wake up until noon. He rested a hand on either side of the bathroom sink and leaned straight-armed over the basin, dropped his head between his shoulders, and closed his eyes. His breathing deepened, and his arms turned to upholstery stuffing. He jerked, listed backwards, and clutched the medicine cabinet to steady himself.

He drove to the factory with one hand on the steering wheel, the other hand working the carving between his fingers. With all the work he'd been doing, he often forgot what day it was. And the seasons? Forget it. Today the cherry tree blossomed, and green wrapped the east foothills. When he'd lived with Grandma, their entire lives revolved around the outdoors—her rituals and little kitchen garden, hunting and fishing, and getting by. With the schedule he was keeping, Billy worried how he was going to be able to give the good parts to his daughter.

At work, he ran goo along the inside of the headliner and screwed it in, just like he did the one before that and the one before that and all them he'd done last week and all the months before. He didn't even notice, his mind crowded with dreams of buying a station wagon and trying to estimate when he'd have enough money saved up to give Grandma a new roof, his life filled with a hundred ambitions.

"Billy. Billy Wayman. That was the break whistle."

Startled, he leaned back on his haunches and blinked up at Malakaton.

"You all right?" asked Mal.

Mal put a hand under Billy's arm and boosted him to his feet in a shot. Mal shook him a little as if to help straighten out his joints.

A guy with red hair and a freckled face stepped over from the next line and leaned in on Billy until he was pressed against the car he'd been working on and couldn't go any further. He smelled stale coffee on the guy's breath. Billy cleared his throat and gave his immediate attention. Feeling for the carving in his pocket, he hoped this wasn't going to turn out bad.

"Billy, Red. Red, Billy," said Mal.

Everyone was on a break, and the line was off. Still, guys on either side ran drills without stopping. The pattern was different than what they usually followed and could almost be used as a cover for the bloodshed these guys had planned for him. A dull ache bruised Billy's chest, making it tough to breathe.

"We're walking out today. What do you think of that?"

Red spoke so low, Billy had trouble hearing him over the drilling. He glanced at Mal, hoping for a clue. Mal scanned the factory.

"Where're you going?" Billy asked, slumped and suddenly weary.

"On strike."

The word sent a chill across Billy's neck, and he coughed.

"A new facility means a new contract," said Mal.

"Management is threatening to take away benefits, things we fought for and won just a few years ago. Only one way to get them to listen—strike. We had to keep it from everyone until today. If the board finds out before we pull off the strike, they'll stop us cold."

Billy remembered reading something in the union manual when he first joined about the membership voting to strike.

"Hell, that's if it's sanctioned," said Red.

"Then there'd be ballots, and everything would be certified all neat and tidy," said Mal.

"This one ain't going be like that. Hell, this one's going to be real messy," said Red.

Billy was doing his best to understand what was happening and keep his breathing steady at the same time. As fast as Mal and Red threw the conversation back and forth, he felt like he was watching a ping-pong tournament.

"The entire membership walks out at the same time," Mal explained, lowering his voice and choosing his words carefully. "It's the only way we can show our opposition to the factory officials and our elected union officials. They're as bad as management."

Billy felt a quick excitement and heard himself asking, "What about our pay?"

"Strike benefits," said Mal.

"I'm not saying all of us don't pay the price," said Red. "But hell, it's our duty. The union committeemen and board ain't doing what we elected them to do. So, we give them a wildcat strike."

Hemming several times and licking his lips, Billy shook his head.

"Illegal," said Mal, looking over their heads again. "Unsanctioned. And there's only one way it's going to work. Everyone's got to be with us on this. Do you understand?"

"Hell, sure he does." said Red, his voice coming out of a great gaping hole. "You with us?"

Stalling for time, Billy hesitated and started wheezing. Least, if they walked out, he'd have time for that doctor's appointment he'd been putting off, though without enough money to pay for the visit.

"I got a new baby. I'm barely making it as it is," he said, surprised to hear himself put his business right out in the open.

There was a pause, and then Red grunted.

"Didn't figure you for a family man, you being so young and all. Sure, it'll be hard. You don't have to tell us that."

"What if you get hurt on the job?" asked Mal. "Stripped of all your benefits, then where'd you be?"

"Back to before," Billy muttered.

Leroy, at his old job, died from burns a month after the foundry explosion, and his family got nothing. Billy couldn't do nothing about that. Here he was being given a choice. All the other guys with families were in for this. Seemed he had him two options. Play safe, which meant he was a broken man and might as well give up on life right then. Or, feeling reckless, Billy could follow the path of the wolf.

"What do we do?"

*   *   *   *   *   *

At five fifteen the factory official handed Billy his check. Billy avoided looking the official in the eye, afraid he'd know what they were up to. Mal only talked about what happened if the UAW officers learned what they aimed to do. Billy didn't even want to imagine what the guards and company men would do to them after firing them first. Then, there was Brenda. She was going to have a wall-eyed fit when she found out this was his last full paycheck for a while. He was going have to get him another job, maybe two or three, until the strike was over.

He slipped the check in the pocket with his carving and glanced at Mal. The two of them looked at Red, who nodded. Billy walked in silence, following the line of yellow paint running down the aisle to three guys adding windshield wipers, the battery, and front bumper to the same car. When they saw him, they dropped their tools. In the pit beneath the car, three guys stopped attaching the gasoline tank and greasing the chassis, and scrambled out.

Rubbing the carving for luck must be working because all the guys in line were raring to go—which sort of surprised him, what with Christmas coming before long. He whispered for them to wait until he was at the end. When he started back, they would meet up with the rest of the guys in the middle and walk out together, just like Red said.

Getting hotter by the minute and trying to breathe, he hurried past the guys who tested the headlights and turn signals and put gasoline in the tank. He'd never given much thought to the three-foot shadows encircling the guys on the line. Only now, up-close did he realize they weren't shadows. Each guy stood in his own puddle of sweat.

Everyone called Harvey—the very last guy on the line—Skypiece, for the felt hat he wore off-duty. He was a real old Negro, and liked nothing better than telling Billy how he'd been working on the line longer than Billy had been alive.

The little pouch on Skypiece's belt for his punch tool was open, and he punched the final inspection card for the bright orange GTO without acknowledging Billy. Skypiece was a real loyal type of guy and, knowing how he felt about the place, Billy figured he best go slow. Though with sweat pouring off his face, and his shirt sticking to his back and steam clouding his eyes, he'd have to be careful not to boil over.

"Nice car," Billy said, wiping an arm across his forehead.

"Custom job for some kid's birthday," said Skypiece.

Through the open car door, Billy smoothed a hand over the leather seat, watching Skypiece work in silence, circling chalk around a ding Billy couldn't even see. Usually, repairs were made after the car left the line, custom cars always first. With everyone walking out, he wondered how long before the dent got fixed. An impossible question, just like how to convince Skypiece to lead the guys out was an impossible question. Billy's breathing was so bad the pain hammered his chest.

"My daddy lined up every morning at the factory gate in the thirties," Skypiece said, testing the door by swinging it back and forth. "Company prizefighters and goons enforced the rules and were always a lot harder on colored workers than whites. If Walter Reuther hadn't come along, there wouldn't be a UAW. And without the UAW, we wouldn't have the benefits we've got now. They protect all of us. A wildcat strike messes with the order of things."

Pushing Billy aside, Skypiece thrust out a grease can for him to hold, and smeared a dab of the black lubricant across the door hinge.

"You okay, kid? You look a little pale," said

Skypiece, still working.

Unable to restrain himself any longer, Billy dropped the can. With sticky fingers, he rubbed his good luck piece with a vengeance and asked for Skypiece's decision by raising his eyebrows, *now or never.*

Skypiece tossed the inspection card on the dashboard. "Surprised, huh?" he said, pulling his favorite hat from his back pocket. "Look kid, someday a moment will present itself to you. When that moment comes, don't turn your back on it because you're scared of losing what little you got. If you do, you'll spend every day after regretting it. Every man is best suited for one job only. This one's mine. You still have yours to find."

Skypiece turned up the felt edges of his hat. "Let's go!" he exclaimed and slapped Billy on the back.

The wolf carving popped out of Billy's hand. He reached out for it and missed as it sailed through the car window and landed in the gap of the passenger bucket seat.

"Company driver's coming. Let's get out of here," cautioned Skypiece.

Leaning through the window, Billy stretched for the carving. Just out of his reach, he grimaced at the time he'd lose opening the door and grabbing it. With regret, and refusing to look back, he hustled to join forces with the rest of the guys—rubbing black goo that was stuck to his fingers across both his cheeks. A rush of adrenaline shot straight up his spine.

War paint.

THE WOLF

A month after Maj's sixteenth birthday, Daddy turned into the brand-new, and nearly empty, high school parking lot driving a bright orange GTO. From where Maj stood on the sidewalk with her friends, the car looked like a sleek and powerful wolf.

Jumping up and down, her friend Linda waved her arms over her head. "It's here!" she shouted.

Standing behind Linda like a screen, Sam caught one of Linda's arms. Dana held down the other. Linda chewed gum a hundred miles an hour. The four of them had been smoking pot together, and when Linda got high, she tended to overexcite.

The car roared. Gravel spit. Sweeping hair from her face with a wide cloth headband, Maj took a better look at the car Mother believed would teach her assertiveness and confidence. It was gigantic compared to the tiny brochure picture, and appeared as if it could crush anyone who tried to hurt her. In an arousal of aggression, she imagined mowing down mean people and making the world a safe place. The car looked equally capable of devouring her, too.

Daddy steered toward them. From a deafening growl to grumbling, when the car was right in front of her, the engine nearly purred. He turned off the key. The car leaped forward. Maj grimaced.

As excited as she was about having her own car, driving a stick shift was tricky. Even the few months of extra practice with Daddy because of problems at the automobile factory, something about a strike, she shuddered at the thought of taming this beast.

Cool and spring-like in a blue seersucker suit, Daddy pushed up his black-rimmed glasses and held the car door open for her. Dana ran to the other side, Sam in her wake.

"Happy birthday, kiddo," Daddy said.

Six different things Maj wanted to say became one simple smile. After years of speech therapy, she spoke well enough to be understood. The difficulty now was deciding which were the right words to pluck out of a mob of confusing feelings. She recognized fear and didn't know how to ask for help.

At the sweep of his arm, she slipped into the driver's seat, hoping he wouldn't smell the pot. Then again, if he knew she was loaded, he'd insist on knowing where she'd gotten it—Brad, star quarterback and her snazzy dresser boyfriend in color-coordinated golfing attire— one day all purple like a grape, another all green or yellow or red, strutting around school like a peacock. Daddy would make sure she never saw Brad again, and he wouldn't let her drive. Maybe she could use that as an excuse to get out of driving this brute.

Inside, the car was close and intimate, like the cockpits of Daddy's friends' private airplanes. The leather smelled like a new doll, and the familiar scent made her giggle. She wrapped a hand around the wooden gearshift knob and practiced flicking it from side-to-side. Her smile faded at the car keys dangling from Daddy's fingers as he stood by her door.

He looked as doubtful as she felt. "Ready?"

"Let's go!" Maj shouted.

Linda pushed past Daddy and hopped in the back seat. She licked her tongue against the leather and scrunched up her face.

Daddy gave Maj a reassuring smile, shut her door, and made his way around the car to the passenger side.

"We'll cruise the strip in style!" shouted Dana, climbing in the back seat wild-eyed and leaving Sam alone outside.

When Daddy came around the car and spotted Sam standing there, he stopped. She had been standing there all along, but with the car hiding most of her, this was his first real look. Sam wore only a two-piece bathing suit.

"Hello, Mr. Hawthorne," said Sam.

Maj held her breath. Dana and Linda crowded to the side window to watch Daddy and Sam outside. His eyebrows shot up and his thick black glasses fogged over. He stuck his hands in his pockets, staring steadily into Sam's face, not once dropping his gaze to the rest of her. Sam's laugh was deep like a man, her body curved like a woman. She could never be a high-fashion model with a figure like that. Not that she'd want to anyway.

"Challenging the system, sir," said Sam.

Sam's act of defiance in wearing a bikini to school came out of a committee Maj and her friends had served on together the summer before their freshman year. As a group, they decided things about their new school, like the colors: red and gold; mascot: mustangs; motto: freedom means responsibility; and the rules: none. If they wanted to, students went to class. If not, they didn't. Mother's influence had assured Maj a spot on the committee. She wasn't expected to say anything, and she liked serving. At the time, she and the others believed the principal and their parents would never agree to their no-rules policy. Now, their freedoms seemed natural, and having a car of her own added to the possibilities.

Daddy cleared his throat. "Does your father know about this?"

Sam turned pale. "I'm sure he will," she said, raising her eyebrows and joining Linda and Dana in the back seat.

Still standing outside the car, Daddy glanced at Maj's three friends and more slowly to Maj.

She flushed and avoided meeting his eye. "Come on, Daddy."

She switched on the car radio and spun on high Bob Dylan singing *The Times They Are A-Changin*. Motioning to Daddy, she smoothed a hand across the soft brown leather passenger seat. Bumping up against something buried in the gap, Maj wrapped her fingers around a tiny piece of wood, no larger than the bristly part of a toothbrush.

Daddy slipped into the car. With eyes glittering, Maj showed him the small carving.

He held up to sunlight a howling wolf. "You found it in the car?" He looked at her oddly and thrust out his chin like nudging her awake.

"Stuck between the seat," Maj said after a pause, her heart pulsing in her ears so hard she could barely hear herself talk.

Pinching her thumb and forefinger together, a vision flashed like a mirror in the sunlight. Curious, Maj smelled a faint hint of grease on her fingers. Wondering how the little guy got so tacky, she tried to recover from the unexpected thrill of finding the carving.

The tip of the wolf's tail was missing, and a tiny crack ran from snout to forehead. The wood inside the split was redder than the polished patina covering the rest of the piece. His ears plastered back, worn and smooth and tiny. His front stance was solid, one foot a bit in front of the other.

Daddy wiped the carving with his handkerchief and dropped it in her outstretched hand. A feeling of hope warmed a rod of loneliness inside. Two months ago, a month before Maj's sixteenth birthday, MorMor died in her sleep. Mother retreated to her bedroom, leaving Maj grieved and on her own. Before long, Great Oaks withered into a lonely place to live.

"Your mother wanted to be here, but she's flying out tomorrow," said Daddy. "There was a last-minute cancellation for that painting retreat in Spain she wanted to attend. The trip will do her good. Take her mind off MorMor. She's packing now. She said to be sure to tell you she'll be at dinner tonight."

Straightening his long, narrow tie and positioning the tie clasp just so, Daddy was completely composed in the constrained way he acted when he was uncomfortable and had to face Maj with disappointment.

Maj was so startled at the news of Mother leaving the country that any response she may have pulled from her mind completely vanished. She pushed back tears, and then wondered why she cared. Depending on Carmen and Ramon to greet Maj when she got home from school, Mother had been absent from Great Oaks in the afternoons for a long, long time.

The recess bell echoed off the hill behind the parking lot. In seconds, kids would parade out of temporary classrooms. Brad's debate class was near enough to the parking lot that, if he were looking, he was likely frowning. Not at all keen about Maj having her own car, he preferred that she depended on him to drive her.

She slipped the wolf in the pocket of her Capri pants and, not feeling so all-alone anymore, turned the key and punched the accelerator. The car roared. Linda screamed.

Daddy grabbed the dashboard and pushed up his glasses. "Alrighty now, kiddo."

"Let's go!" cried Maj.

She rammed the gearshift into first, lifted her foot off the clutch, and pressed down on the gas. The car stalled. On her third try she got the car going, tires squealing all the way out of the parking lot.

* * * * * *

Two days later, the weather was cool and windy. Before dressing for school, first Maj slung over her head a long necklace she'd made with a rawhide cord Ramon cut for her, and she had managed to push through a tiny hole at the top of the wolf carving. MorMor had said once that in Sweden, the spirit of growing crops took the form of a wolf, and when the wind rippled like waves across the ripening fields, a wolf passed through. A sweet feeling blossomed that the wolf was a gift from MorMor destined for her.

Over the necklace, Maj wore the same sort of shirtwaist dress, buttoned all the way up, that Mother liked. But where Mother's dresses were monochromatic pastels, the dresses Maj wore were shorter and richer in color. She threw a ribbed cardigan over her shoulders.

Feeling confident with the wolf around her neck and her newfound independence, she trotted down the hallway to breakfast, only to find Daddy had already left for work. Though she shivered at the thought of driving her new car to school alone, she'd survived the drive all the way to San Francisco yesterday, and besides, all her rehearsals to borrow Mother's car sounded ungrateful to her. She should have just let Brad drive her to school.

Mother had flown off, even knowing she'd promised to go with Maj to the modeling job Jimmy had assigned. Ever since Mother's surprising show at the photographer's studio years ago, she'd been separating herself from Maj's modeling career a little more each year. Maj had started this in the first place to please Mother. Now that Mother obviously couldn't be bothered at all, Maj couldn't find any reason why she should bother.

On the wooden bridge, leaving the ancient and rambling Great Oaks estate started by Daddy's great grandfather, the car jerked and came to a stop. Ready to give up and ditch the car, Maj drew strength from the badgers' and beavers' and bears' totem pole faces grinning at her from either side of the entrance to the bridge. She took a deep breath to start again just as a turkey vulture soared over the greening hillside. The giant bird swerved, caught a wind current, and disappeared into the haze.

Maj got the GTO started. Traveled inches. Stalled again. She squished her left foot against the clutch, shoved the car in gear, and popped up on the clutch. The car died. With her confidence fading, she thought about leaving the car and hitchhiking the rest of the way to school. She nailed her foot against the clutch, restarted the car, and pushed down on the accelerator. The louder the car screamed, the hotter her face turned.

Daddy's voice came to her from a long tunnel. "Ease out on the clutch. Slooooowly."

Her neck snapped back, and she was off like a shot

At school, Maj cut third period with her friends, and together they hiked up the hill behind their high school. The others tossed their books under a giant live-oak tree and sprawled in the grass. From the pocket of her shorts, Dana pulled a long, slender package of marijuana and rolling papers. Her latest hairstyle—an asymmetric, five-point cut—swung forward, covering an eye.

More slowly, Maj sank to her knees in the crushed, wild mustard meadow, with her chemistry binder clutched to her chest. Not studying molecular structure last night put her way behind. Just as MorMor had warned, Maj had lost her way in school. Modeling was to blame. She was done with her agent and with Mother's insistence that she model.

She let her hair fall forward and hid her face like a waterfall.

"I'm never modeling again," Maj said quietly without looking up.

"Why?" asked Dana, surprise in her voice.

"Never, ever, ever again."

"What happened?" said Linda.

The words out of Maj's mouth were not the ones she'd shouted in the car all the way home yesterday, after losing her way about a hundred times. They were not the words she repeated all night, or the words that awoke her this morning. Rather than all that practice helping, now she couldn't remember even one of the cover-ups she'd made up to hide the humiliation and betrayal she'd felt at the fashion show yesterday.

Irritated for not being as composed as she'd planned, at least the disaster made Maj's decision easier. From now on, school came first, and modeling plunged to the bottom of the list. The wild rhythm of her heart pointed to her apprehension telling Mother of her plans and Maj's doubts she could pull her grades up enough to qualify for college.

Absorbed in her own thoughts, Maj looked up. Surprised to find the three of them staring at her, she blushed.

"Mother promised I'd never have to model in front of people staring at me," Maj said, faltering. "She lied."

Cameras didn't scare her. Posing for photographs was the one place Maj felt in control of the people around her. Runway modeling was awful. From the moment she'd entered the wide arch, formed by rows of Corinthian columns at the Palace of Fine Arts behind a long line of discreet limo sedans, Maj felt ambushed with a horrible sensation that whatever happened was going to end poorly. Mother disappeared, so she didn't have to look Maj in the face and tell her to do something they both knew she was sure to fail.

"The show in the city?" asked Dana.

Maj nodded.

"That's so boss!" exclaimed Dana. "I heard about it on television last night. Designers from all over the world. A fund raiser, right?"

"The only good thing about it," Maj answered, feeling dejected.

"The Palace is being torn down and a permanent copy built," Dana explained, sounding like an expert.

The Palace of Fine Arts was one of the temporary

buildings hosting the 1915 Panama-Pacific International Exposition, an event Daddy, his family, and most San Franciscans felt represented the city's resurrection from the great earthquake of 1906.

"Driving took me forever to get there and then... I don't want to talk about it," Maj blurted after a quiet minute, wondering how she would ever get up enough nerve to tell Mother she wasn't modeling anymore.

Clasping her cold and clammy hands together, Maj drew up her shoulders and sighed. She must have sighed louder than she intended because her friends looked at her uneasy, and Dana passed her the joint.

Smoke filled Maj's lungs, and blood beat against her eyelids. She drew again and then again until her mind stilled. The past melted, and the future vanished. She tilted her face to the sun and felt its warmth on her shoulders. The instantaneous release of tension sent her floating.

"You sure you're okay?" asked Sam.

"Please, just stop looking at me," Maj said in an overly tired voice. "I'm quitting, so I can devote my time to my studies. College."

"But you're good at modeling," cried Linda, her eyebrows popping up.

"You don't need college. Brad will marry you right now," pressed Dana.

"College," Maj repeated, with a warning in her voice and feeling ill at ease. She was grateful when they didn't discuss it any further.

As her friends smoked pot and messed with their make-up, Maj shook back her head, embarrassed by her tears and show of emotion. At least when she modeled, she hid behind layers of makeup, and no one could see her blush.

Waiting for her face to cool, Maj tucked her hair behind her ears and pulled out her notes, hoping for last-minute help. Down the hill, the football team scrimmaged on a muddy field. Brad was easy to spot.

After his game last night, he took Maj home and parked on the street side of the bridge to Great Oaks to smoke pot and make out. He kept saying he wouldn't do anything Maj didn't want him to do, but every time she pushed his hand away, he clawed his way back, pinching and clutching and kneading her skin like a football. It took her nearly an hour to get out of the car, and today she felt beat-up and sore all over. Maj was beginning to wonder if all guys were untrustworthy.

Dana flicked a match and Maj watched her light another joint. Hoping the carving helped her do well on her chemistry test today, Maj retied the rawhide cord like a choker, with the excess cord falling down her back. Instead of bringing the peace like when she found it in the car, today the wolf at her neck trembled, making Maj feel she was standing on shaky ground.

"None of the teachers fell over themselves about my bathing suit like your dad did. I think it's sweet he's such a prude," said Sam. "Your dad is the coolest."

Today being too chilly for something as skimpy as a bikini, Sam wore a traditional cardigan twin set. Having borrowed her mother's cat's-eye sunglasses, Sam pushed back a bob haircut.

Barely able to make out her chemistry notes with her friends' conversation playing in the background, Maj had trouble focusing on the upcoming test.

"I know why Amy's not in school anymore," said Linda, squeezing between Dana and Sam, and smacking her gum. Linda's eyes were glassy and her face shiny in the bubble she blew. The bubble popped.

"She's pregnant!" exclaimed Dana, holding back the swag of hair from her face, taking a long drag and letting out her breath all in a rush.

Dana was obsessed with the idea of going all the way with her boyfriend and terrified of getting pregnant. A wispy cloud settled over them. Dana coughed and handed the joint to Linda.

Linda's eyes were huge. "You think so?"

"You're telling the story, Linda," said Sam, laughing.

Barely listening, Maj flipped through her notes, her fingers leaving sweaty streaks on the pages.

"Amy's dad says our teachers are Communists and corrupting us," explained Linda. "My dad thinks so, too, but he'll let me stay as long as I'm a good girl. A Communist is someone who's brainwashed, right?"

Their experimental high school was radically different than the more established high school across town. Mother had fought John Birchers when they wanted to shut down their new high school.

One teacher had transferred from the old high school. The rest of the teachers were recent graduates from the University of California at Berkeley, the university Maj dreamed of attending in a couple of years. Mother viewed all institutions of higher education as prime locations to snag a rich husband.

"'He loves you, yeah, yeah, yeah,'" Dana started singing. "'With a love like that, you know it can't be wrong.' Are you going to let Brad do it, Maj?"

Even with all three of her friends looking at her, Maj didn't bother answering the same question Dana had been asking about 150 times a day lately.

* * * * * *

Maj watched Brad's scrimmage break up below, and the football team head for the locker room.

Sam eyed Maj through the smoke. "How was dinner with your mother?"

Maj thought before answering, gazing off into the mass of oak tree branches above her.

"Brad was furious she invited Clay instead of him," Maj said in the silence that followed.

"It's weird the way Clay is always hanging around your house," said Linda.

After years of hating and despising how everyone, Mother and Daddy especially, were so taken in by Clay's transparent act: charming to Mother, forthcoming and polite to Daddy and sweet and inviting to her friends, Maj was relieved someone else saw what she already knew was weird, very, very weird and creepy and cruel and wrong.

"I mean he's out of school," said Linda. "He has his own parents."

"I agree," Maj said with much bitterness and nodding her unmistakable agreement.

Sam chimed in. "Weird?" she said. "You've got the coolest parents ever, Maj."

"Did Clay ever try to do it with you, Maj?" asked Dana, on her knees.

A buzzing sounded in Maj's ear.

"I'm telling you straight out," Dana cried, not waiting for Maj's answer and continuing in a whispery voice. "This weekend I'm going all the way with Ronnie."

Dana squealed and pounded both fists on her knees.

Linda leapt to her feet and danced the twist.

Maj had to laugh.

"It's not all you think it is," cautioned Sam.

As the sun crept across the long green football field, and the time for the test was nearly upon her, Maj's stomach curdled.

The lunch bell reached them. Nothing happened below, and then their classmates streamed from buildings like busy ants.

"I've got to ace the test," Maj protested, collecting her papers in her binder and getting to her feet.

"We're coming too," said Linda.

The four of them hiked down the hill together.

"Why don't you like going all the way, Sam?" Dana went on about going all the way like it was going out of style.

"My mom says if I want to marry wearing the white of the Virgin Mary, I have to save myself for my husband," said Linda.

"The white of a virgin," Maj repeated, the buzzing in her ears now a pulsing beat.

"You want to wear white on your wedding day, don't you?" asked Linda.

Maj nodded.

"Then you have to be a virgin, silly," Linda explained.

"Says who?" probed Sam.

Linda spit out her gum and peeled a fresh piece. "Father Frances."

Maj blushed and took a step back, tripping on a dirt clod. Sam steadied her.

"You won't go all the way because Wally will only marry a virgin," said Sam. "Even if he takes it from you, he won't marry you, Linda."

"My virginity is my gift as a bride to her husband."

Linda spoke like an expert.

Dana snorted. "You and Wally do everything else. Doesn't that count?"

"So long as my hymen isn't broken, I'm okay," answered Linda. "In case you don't know that either, Maj, the first time your boyfriend enters you, he breaks your hymen. The spot of blood is a sign to him of your virginity. My mother says that in some countries, people parade the bloody sheets down the center of town for everyone to see."

Linda's words jolted Maj. The white of a virgin. The first time he entered you. Ruby red blood. The smell of burnt metallic. Clay had unleashed *Loki.* When Maj was young and she understood Clay wasn't going to stop, she'd turned into an escape-artist at the first slap of his shoes on the Mexican tiled foyer. She'd sneak to one of her favorite hiding places—protected in the arms of the massive oak tree shading the front of Great Oaks or hidden in Daddy's prized Caddie or tucked inside the ironing bag filled with snowy clean clothes where Carmen often found her sleeping as she pulled out pieces to be ironed.

The few times Clay had caught Maj off-guard, he buried enough dirty feelings of shame and humiliation to remind her just how evil *Loki* truly could be and left her ashamed and unworthy of love. Maj had never considered that he might have taken something that was rightfully hers to give. If Brad knew she wasn't a virgin, he'd likely drop her for head-cheerleader Sara. Maj touched the wolf carving at her neck not to cry.

Dana looped an arm in hers. Maj's ironing board body relaxed, and she let her friend in near.

Brad broke from the crowd with a wave. In his yellow sports shirt and yellow slacks and loafers, he resembled a banana.

"Sam told us when she did it," said Dana, with a sideways glance at Sam. "I'm telling you, I'm doing it this weekend. Linda's still a virgin. You probably are, too. Right, Maj?"

Startled, Maj looked up and winced. After thinking about it for a second, she disengaged from Dana. Taking a long breath, Maj glanced over her shoulder with an expression a photographer had once called coy.

"Wouldn't you like to know?" Maj said, speaking so easily, she surprised herself.

Then she whirled around and ran from her friends, even knowing the bad feelings were all her own fault and not theirs. What happened was a long time ago.

She reached Brad and kissed him hard on the lips.

His face shifted and he roamed her body before linking eyes with her.

"What was that for?" he asked, holding her tight.

"Still want to go out tonight?" she asked.

"I thought you couldn't."

"Now I can," she corrected him.

Arm-in-arm with him to chemistry class, Maj smiled sadly with no reason not to give Brad what he wanted. The pressure of the rawhide cord around her neck made it difficult to swallow.

PART FOUR

DURING

1968 - FEBRUARY

i.

The wildcat strike at the automobile factory taught Billy one thing. Never underestimate management. The workers had gotten so fired up that if their guys had known they were being filmed, even more of them would've jumped on car hoods hollering and screaming. As it was, ten men were fired for the illegal strike, and not one of the changes they went out for came even close to happening.

Now three years later, Billy was the father of three and in worse financial shape than he had been then, except that now he was a union representative and had the added responsibility of taking care of, not only his family, but the guys too. The decision he was expected to make for all them today could break him.

He flicked his cigarette out the car window. The wind sent an ash back into his eye. Squinting, he rolled up the window against a cold February morning. His foot on the accelerator and using his knees to steer, he cupped his hands against his mouth, hoping to warm his blood. Could be the cold making his hands shake or could be the six cups of coffee and fistful of Bennies he'd taken to wake up and get on the road well before dawn and his family stirred.

The idea of tracking down his good luck charm hadn't occurred to Billy until lately, probably because of the pressure he was under. The urgency to feel the wood grain of Grandma's carving against his fingertips had helped him to convince the factory ladies in shipping to give him the address of the orange GTO buyer. That the special order could have come from anywhere in the western states; to find the bright orange GTO so near had Billy speeding.

Nearly at his destination, he pulled off the highway and onto a country road shaded by giant live oak trees. With only a post office box address in Diablo, he practiced what he planned to say to get a postmaster to give him directions to a Hawthorne residence.

The brake lights of the car ahead of him blazed, forcing him to slow down, and then to come to a complete stop. Road construction ahead. He drummed his fingers on the steering wheel, waiting behind a long line of stopped traffic.

After fifteen minutes of waiting and with no sign that the flagman planned on waving them through any time soon, Billy turned around. As tempting as it was to wait as long as it took, just knowing that the answer to what happened to the carving could be within driving distance lightened his mood from abysmal to grey. The decision he had to deliver at work pulled him back to Fremont with the promise he could try again tomorrow.

Aware that the GTO could drive up right beside him at any time, Billy found himself looking for it.

* * * * * *

When the clock on the dashboard showed fifteen minutes before his meeting, Billy was finally forced to give all his attention to the unanswerable dilemma of who to fight management for and who to throw under the bus.

On the other side of the street up ahead, a guy walking a dog suddenly stopped and yanked the leash hard enough to knock the dog off its feet.

"Hey!" Billy shouted.

The guy was an asshole. A quick and mean one, too. Billy slowed down the car.

The guy yanked the leash again and hauled up the shepherd, so it was just hanging there strangled by a choke chain collar. The longer he held the dog in the air, the redder the guy's face turned, and the madder Billy got. The dog had a real pathetic look on its face.

Fuming, Billy stopped the car in the middle of the road and rolled down his window.

"Hey, man, what's the point of that?" Billy worked to keep his voice neutral and spoke only loud enough to be heard. Not in his usual neighborhood, he didn't want to cross any lines, visible or otherwise.

The guy dropped the dog to the ground. "What's it to you?" he said and stomped away, dragging the dog behind him.

The guy was right. The dog was none of Billy's business. Besides, he couldn't afford to be late to his meeting with management this morning. If he hoped to survive as the new union rep, Billy had to be on time with the right decision, and he sure as hell didn't know what that was.

In his rear view mirror, Billy saw the guy yank the dog in the air again. This time, he kicked it in the gut.

Billy threw the car in reverse, tires squealing, and turned the wheel into a skidding stop—cutting off the guy. Billy jumped out of his car.

"Maybe you didn't hear me before." Billy made his voice louder and tried not to wheeze. "I asked you, what's the point of that?"

Now that Billy was standing outside his car, the guy didn't look so tough. As a matter of fact, he looked scared. Billy stood his ground, waiting for the guy to let down the dog, not much older than a puppy. Ready to hit someone, instead, Billy dug his hands in his pockets where he wished for the millionth time he'd find the wolf.

The guy lowered his arms until the dog was back on its feet again. He put both hands in the air and backed up.

"I don't want any trouble, man. You want this piece of shit, take it." The guy threw the leash at him and ran back the way he'd come.

Billy looked down at the dog. He swore it smiled up at him.

"Damn," Billy said, with too many dependents as it was. "Me and my big mouth. When am I going to learn?"

The dog jumped in the front seat of his '58 Chevy without being invited and together they raced to work.

The automobile factory looked like a prison, just how management intended. Security guarded gates in and out. The guys even marked their time working inside according to prison time given for crimes. He wasn't planning on being a lifer, hoping to get out in ten to twenty—grand theft.

Billy drove to the front of the three-mile parking lot, found a spot only about a half a mile away from the factory's front entrance, parked, and opened the door.

"Go, Sister Wolf," Billy said. "Be free."

The dog didn't budge.

"Out," Billy growled. "Git."

The dog still didn't budge, so Billy rolled down his window for her to escape. He reached across to roll down the other window, too. The dog slapped a wet tongue across his ear, leapt over the front seat, and landed squarely in the back. Not wanting any more dog slobber, he left the back windows up. Partway to the guard shack, he looked back. Sister Wolf had her face smashed up against the rearview window. Billy groaned.

* * * * * *

Billy found Webb waiting for him on the catwalk, and together they entered the union office smack in the middle of the plant.

When his buddy from the old neighborhood returned from two tours of duty in Vietnam last year, Billy had convinced Webb to hire on here. As kids, they'd taken to each other right off, and time hadn't done nothing to change that. When union elections came up, damned if Webb didn't get elected union rep himself.

Billy shouted over the noise of the factory. "Where is everyone?"

"Meeting's off," said Webb. "Word has it Alabama's looking for you."

Billy groaned and steeled himself.

"Here he here now." Webb spoke under his breath. Billy's heart stopped in the time it took him to breathe and then sped zero to sixty in a tenth of a second. He lighted a cigarette. Seeing his hands shake slapped sense into him. He sat down so as not to pace. Last thing he wanted was for Alabama to see him nervous. With all expression wiped off his face, Billy swiveled and faced the guy responsible for making his life miserable.

As a matter of prejudice, Alabama would never enter the office with Webb inside. Or so Billy hoped. With the door open, factory noise hammered his ears but didn't interfere none with Billy watching for the knife Alabama managed to smuggle past the guards, just like he slipped inside the factory.

"Being here is only going to make things worse for you," warned Billy.

Alabama nodded toward Webb, his eyes darting from one corner of the factory to the other. "Make him leave."

"We can talk from here," replied Billy, as calmly as he could muster.

Alabama was a painter and a white supremacist. Every faction in here had their supremacists—whites, blacks, and Chicanos alike. The rank and file Alabama controlled were a group of white conservatives, Hells Angels, rednecks, and hillbillies from the valley. Most of the guys Billy represented were part of the two hundred men on the frame line, trim line, and body shop. As Alabama's committeeman, Billy's job was to negotiate Alabama's suspension—when what Billy really wanted was to have Alabama terminated.

Alabama put his hand in his pocket. "I ain't got time for your squawkin' an' talkin'. I want my suspension lifted an' my job back." He flicked the knife from his pocket, still standing on his side of the threshold.

Angry now, Billy scooted to the edge of his seat and scanned the shop floor. The all-glass room felt like swimming in a god-dammed fish bowl. Windows on either side looked out at hanging air guns and metal crossbars, welders, and wires. Lines of cars and trucks and men stretched all the way around in a circle. No guards, of course, but Alabama's guys were out there watching, the rank and file going about their business— some scowling and others grimacing, always with an eye on what was going on in the office.

"I know what I'm doing," said Billy. "Now leave the property before you make a fool of yourself for the second time with that fucking switchblade of yours."

The break whistle blew. Alabama's men gathered on either side of the office.

"You got no call to speak to me like that after what me and my boys did to get you elected, okie-boy," warned Alabama. "You forget what color you are?"

"I appreciate all you did for me in the election," said Billy. "Don't get to thinking that means I'm going kiss your ass. Theirs neither. I ain't."

Alabama's eyes turned dark as he stepped over the threshold. A lead weight slammed against Billy's lungs. Webb didn't move.

Billy spoke as lackadaisical as he could with his heart racing and no breath. "The Hall. An hour."

"You best be careful, okie-boy," said Alabama. "Real careful."

Alabama left and Billy wondered how much more messed up his life could get.

ii.

A half an hour north, lost in her studies, Maj vaguely heard the telephone ringing. She didn't bother getting up to answer it.

"It's for you, Maj!" shouted Nancy.

The upstairs telephone hung on the wall across the hall from Nancy's bedroom, in the Berkeley Victorian Maj shared with two other college roommates.

Maj shouted over *Jimmy Mack,* by Martha and the

Vandellas, on her stereo. "Take a message."

"Maj!"

She threw down her pencil, and left the Greek mythology report due in a couple of hours, with crumpled papers spread haphazardly over her desk. Refusing to look at or acknowledge the poison letter she'd pinned on her bulletin board from her academic advisor, Maj stomping to the telephone and tripped over a pile of books.

The hallway was long with ceilings that soared into darkness in a house once grand and historic, and now old and rundown. The only way to get hot water in the upstairs shower was by running the kitchen faucet downstairs at the same time. Five bedrooms, a parlor where they stored their bikes in the rain, and a giant kitchen—though no one cooked with the corner market just down the block—the house smelled its age, musty and safe.

Walking slowly down the hallway gave Maj time to carefully arrange her demand that Mother limit her calling. Every single morning for two entire years to nag Maj about moving back home was too much. Besides, Maj loved living in Berkeley. Driving into town the first time, she felt like she was coming home and fit in simply for being her.

Everybody in Berkeley was into their own thing and creating excitement. A sense of expectancy hummed— even at night—compared to after seven o'clock at Great Oaks, where only crickets chirped. The Fates, three goddesses she'd chosen for her class paper, demonstrated that Maj had some say in her future by the choices she made. At the moment, she seemed powerless against the mysterious academic probation letter from her creepy advisor. She could do something about Mother's constant interference.

Maj reached the phone, ready with her demand. "You ca—"

"I've arranged for a car brought around to the photographer's studio at precisely six-thirty," said Mother.

Maj groaned. Jimmy must have already received her message that she planned to bail on the photo shoot this afternoon. This car, or whatever Mother had planned, was her insurance that Maj would be at the studio—doing precisely what Mother wanted, as usual.

Cautious now, Maj spoke quickly before Mother hung up.

"I have to—" Almost saying study, Maj stopped herself. Her lie to cover her night out very nearly exposed what Mother had no clue about, and Maj's gravest deception—that she was attending college.

With a pumping heart and hot face, Maj told Mother the truth about tonight.

"Sorry, Mother. I have a date."

The words sent a flutter of excitement through Maj's body.

"I thought you weren't seeing anyone," said Mother.

Twisting the telephone cord between her fingers, Maj confessed. "Well, not really a date. It's more—"

"I was going to tell you tonight in person."

Maj stopped fidgeting. "What is it? Has he stopped eating?"

Along with language, Daddy had lost his sense of smell in a bus accident on a European holiday with Mother. For a year and a half without the automatic trigger for the breakdown of his food, he'd been steadily losing weight. Mother assumed when Maj helped bring Daddy home, she'd put off attending the university. Maj stayed on to help at Great Oaks only until fall. Then, without telling Mother any differently, she went ahead with the classes she'd signed up for. She kept going toward filling requirements toward an undergraduate degree. Maj was ashamed of lying, but one lie forced another, and before long, leaving out the lectures, labs, homework, volunteering at Napa State Hospital on the weekends, and the probation letter became easier than admitting her dishonesty. Mother only knew Maj modeled. Maj only modeled, so she could afford to secretly stay in college and fulfill her promise to MorMor.

"Your father's medical needs are expensive," said Mother. "The last of his investments and all our money have gone to pay for his doctors and therapy. I've done my best, but there is no money left. Just the house, the silver, and the cars."

Mother's words took Maj's breath away. Gasping, she tried to comprehend, watching as if in slow motion as a dust mote floated on a single ray of sunlight through the transom.

At nineteen years old, Maj was in college learning how to help kids form sounds correctly and string words together in the right order, in hopes of one day becoming a speech therapist. On days like today, when she didn't know what to say, words drifted like dust without substance. Pacing until the telephone cord was stretched all the way out, Maj paced back the way she had come. Her stomach rumbled. She wanted a cigarette. A glimmer of hope broke through the landslide.

"Tell Samuel to unlock my modeling money," Maj said in a rush. "There must be enough in my trust to help out at least for a little while."

"We've already raided your account to pay expenses. I regret having to put such a burden on you and at such a young age. Your father's future depends on you."

"Raided my account?" repeated Maj.

She fell against the wall, unable to keep up with Mother's words. Suddenly cold, Maj hugged herself, wishing she'd thrown on a robe. Anything, just so she didn't have to hear Mother and accept what was being demanded of her—to look at everything in her life differently.

"We'll discuss it tonight," finished Mother.

"I have a date," Maj repeated, holding firm to the one thing she was sure of.

Heat from standing up to Mother rose off her pajama collar, turning Maj from cold to hot as she untangled herself from Mother's words.

"For heaven's sake. The opera is *Beauty and the Beast*," said Mother. "You simply must see it. First production in the city since before you were born."

Carmen must have entered the study where Mother was on the telephone because Mother broke into her own conversation to remind Carmen to take care watering the violets, as if by now Carmen didn't know that violets disliked getting their leaves wet, and replace the vase of flowers in the foyer that were beginning to smell old. Mother ended with what Maj was sure had been Mother's initial and intended message.

"Whatever you used on the foyer has turned the tiles into a skating rink. Clean them again, this time with water. We must be careful Mister Hawthorne does not fall," Mother finished, speaking now to Carmen and Maj both.

"Everyone who is anyone will be there tonight," Mother said, turning her full attention back to Maj in a tone that seemed incredulous how anyone could possibly get along without her guidance. "Jimmy guarantees your picture will run on the society page tomorrow. You know what that could mean to your future."

Determined Maj marry well—nobility, mogul, one of San Francisco's finest men—Mother's ambition shaped Maj's life. Today's scheme, in the constant stream to catch Maj a rich husband, was intended to divert her attention from Mother's real message. Model to support the family. The realization that school would be out this time, for real, spread over Maj like a straightjacket. There must be a way around having to give up everything she wanted for the good of everyone else.

"I'm sorry, Mother," Maj said, feeling sorry for herself, too.

"Jimmy hands you an opportunity for good money and a little fame and you refuse it," said Mother. "But you should do what's best for you. I told Samuel we should just sell the house. It's mortgaged, of course, but we'll gain enough money to pay your father's medical bills, at least for a few months, so long as we find a way to live cheaply. Of course, we'll have to let Carmen and Ramon go."

Words fell over Maj like a net. "You wouldn't do that."

"We don't have a choice," said Mother. "You do. Model, or marry a rich husband. For heaven's sake, we can't support you. We couldn't afford a new dress for you tonight, so I borrowed one from Mimi. She wore it once to a private party, and none of our friends were there. Your father expects you. We'll pick you up at six-thirty. Do your best at the shoot today. All of our futures depend on it. *Hej då.*"

iii.

Finding himself standing in front of the file cabinet in the union office, Billy forgot what he was looking for. Webb rifled through a stack of complaints piled up in front of him, making him appear busy.

"The Panthers are lining up behind Skypiece," Webb said.

Billy stared out the windows—on the lookout now, not only for Alabama showing up with even more of his guys, but also watching for Black Panthers, too. Billy had two cases. He could only get one guy's case through and that was if he fought hard and was real lucky. Skypiece or Alabama? Smothered, Billy looked for something to smash.

"The guys are here." Webb nodded out the window to where Mal and Red headed down the walkway.

If Alabama's guys made any trouble now, Billy would be four strong. The two stopped at the bulletin board, where Red crumpled a paper in his fist. He tripped over a loose board and yelled about the safety hazard. After the wildcat strike, and Mal and Red and Billy and Webb were elected union officials, Red started strutting around like a goddamned bantam rooster, and him being uglier than a junkyard dog. Mal dragged Red into the office.

Mal was one of the few guys who didn't fit neatly into any of the one-third white, one-third black, and one-third Chicano factory divisions. Hawaiian and Chinese, Mal was nearly eighty pounds heavier than when Billy had first met him four years ago. He filled up the entire doorway. Billy recognized the Hawaiian tune Mal hummed as a joyful one, a pretty good sign.

"You two seen this?" snapped Red.

Webb smoothed out the latest hand-drawn cartoon posted by the other side in the ongoing battle of the brown-nosers, management lackies, milk toasts, and yes-men versus Billy's dope-smoking revolutionaries, druggies, and alcoholics. The bulletin showed a guy with his eyes bugged out, a joint in one hand, a beer mug in the other, and a slew of electrical wires strung up behind him—most of them connected to his ass. Anyone could tell it was Red by all the freckles.

The caption on the cartoon read: "Wired tighter than P.G.&E."

Ready to laugh, Billy pulled away from the desk, not wanting to piss off Red.

"We're talking about the Panthers," said Webb, dragging Mal and Red into Billy's problem.

"And…" prompted Red, hanging his pea coat over the back of his chair.

"Skypiece lost a finger, brother," said Webb. "If the company had replaced the coupling, the accident wouldn't have happened. The Panthers want the company to pay all his hospital bills and time off."

Billy waited, knowing there had to be more.

"The Panthers want the company to take full responsibility for his accident, in writing," said Webb.

Billy groaned.

"And, they want Alabama fired," finished Webb.

"How the hell am I supposed to do that?" Billy demanded.

"Alabama's agitating for every last Negro in here to be maimed or killed," said Webb.

If Webb hadn't been so firm about keeping to their childhood promise about keeping their shared Indian background a secret, right about now Webb would be sure to remind Billy how if Alabama even suspected that Grandma was a full-blood, Alabama would turn on Billy in less time it took to blink an eye. Later he'd explain he wanted to see the color of a half-breed's blood. And Webb would be right.

Billy squashed out his cigarette butt. The ashtray was too full. He dumped the ashes in the can and watched a paper fire go out.

"Can you get the Panthers to back off?" asked Mal.

Billy stared at Webb, wanting him to look up from filing a complaint in one stack and turning the next form on a second pile.

"Not if Billy rolls over," answered Webb.

Billy kept his eyes trained on him.

"Maybe I can," said Webb after a hesitation. "But that ain't the point."

"What is the point?" Billy snapped, his body beat and jacked up.

"Point is you're white," said Webb. "You never take none of the money you're all the time offered under the table. Never affiliated with any one group in particular. The factory gave you that test and you blew everyone away when you turned down the supervisor position. Everyone. The guys respect you. Management fears you."

Red and Mal nodded with that, Red with a begrudging frown on his face.

"You're the only one who can do this, Billy," urged Webb. "Skypiece has a legitimate grievance. Alabama deserves to be terminated. The Panthers want you to prove you're the man they think you are, by doing the right thing by Skypiece and getting Alabama fired."

Avoiding Billy's eyes, Webb traced a finger from the middle of the table to the wooden edge and back. Red and Mal said Billy was crazy, but he swore that ever since Webb got back from `Nam, he hadn't once look Billy straight in the eye. Billy was spared the draft, so far anyways. Five years ago, the birth of Lisa classified him as 2A. One year later, Summer Rose locked him in at 3A. Then came Melissa last year. Problem was Billy didn't come from money, and he wasn't a college boy. He was only 23 years old, and this war seemed destined to drag on forever.

Unexpectedly, Webb pushed away from the table and crept to the windows, a Green Beret with a cruel streak he never had before Vietnam and just couldn't seem to shake. He wiped away his breath on the glass and stared out into the factory. Webb might be seeing the men. Or, he just as easily saw a jungle full of enemy fire and burning bodies.

"The election's right around the corner," said Red.

Trying for as much sarcasm as he could sling, Billy countered. "Gee, thanks, Red. I nearly forgot."

"Take it easy, Billy," said Red. "You weren't the only one Alabama helped get elected. We owe him, too."

"This is Billy's decision," said Webb. "Let him do what he thinks best."

Red crossed his arms and stared down Billy.

"Election or no election, we're here to give fair representation to all the men equally," said Mal. "You let management fire Alabama over being drunk and disorderly only makes it easier for them to fire the next guy for something not so crazy. Then come the next time, and termination is from conduct even less offensive. We've got to hold the line."

Outside the windows, a line of base frames moved down the conveyer belt from overhead hoists. A workman dropped a dressed engine into place. Another guy hooked up the drive shaft. By the time the first guy took his hoist back to the line of engines, another chassis waited. Neither worker had been issued gloves or protective eye gear.

"The coupling that hurt Skypiece isn't going to get fixed. On or off the record," Billy said.

"That's why the neglect's got to be documented," said Mal. "Same thing happens again, and we've got us an even deeper pattern of collapse recorded. Setting precedent is what we do."

Buried in the belly of this beast, Billy's body felt like a vibrating riveter, and his breathing was off. A couple of years ago, after he couldn't stand Brenda hounding him about going to the doctor, the damned guy told Billy he had asthma and that it was psychosomatic.

"What the hell does that mean?" Billy had demanded.

"Your poor breathing is all in your head," answered the doctor.

Billy had stomped out of the office with the doctor shouting for him to quit smoking and learn how to calm down.

"I'd like to see you try dealing with workers who don't give a damn about your job and management who doesn't give a flying shit about its workers," Billy had shouted over his shoulder.

Now Billy sat still and tried taking long slow breaths.

*   *   *   *   *   *

"I'm going," Billy said. "Alabama with another day of no pay…"

Billy said he was leaving and then didn't get out of the chair, leaving all the possibilities of what could happen with Alabama hanging in the air.

"Before you go, a representative from the United Farm Workers dropped these at the Hall as we were leaving," Red explained, reaching in his chest pocket and spreading four tickets out on the desk like playing cards. "Their thanks for the check we sent the UFW. It's a benefit. Tonight. The Fillmore. Us four are going to listen to this here Carlos Santana and his blues band."

Proud of himself, Red settled in the chair with his hands behind his head. The freckles across his face looked like scattered jigsaw puzzle pieces.

"We are, are we?" said Webb, picking up a ticket and looking it over.

"Hell, you want to support Cesar Chavez and the farm workers, don't you?" Mal slid two chairs together and sat down. "We found out real quick during the wildcat strike what it's like when strike funds run low. Morale suffers. The cause falls short. The United Auto Workers in solidarity with our fellow United Farm Workers brothers. The concert tonight will be good for you, Webb. It'll be good for all of us."

Webb opened his mouth to answer back. Billy stood up first.

"The four of us are going," insisted Red, stopping Billy and slipping the tickets back in his shirt pocket. "Tell them why, Mal."

"I scored."

The furnace kicked on. Stale cigarette smoke rode in on a wave of dry heat.

"Scored what?" Billy asked in the silence.

"Four hits of Ozly's Blue," answered Mal. "Jimmy Hendrix's acid of choice. Made by a San Francisco chemist."

"Count me out," Billy said and left.

"Billy, wait," called Mal. "You know you have a dog in the back seat of your car?"

Billy groaned.

iv.

At five forty-five, Maj lighted yet another in a long line of cigarettes, hoping to quiet her rumbling stomach. Last year Twiggy, a British waif-like girl with big eyes and a flat chest, dominated the cover of every major fashion magazine. Since then, Jimmy wanted Maj skinny, and said cigarettes would curb her appetite. Jimmy was right. If she quit smoking pot and didn't go on any more fooders, cigarettes probably would work a lot better at keeping her—as Jimmy said—all eyelashes and legs, but Maj liked the way she looked. She didn't want to be skinny.

The photographer dragged Vaseline though the length of Maj's hair. Squirming as the minutes ticked faster, she wished Neil would hurry. Otis Redding's voice filled the empty studio with how good his girl made him feel. The palms of Maj's hands turned the gloves damp.

"Six-fifteen," Maj reminded.

"Loosen up," complained Neil.

Showing up for both the modeling job and going with Raul to the Fillmore seemed a doable compromise earlier. Now Maj was convinced that Mother would show up even in spite of the message Maj had called home and left with Carmen. Maj would not be joining her parents at the opera. On edge and ready to burst like a smashed melon, she tilted her head to the side and then up, her face always looking for the light and her heart searching for meaning.

Modeling to put herself through college was a secret

tribute to MorMor. Modeling to pay for Daddy's treatments would be difficult, but Maj believed she could do it. She wasn't entirely surprised about his lack of money. Great Oaks was vast. His great-grandfather had struck it rich as a gold-miner and paid a sack full of gold nuggets to have the massive house built. A wing on either side, like a butterfly, each was two stories tall with a hardwood ballroom taking up the entire second floor of the east wing. He'd built Great Oaks for Jenny Watson, his one true love, Maj's great, great-grandmother.

What Daddy hadn't told Maj, she'd overheard as a kid playing dolls outside his office. Much of his personal mutterings made no sense but she loved the sad, velvety sound of Daddy's voice. A crooked business partner. An earthquake. A giant crash. His father closing off both wings of the butterfly house. Daddy often emerged from his study drawn and pale and never talked about what was bothering him. Now, with his head injury, he hadn't worked for more than two years. Though she no longer danced and played as a child to brighten his mood, Maj could give him this.

Modeling to support Mother's lifestyle was something else entirely. One thing Maj was sure of, she wasn't going to devote her life to work she didn't love, nor would she quit school just so Mother could hire a limousine for the night. How dare Mother raid Maj's trust fund without first asking her permission?

"Anger. I like it," said Neil.

Jittery from black coffee and cigarettes, Maj rolled her eyes, imagining Mother's admission as simply a ruse to manipulate Maj into opening up for the camera again. Mother was crazy if she thought that using fear and coercion would crack the lock. Still, if there truly was no money left, giving only enough to get by wasn't going to work anymore.

*　*　*　*　*　*

Next thing Maj knew, she was tying the wolf around her neck and catching her breath as Raul's truck lurched toward San Francisco. Speed washing the Vaseline out of her hair and changing into street clothes, she had ditched the studio at six-twenty-five. Proud she'd said no to Mother, Maj knew that relaying her opposition in a message didn't really count much as progress.

Trucks and cars and cabs streaked past them in the slow lane.

"I hope I didn't make us late for the concert," said Maj.

With the corners of his mouth turned up, Raul shook his head.

"Dolores Huerta speaks after the first set," he said, his voice thoughtful and quiet. With not much differentiation between s, z, c, his speech sounded soft and exotic. "You'll like her. Carlos Santana plays before and after her speech. You'll like him, too."

Out of the noise of the wind rose Raul's excitement. She and Raul had met a few months ago at Napa State Hospital on Maj's first day volunteering with autistic kids. Raul interned on weekends as a social scientist. Other than at the hospital and a philosophy class they shared, this was their first time out and their first time together at night. Maj smelled open skies and dusty trails when she was with Raul.

Raul kept his eyes on the downtown traffic as they exited the bridge. Dusk, when the real world intersected with the world of the trolls, turned the city gray. At the bottom of the off-ramp, a green Muni bus approached the cross-traffic signal. Light inside the bus fell on commuters, hunched together like tired props in a raw photograph. Afraid the part she played in Neil's work of art tonight wasn't good enough, Maj had fled the studio before hearing his verdict.

The red traffic light glowed, and the truck came to a stop.

"Professor Hicks' lecture today. . . " Embarrassed and unsure what she meant to ask, Maj looked away.

Raul's eyes flicked from the road, and he touched her arm. An Indian-style kerchief across his forehead sent a shadow over his eyes. Headlights from an oncoming car found his eyes and made them shine. They were both quiet for a long time.

"Nietzsche's parable," said Raul finally.

"I must've missed something," said Maj quickly. "Did Professor Hicks say how to slay the Dragon of Thou Shalt?"

Raul shook his head. "I was hoping for the answer, too."

He grunted as he rolled down his window. The light changed. Raul stuck out his arm to signal a right turn onto Van Ness Avenue. The Opera House came into view, lit in wavy, yellow lights with long tails floating from the square building. The thickening fog intensified the effect of the spotlight up close as it circled the sky, announcing the opera to the galaxies. Television crews and lines of limousines made Maj's stomach hurt, and she suddenly remembered the required speech for tomorrow's class. She should have said no to Raul and Mother both, stayed home and practiced.

On the other side of the familiar landmark, Raul pulled onto a side street and into a parking lot and turned off the engine. Maj sank into herself, wishing she could magically slip through the seat cover and disappear.

"Why are you parking here?" she asked quickly, scanning the lot.

"The Fillmore is over there." Raul pointed across the street where music blared from a two-story building.

A hole in one of the painted-black windows of the building sent out a kaleidoscope of colors. She easily could have gone to the opera, she sighed to herself, snuck out and met Raul, too.

She slid off the front seat, self-conscious in her faded jeans and bare belly under her favorite jacket, just as a Jaguar sedan parked beside Raul's dented 1951 Studebaker truck.

Not sure what kind of car Mother rented, Maj ducked her head.

A man in a tuxedo exited the Jaguar and offered his hand to a woman in a long gown of pink chiffon. The cotton-candy color pulled out the yellow in the woman's skin and made her look older than she probably was. The man opened the back door and out swept a girl about ten or twelve. Not the least bit self-conscious in a gown that matched her mother's, the young girl glided alongside her parents under the spell of her first opera.

Maj, on the other hand, was a mess, afraid of getting caught, always afraid of getting caught and getting hurt or in trouble.

A guy with long, frizzy-red hair strolled by, whispering out of the side of his mouth. "Acid. Grass. Mescaline."

The crowd of concert-goers and opera-enthusiasts

arrived together at an appliance store on the corner, where Walter Cronkite's face spread across every television set lining the window shelves. Rice paddies filled the screens. A bomb exploded.

The two crowds split and went their separate ways.

At a poster-splattered door, Raul handed tickets to a guy with spinning eyes like pinwheels. Maj peered back to the bright lights of Van Ness Avenue. Safe now, she wondered how much Mother's limousine cost. And, the opera tickets? Maj had no idea how much money she made from the shoot today or even if it was a paid gig. Jimmy gave the money she earned to Daddy's attorney who sent her an allowance every month. Before leaving for the shoot earlier, Maj had left messages for both Jimmy and her attorney, asking for answers.

v.

In the factory parking lot, Billy convinced Mal he needed a dog, and was relieved when Mal took Sister Wolf.

Billy spent the rest of the day unable to breathe, pacing the union hall, and cringing at every other sound—sure Alabama was creeping up from behind to clobber him. After miraculously avoiding him, Billy finally accepted that he wasn't going to be meeting with the company men until morning. Knowing the delay bought him even more time to think was not something he was particularly looking forward to. Thinking and planning and logic weren't going to get him out of this one. Someone was going to get hurt.

He wound down the quiet tree-lined street to his two-bedroom house in Fremont. When he found himself white-knuckled, he tried easing up on the grip he had on the steering wheel. The driveway was littered with tricycles and toys, so he parked on the street under a tree with no leaves. The sky was gray, matching his mood exactly.

The smell of meatloaf and potatoes and the whine of Elvis met him at the front door. His shoulders relaxed and he felt contented in this tiny bubble called home, far from the pressures at work.

Lisa saw him and screamed.

"Daddy, Daddy!"

His little girl jumped into his arms. Billy held her close. Brenda walked in, beaming to beat the band. From the way she kissed him, right off he knew he was in trouble.

Brenda prodded him with a smile and a nod.

"What'd he say?"

He looked at her bleakly, sensing a trap.

"The interview," she reminded him. "In Oakland."

With the sweetness of her kiss still fresh on his lips, Billy groaned.

"Oh, baby, I'm sorry," he said.

"You didn't go." Brenda anchored her fists to her hips and glared at him.

Even after three kids, Brenda's body was just as tight as when they first met five years ago, back in the days when there was nothing better than sex. Still wasn't, but he didn't get that much anymore. When he finally caught on how untrustworthy she was about taking the pill, he started holding himself back. Now that he didn't ask for it anymore, things between them were pretty tense. Letting her down only made life worse.

"I know how much it meant to you," he said, feeling like a real heel.

"How much it means to us, Billy," she urged. "To us as a family." Frustration carved shadows under her eyes.

"You're right. I got caught up with things at the factory . . . " Billy stopped when he saw she wasn't interested.

"I'm sorry. Tomorrow," he promised.

Starving, he checked the kitchen. Overturned plates of food smashed all over the table showed the kids had eaten. There wasn't a plate set for him.

"Wash your hands. I'll fix you something."

He swung Lisa onto his back. Even with his troubled breathing, he galloped past Brenda to the stereo with his little girl kicking his sides. Winded, he leaned over the hi-fi, dipping farther than he needed. Lisa squealed and tightened her grip from sliding over his head. They laughed together as he lifted off Brenda's Elvis '45, put on the Doors, and cranked up the volume.

The little girls howled from their bedroom.

"Now look what you've done," snapped Brenda. "And just so you know, the kind of man you want to be doesn't listen to that kind of music." She stomped to the kids' bedroom.

The telephone rang. Hoping to catch his breath, Billy pried Lisa off his back, but she tightened her grip around his neck and dug her knees into his sides. She didn't say anything. Neither did he.

The silence between each ring was filled with the Doors imploring him to wake up. His stomach growled. Summer Rose spotted him and zoomed his way. Brenda snatched the telephone as Summer leaped into his arms with Lisa still stuck to his back. The girls smelled clean. They were happy and well fed. Brenda was a good mom. She called him The Iceman on account of Ma and the way he was raised. He admitted he was chilly sometimes but guessed Grandma's theory was closer to the truth. He had him a wolf caught inside.

Billy put down Summer and went to wash up, wanting to make Brenda happy.

Brenda hung up the telephone. "Now, don't go and get all upset. My sisters are stopping by after dinner."

"Not tonight," warned Billy.

"They're not planning on staying long."

"I'm not going through another night with Carol harping on me."

Billy's throat turned bitter as the two of them stared at each other. Lisa slid down his back, choking him. He snatched hold of her arm, and she let out a gasp. Aware of how skinny her arm and how tight his grip, he put an arm under Lisa and hoisted her higher. She leaned her head against his back. He felt her heart beat and coughed.

"Let's don't do this," said Billy.

"What?" accused Brenda. "Talk about how you never keep your promises?"

"I said I was sorry."

A car horn blared from the street. Balled up, Billy forced himself to move away from Brenda and stepped over Melissa. Out the front window, Red's car idled with Webb in the driver's seat and Mal in the back.

Lisa shouted right in his ear. "Daddy, Daddy. It's Malie."

"What are they doing here?" demanded Brenda.

Billy put down Summer and helped Lisa off his back. Lisa shoved her face up to the front window, waving both her arms over her head.

"There's union business tonight," said Billy. "I told them I was staying home."

The doorbell rang.

"I'm going to see if Malie brought his ukulele, Daddy," squealed Lisa. She opened the door with both hands and streaked past Red at the doorway.

Summer took off behind Lisa. Red caught Summer and held her back. His face reddened when he saw Brenda. "Brenda." Red nodded. "Hell, I'm sorry to bother you, Billy."

Melissa, who'd nearly made it to the window before her sisters ran away, started crying. Brenda picked her up and dragged shut the swinging kitchen door with such force it thumped back and forth.

"Hell, we thought we could do without you," said Red, loud enough for Brenda to hear in the kitchen. "Looks like we need a vote. You make a quorum," he finished, slicker than owl shit.

"Daddy, Daddy," screamed Lisa from outside.

Panicked about his little girl, Billy pushed past Red. Mal had the damned Sister Wolf by the leash and was doing his best to keep the dog from jumping on Lisa.

"Look, Daddy, a dog. A dog," Lisa said, making a face that asked, *I believe in miracles, do you?* She sighed for emphasis and leaned forward with a fist to her heart.

Red raised his bushy red eyebrows and jerked his head toward the car, letting Billy know a vote was not at all what he had in mind.

Brenda shouted a warning as if reading Billy's mind. "Billy!"

"What are you doing with the dog, Mal?" Billy asked, trying to breathe.

Under one arm, Mal had a giant-sized sack of dog food and a pillow, and clutched a kennel in his other hand.

Brenda came out of the kitchen.

"I'm sorry, Brenda, Billy," said Mal. "She only

stopped barking when we got here. My roommates said no."

"Now what do I do?" asked Billy.

"Better put her out back." Mal gave Billy the leash and nodded at the girls rooted in place, wide eyes glued to the puppy as it reared up and fought against the leash to flatten them. "Let her sleep in the kennel next to your bed, or she'll bark all night."

Mal ducked his head and put the kennel in the hallway, then headed back to the car with Red.

"I'll find it a home tomorrow," Billy said to Brenda who was as frozen in place as the kids were.

He took the dog out back, threw the dog bed on the ground and slid the glass door shut. The girls plastered their faces to the glass door, making the dog bark. Lisa rapped her knuckles against the glass. She shook her finger.

"No, no, Sadie," Lisa said.

The dog whimpered and settled down.

Lisa looked over her shoulder. "I named him, Sadie, Daddy."

Billy glanced at Brenda. She turned away.

"Go," Brenda said. "Just go."

"Wait up," Billy called to Red.

vi.

Inside the Fillmore, the dark cavernous room was filled with clusters of men mingled with a mass of arriving college students. Raul grabbed Maj's hand, and together they swept across a ruby-red carpet and sloshed up the stairs as part of a huge wave ascending into a smoke-shrouded hall of flickering bright lights and loud music.

Feeling like they were being followed, Maj slowed

down. A girl overtook them and disappeared into a crowd of gyrating kids, mostly her age. Overstuffed chairs and velvet sofas lined the walls. Beneath Maj, the floor vibrated to the music.

Raul grinned. "I'm glad you came."

Colored lights keyed to blues music flashed in his face.

"Me, too," Maj said, happy.

Raul pointed to the stage. "Carlos Santana."

Smoke hung above a man stooped over a guitar. Surrounding him were a keyboardist, a bassist, and a drummer behind a drum set like the Beatles'. Another drummer—with his fingers taped white—sat off to the side of the stage with a long, narrow conga drum between his legs. Carlos Santana tilted his face, and his ponytail slipped between hunched shoulders. Furrows cut across his forehead like a fertile field. A black mustache wound down either side of his mouth and covered his chin, as if a mask had slipped and landed there. He wore cowboy boots made of a patchwork of colors.

"I need to see some people backstage." Raul spoke close to her ear.

Maj cringed at the thought of meeting new people, preferring to be surrounded by strangers.

"Is it all right if I stay here?" Maj spoke softly, not wanting to draw attention to herself.

Raul hesitated.

"Sorry." Maj shrugged and then said brightly. "That's okay. If you think I should."

Not wanting to cause a fuss, Maj gave in with the word "should" echoing in her head—"unless you think I should." It was as if Mother stood right alongside Maj, armed with all her "Thou Shalts," all her better ways of doing things.

Raul motioned for Maj to follow. Instead of going backstage, he stopped at an empty sofa under a colossal banner ornamented in gold and emblazoned with huge black UAW letters. They were about twenty feet off to the right side of the stage and way up front.

To Maj's amazement, Raul nodded, encouraging her to sit. Then he left. Maj wasn't much familiar with asking for what she wanted and especially not with getting it, except from Daddy. An electric thrill sparked the air. She touched the carving at her neck, her fingers trembling. The smooth feel of the wood brushed aside her speech assignment tomorrow, her guilt for letting down Mother and Daddy, and the layer of shame always just beneath the surface of her skin. The wooden wolf wrapped her in a cocoon of throbbing music and light.

vii.

Webb steered Billy away with a nod to the dance floor. Secret moves smoothed into quiet. A guy at the microphone whispered words of justice. Fins of turquoise and red bled into a girl with her back to him. Swaying back and forth, long yellow hair flowed like a river. Her movements slowed as the music slowed. The air turned sweet.

"She's his," said Webb, and nodded.

A Chicano walking away from the blonde wore faded blue jeans, and his long-sleeved snap-down shirt tapped at Billy like a mind-finger. He'd picked cotton alongside Mexicans dressed in the same kind of cowboy clothes minus the cowboy boots. The two biggest things Billy had learned from the Mexican workers was that as poor as he and Grandma were, they were poorer still, and that those with the least always seemed to give the most.

Light-headed, Billy leaned back. Pillows wrapped themselves around him. Grandma and him. Mexicans and him. Auto workers and farm workers. All of them shared one thing. The crumbs.

A speck of red like a pin-prick of blood, flattened against the back of his eyelids. It changed from the color of new brick to the color of the tree bark where he grew up. The same color as the path his great-grandmother Martha turkey-gobbled on her drunken walk home.

A path cleared.

viii.

Psychedelic colors twirled around the room, gyrating everyone's movements wild and jerky. A man as huge as a giant offered Maj a joint. She shrank from him until she spotted the merry eyes and rosy cheeks of Olle-the-Loyal. Next to him stood a Negro who looked like Tjovik-the-Wise from the same tale. The only one missing was the queen's choice—the handsome prince. Maj looked for him without success.

Olle-the-Loyal blocked the crowd like a standing sentinel. Someone else was there, too. A presence Maj sensed but couldn't see. Loaded, behind her eyes, points of light became stars. An urgency shot through her. A lesson waited to be learned.

Giant speakers loomed from the stage like great black crows. The one in front of Maj undulated and began to sizzle. The room turned hazy.

Beneath her, the floor trembled. Vibrations shuddered. The colored lights clicked off to darkness. Music stopped. The stage turned black.

Shaking beneath Maj grew to a fevered pitch, like a herd of wild ponies tramping, stamping, and panting across the floor. Heartache and happiness, fear and wisdom, sparks flew and depths opened.

Maj listed to the side, stumbled and threw out both arms like a trapeze artist as the floor beneath her feet creaked and moaned and shifted erratically.

Someone clutched her elbow. Through his touch, Maj found her balance. She turned and, blushing hard, drew in a shuddering sigh at his slow and brilliant smile.

The boy from her childhood, now a man, concentrated on keeping her upright. Then his brow turned from serious to amused. He chuckled softly.

No one ran from the room. No one breathed a word.

His touch, warm and steady on Maj's elbow, was all there was and all there ever would be.

ix.

Shaking ended and the earth turned still.

Someone gave the delayed shout. "Earthquake!"

Lights flashed on, then off, and on again, making Billy dizzy as if he'd caught a glimpse of his entire life, watched as he dissolved into nothingness, and came back out of the void. The light show started up. Music began as if it had never ended.

With his hand cupping her elbow to keep her steady, a grown-up version of the scrappy yellow-haired girl who'd appeared out of nowhere on Grandma's stretch of highway, again on a shared Oakland sidewalk, and then in Golden Gate Park stood before him as if they'd arranged this meeting together long ago and every moment had steered them to this exact place at this exact time.

He sucked in his breath and took his time exhaling, enthralled by watching the blonde's eyes wake up. A flame burned, catching fire to a hanging iridescence behind her eyes. The blaze burned brighter.

All the blood rushed from her face, and she went from red to white.

Billy smiled, watching her struggle to breathe properly with her hand at her neck. Silver confetti dripped from her eyes. She'd changed since the last time they'd touched, but much of her was exactly the same. Her face still radiated joy and was determinedly brave. She'd grown taller with the same matter-of-fact acceptance and surety that they belonged together. Her lips parted. Neither of them spoke. They both knew.

Heat traveled from her hand, warming and flattening and elongating their grasp like pulled taffy. She started to raise his hands to her lips like when they were kids. Suddenly, she was reaching for him. Pulling him to her, she rewarded him a kiss.

A spark from his mouth turned her self-conscious. She ducked her head.

"Again?" Billy murmured, lifting her chin and kissing away a tear, her breath soft on his neck.

He started to smooth back hair that had fallen in her face, and then he dropped his hand. No longer able to differentiate between what was real and what was the high, Billy did know that a married man kissing a girl who wasn't his wife would only lead to trouble for both of them.

x.

"Who are . . . " Maj started, a rusty iron gate creaking open after years of hiding from him and now with no desire to run.

She watched as the eyes of the boy-turned-man glazed over, and he separated from her. Shutting her out, he left her just as Maj once had closed him out. He looked over her head. Like when they were young and he saw Daddy coming for her, his eyes flashed. The grown-up prince dropped his hands from her shoulders and backed away.

Raul appeared beside her.

In a daze and without even knowing the man's name, Maj opened her mouth to call him back and beg him not to leave. He disappeared into the horde of people like a puff of smoke, a magician's trick.

"You all right?" asked Raul, peering into her face. "Quite an earthquake. Were you scared?"

Torn, Maj wanted to run to the man, find out who he was, and why he kept appearing in her life. Feeling disloyal to Raul and to the boy-turned-man from her childhood, it took all her strength and attention to return to Raul. She shook her head, confused how to say yes and no to Raul's questions. He stood so near, she felt his breath. They did not touch. As the pressure of the boy-turned-man's lips glowed against her lips and settled into her heart, she started to explain.

Raul stopped her by pointed to the stage.

Grateful not having to make sense of the impossible, Maj tucked what just happened in a secret vault in her mind for safe-keeping until she had a chance to relive the moment and that kiss in quiet and privacy. The man's lingering touch, like a magic wand, rendered her whole and complete. She blushed, remembering him watching her look over his lined face and lean and muscular body. Happy he no longer went shoeless had her shaking her head and grinning like a love-struck little girl. She sensed he remained nearby.

As the music stopped, clapping and hollering encircled Maj, and tears wet her face. She tried scanning the room, but it was too hazy to make out people in the dark. Instead, she turned to watch the furrows in Carlos Santana's face relax. Sweat reflected off of his forehead and he peered across the room as if awakening from a dream.

A spotlight snapped on. Carlos, near in age to the man from her past, shaded his eyes against smoky white light running from the stage to the ceiling, a stairway to heaven.

Like the king's escorts, Carlos's band members lined up behind him, slapping each other on the back, grinning and even hugging chest-to-chest—something Maj hadn't see between men before. Friends united by a cause.

Gigantic red flags hung from flag poles on either side of the stage, emblazed with the same black Aztec eagle as the bumper sticker on Raul's truck.

"*Viva la causa,*" shouted Carlos, his black mustache twitching and his patchwork boots glowing.

The crowd followed, their excitement coursing through Maj's body. "*Viva la causa!*"

Feeling as if the world were broadening and deepening before her, Maj shouted with abandon along with everyone else. Overflowing with gratitude to Raul for bringing her here, she smiled at him. Raul showed no emotion. Instantly, Maj went quiet, too.

Standing beyond Raul, a girl stared at Maj, her look dagger sharp. It was the girl who'd followed them earlier. Maj's stomach stung like from a dragon switch. She rubbed the carving at her neck with the distinct feeling she wasn't wanted here.

Self-conscious, Maj slouched, wishing she were

invisible, and looked for the man. Did he belong here? Was this his cause? She spotted Olle-the-Loyal. No crowned prince.

Carlos motioned to someone off to the side of the stage. Maj leaned forward slightly and, without actually moving her head, looked again. The girl still stared at her. Maj arched back. Uncomfortable and not knowing what else to do, she concentrated on what was happening on the stage.

"Cesar Chavez is too weak from his fast to be here tonight," said Carlos. "From the beginning, he and Dolores Huerta have fought side-by-side for farm workers' rights."

At the name of Cesar Chavez, a ripple of admiration flowed through the crowd. Maj had forgotten the exact date Raul told her Chavez started the grape picker's strike. She did know that Chavez's cause had spread to a national strike and made the purchase of wine a political act. Before Daddy's accident, and when Mother still threw black-tie cocktail parties and dinner gatherings, the affairs inevitably ended with guests clutching wine glasses in a hot debate over table grapes and Mexican farm labor.

Carlos adjusted down the height of the microphone for Dolores.

"Let's show Carlos and the guys how much we dig their music," Dolores shouted.

Everyone cheered. A chant went up. "We want Carlos. We want Carlos."

Alone on the stage, Dolores' eyes were soft and patient. Suddenly irritated, Maj fidgeted, wishing Dolores would just ask Carlos to speak for her. Instead, the woman wrapped both hands around the microphone stand and, even as the murmuring from most of the people in the crowd grew louder, she began speaking.

Maj shuddered. Raul wrapped his arm around her. At his touch, she tensed. To hide it, she moved a little closer.

"Pedro, put up your hand," started Dolores. "There, in the back. Pedro gives an honest day's work, six days a week. So do his wife and children. We believe they deserve an honest day's pay. You believe that, too, don't you?"

Grunts tossed about here and there, low and reserved like a bass guitar. No chance for a full embrace. Maj's armpits turned sticky like she was standing up there in front of everyone and imagined speaking in front of her entire class tomorrow.

"Would you call a one-room shack made of sheet metal where Pedro and his family live, fair?" asked Dolores. "No running water, no bathroom, no bed, fair? Pedro doesn't complain. He is one of the lucky ones; his family has one lone gas burner to cook on."

Dolores pulled Maj out herself, speaking clearly and simply about men and women working toward a better life. People who picked this country's fruits and vegetables with callused hands and aching knees, broken dreams, and lost hope deserved better. That their kids breathed crop-dusted poisons kindled Maj's indignation and incited her outrage. Never again would she see Carmen and Ramon in the same way, and Maj truly believed that when everyone heard about this, the deplorable conditions would improve immediately.

Dolores' weariness gave way to strength, and she grew larger. Maj imagined delivering a similar speech. Scrambling through her imagination for less than a moment, she took on the needs of autistic kids as her cause.

Head erect, arms at her sides, and feet firmly planted shoulder-width apart, Dolores was not one to give away power or deflect it.

Imitating her stance made Maj suddenly aware how seldom she actually stood up straight in public. She was surprised to find that she was taller than Raul.

"Cesar Chavez goes without food to remind workers of their pledge for nonviolence," continued Dolores. "He also reminds growers that we, at a mere eight thousand strong, are no match for the farm owners."

Olle-the-Loyal cupped his hands around his mouth. "The UAW stands in brotherhood with the UFW!"

Startled, Maj hadn't realized Olle-the-Loyal was still so near. Goosebumps shivered across her arms. Satisfied just knowing her mystery man was in the same room with her, she could be patient. If his withdrawal was anything like hers, she didn't expect to see the man again until he was ready. So far, the timing of their chance connections seemed fragile and awkwardly off, like coming in for a landing and missing the tarmac. A lesson seemed to be forming for Maj to learn to trust that chances were never over and would always come again.

MANAGEMENT

Billy awakened, the blonde curled beside him, her breath warm against his chest. Before he opened his eyes, she vanished like vapor on asphalt. Awake and asleep—both at the same time—he felt the cars and trucks whizzing by on the highway move through his body, connecting him to the wet, pulsing center of life. He wasn't confused, more disoriented. Memories came in fragments. Last night, he was kissed whole and complete.

The alarm clock shrieked. Skin leapt off his bones. Billy snatched the clock and squeezed it with both hands, fingers fumbling for the knob, his heart slamming against his chest. Even after it was off, the noise bounced in his skull, making him woozy. He felt the bed next to him, making sure Brenda hadn't left him yet. Relieved to find her there, he closed his eyes.

Brenda's breathing slowed. The little sucking noise she made in her sleep brought Billy to an old Wilson Pickett song and all the things Brenda used to do to him in the midnight hour.

Pre-dawn turned their bedroom dingy and small. Sadie whimpered as Billy stumbled out of bed. The dog looked out from the kennel and smiled. Billy went in the bathroom, crouched over the faucet, and slurped like a parched hyena. Then, greeted with a slobber face-washing, he chased Sadie outside and fed her.

* * * * * *

At the guard booth, Billy pulled his identification from a plastic wallet Brenda gave him last Christmas, saying it was from the girls. The guard glared at him. Billy scrunched his eyes, a shield against the guy stealing a chunk of him, and flashed his badge. The morning, cold as a well digger's ass, wasn't entirely to blame for his vibrating fingers. After being frisked for knives and guns, Billy slipped his wallet in his pocket and wondered whatever happened to the genuine alligator wallet he stole. Twelfth birthday. Hanes Department store. The girl.

Rather than a life of thievery, that day presented a future different than the tough, closed-off, pissed-off, son-of-a-bitch Billy had wrapped himself in. That wasn't to say he wasn't still tough. Closed-off. Pissed-off. A son-of-a-bitch. He was, yet in those few fleeting moments with the blonde, Billy wanted to do better. Be better. More. Acid might be making him think in shorthand, but it wasn't responsible for conjuring the blonde up last night. Her being there, right beside him, wasn't random. Four times. Meant something. Four times. Not a coincidence.

Billy shook off all thoughts of her, as he walked as normally as possible inside the factory toward the stairway to management offices. Rising out of the bowels of the plant, the morning whistle was the saddest sound he ever heard. As he considered things now, the battle wasn't between Alabama and Skypiece or the Panthers and Whites and Chicanos inside. The true enemy was the establishment. Not necessarily out to *destroy* all union workers, their constituencies, customers—and even the country itself—still, politicians and management were, and always would be, out to protect themselves and their shareholders first and foremost. Period. End of story.

On the second floor, Webb stepped out of the shadows. He'd changed his hair from tight against his head to so bushy that Webb appeared to have grown at least two full inches since last night. Seeing Webb's profile showed Billy his old friend again. No longer a guerilla fighter for Special Forces and part of the counter-insurgency. No longer responsible for burning down huts and poisoning the water of people he didn't know. Last night, colors from the light show flickered across Webb's face, and all the past that had been messing with Webb's head so bad were gone. The past vanished, making Webb pure again, like when they were kids together. Billy wondered if that was really true.

At the Fillmore, life had clicked into focus. Billy wasn't ever going to be a bank teller. That was what Brenda wanted, not what he wanted. The loss of her dream could change everything he had here and life as he knew it.

Webb was still in 'Nam during the wildcat strike, but the rest of them who served on the picket line had been given union history lessons from Skypiece, whether they wanted it or not. Daily, Skypiece would read aloud all about Walter Reuther from a biography about the founder of the UAW that he'd checked out of the library. Billy memorized a quote of Reuther's: "There is no greater calling than to serve your fellow men. There is no greater contribution than to help the weak. There is no greater satisfaction than to have done it well."

Last night, when Huerta declared that no one was free until everyone was, Billy knew he was born to lead the workers in this factory.

The second whistle went off. From the third floor landing, it sounded more like a burp. Crowded and dirty, under-lighted with broken and rusted equipment, fractured bones and ten-hour shifts—sometimes up to six and seven days a week—none of it was visible from up here at the management level.

Cesar Chavez gave dignity to people who were invisible to society. Billy vowed to do the same for the autoworkers. He planned to piss off management and be a continual thorn in their side, starting this morning. Take care of his, and that included these guys in the plant, and the rest would fall in place.

Billy pinched the filterless end of his cigarette, took a last hit, and burned his fingers. He mashed out the butt under his boot heel on the catwalk's metal grating. Last night, Dolores Huerta reminded him of his grandmother's prediction that one day he would lead men.

Today just might be that day.

*   *   *   *   *   *

Two hours later, Billy and Webb blasted out of the meeting room, nearly plowing into Mal. Billy's heart sped like a car engine with a stuck throttle. He had him the urge to kick something. Mal lorded over the door with his arms folded like a sentinel, staring down guards who glared right back at him.

"Red's still tripping from last night." Mal spoke low and out of the side of his mouth, as the three of them made their way down the stairway. "He said he'd get here just as soon as he's able."

"Everyone's taking odds how much higher Webb's hair can get," Billy said in a light-hearted tone, trying to control the buzzing vibrating through him and knowing ears were listening.

Mal chuckled. Webb stared straight ahead. Mal and Webb moved as a unit, pulling Billy along between them. Wound tight and finding the feeling irresistible, Billy wondered if they could feel his heart popping.

One of the soft-trim guys shouted. "Way to go."

Already word of Billy's meeting was ground into the noise of the line starting up. The guys turned back to their jobs with their spines a little straighter, though that may have been just Billy's imagination.

Webb and Mal navigated Billy through the plant, his arms pinned at his sides between them. He wasn't sure if they were trying to keep someone out or him in.

"I didn't give up anyone," said Billy.

"At the hour and a half mark, I figured you were holding tight," said Mal.

"It wasn't like that." Webb's voice was hoarse, like he was talking in church. "You should have seen him, man. Billy Wayman stood them down. I can't hardly believe it, and I saw it with my own two eyes."

Billy tried to look at Webb. Wedged between Webb and Mal like he was, it was easier for Billy if he kept his eyes straight ahead on the guys on the assembly line. Knowing Mal wasn't going to let him go until Webb and him told everything that happened, Billy let himself be pulled out of factory and into a light drizzle. The three of them walked past the guard shack to Billy's car, so he could go break the good news to Alabama.

An assembler raised a hand at them. "We're behind you, kid."

Even guys on the three-mile hike through the parking lot, who hadn't even been in the plant yet, already knew. The old guys didn't look as winded as usual.

At his car, Billy dislodged from Webb and Mal and dug out a ring of keys from his pants pocket. Taking his time, he flipped through the wad before picking out the key to his Chevy.

"I saved Alabama his job," Billy said.

Mal nodded.

"Skypiece will be paid for the time he was out," Billy continued. "That, and all his hospitalization. He gets his money, and we get it in writing."

"What'd you have to give up?" asked Mal.

Off in the distance, a line of haulers loaded brand-new cars fresh off the assembly line and ready for marketplace.

"Made me listen to a bunch of horseshit about getting along and keeping things calmed down," replied Billy. "The importance of keeping people in line."

Webb grabbed hold of both Billy and Mal.

"Don't you get it? Billy Wayman Wolf is a ghetto boy, fair-minded to Blacks and Chicanos alike. Even the Panthers and the parolees like you. Sure, Billy's part in the '64 strike played into it, and it was brilliant the way you slipped that in as a reminder. But that's not why the company caved. You opened their eyes to the likelihood of an all-out war inside. Management is scared. They believe you're the only one with the power of the rank and file behind you who can stop it."

The thorn. Planted. Now. Keep it sharp and firmly stuck in management's side, Billy thought to himself. That part wasn't going to be easy.

SPIDERS AND TOADS

The following night, Maj knotted an orange kerchief behind her head and returned to the Fillmore alone. Unable to spot the boy-turned-man, she returned the next night, both times wearing the same scarf and both times holding-her-breath-hopeful. Even after trying several times and still not finding him, she wasn't surprised. He wasn't ready. She accepted that. Her heart, on the other hand, refused to leave her alone or believe that their encounters were simply coincidental. The tingling in her spine, a faint sensation of deja vu, the two of them didn't just float to the exact same place, at the exact the same moment by chance—four times in twelve years.

Unsuccessful at finding him at the Fillmore and longing to ask if he knew why they kept meeting, Maj changed course. She stayed home and called the operator for help identifying the UAW from the banner at Carlos Santana's concert.

"The initials stand for the United Automobile Workers Union," said the operator. "There is a local chapter in Fremont."

Maj tried on several outfits before deciding on a simple cotton fitted dress, with a wide lapel collar edged in lace and long sleeves, confident today she'd learn something about the man—anything solid that made him real. Grinning at the chance of even knowing his name, Maj did a little twirl around her bedroom.

She stumbled, well aware that as magical as each of their meetings had been, afterwards, awful things seemed to follow. Now, plagued by the poison letter from her academic advisor, she was going after good fortune instead. The memory of the boy-turned-man's touch gave Maj the shivers.

A floppy hat covered her eyebrows and made her feel safe, like hiding behind a mask. Mother believed women were supposed to have eyebrows and, since Maj's were too blonde to show, she should paint them on. Mother didn't know Maj had stopped wearing a bra, and she wasn't around to complain about Maj's dark circles. Mother would absolutely freak out if she knew Maj had stopped wearing make-up, like the girl working at the Fillmore refreshment stand.

Mother's morning calls had been absent for more than a week as if, so long as Maj said yes to every job Jimmy called her about, she'd miraculously earned her freedom. So far Maj was keeping up with both studying and modeling, but with school demands getting harder, all the modeling jobs piling up had her worried.

Maj stuffed the map of the Bay Area, with her route to Fremont marked in red pen, into the green and yellow macramé purse she'd knotted herself. Checking for the GTO car keys, she opened the front door and came face-to-face with her academic advisor.

A wave of distaste broke over her. With him standing so near to the door, Maj smelled his stale cigarette breath.

"Well, well, well," her advisor said, tapping his clipboard with the tip of his pen. "Time for your one required surprise visit." He lifted his voice at the end of the sentence, like a kindergarten teacher to a room of excited five-year-olds or a circus ring-master to a rapt audience. Sweat covered his temples.

Maj stepped back. Uninvited, he followed her inside. His presence in her house made her feel like she had been dousing with a bucket of spiders and toads.

This wasn't the first time her advisor had shown up unexpectedly. Calls to the house, soon after Maj received his letter about her probationary status, quickly turned into him showing up outside her house, revving his black Corvette Stingray just as she was leaving for class. Insisting he drive her to school, her advisor would agitate Maj about her classes the entire time and not let her leave until he showered her with so-called compliments about how fond he was of every little thing about her. Her dislike for him deepened further when he started showing up after class. Though he never acknowledged her professors, her guidance counselor was quick to recount their below-average performance assessment reports of her.

"Which," he often said, wagging his finger in front of her nose, "isn't going to get you off probation anytime soon."

Maj hated most when he made her sit with him while he showed her what she was doing wrong, making no sense, leaning in a little too close and breathing just a little too hard.

This was the first time he'd been inside her house.

"I'm late for an appointment," Maj made up quickly, shrugging her shoulders against what felt like bugs creeping up her back. She wished her roommates were home.

Checking his papers, her advisor scanned the entry

hall and then peered into the parlor. His black rimmed glasses, tweed jacket, button-down shirt, and loafers made him look scholarly and on the way up. In the sunlight, another story revealed yellowing at the collar and a frayed lapel and glasses that appeared to have no lenses. Not simply an underpaid college employee, he looked slovenly and rundown.

"I'm here to ensure your living environment is conducive to studying," he reported.

Confused as to what she'd done wrong and considering how much pot was all over the place, Maj cringed.

"My roommates are due home soon," she made up quickly. "I prefer they be here."

He looked away abruptly and tsked, marking a paper on his clipboard. Maj tried looking over his shoulder, but he rotated away.

"A mark against you for this mess," he said.

A black flash twisted her heart as he motioned toward the parlor that reeked of wet wool socks and was cluttered with bicycles and jackets, random shoes, an old bucket to catch rainwater, and Nancy's art project for her final that was leaning up against the wall.

"Oh, no, I study—" Maj started and then ripped off her hat and ran after him, disadvantaged by his abrupt and unpredictable shifts and moves.

She caught him upstairs going straight to her bedroom door, making her immediately suspicious. Lucky guess? Or, had he somehow already known where she slept?

Intending to stop him from entering, she slipped in front of him.

"I've got to run. I don't want to be late to my appointment," she said in a rush, fighting the urge to shove distance between them, as she waited for some response from him.

He wrote on his clipboard and paused, his pen poised for more. "School related?"

"School related?" Maj repeated as the bottoms of her feet tingled.

He cocked his head with his eyebrows up, as if amused by her discomfort.

"Why… no… no, not school related, really," she stuttered.

Her advisor walked around her into her bedroom. With sunlight flooding through the windows, she saw his thinning hair and dandruff on his shoulders. With his back turned—and before he spotted the ashtray, with not only cigarette butts, but a joint or two—Maj blocked his view, trying to act natural and not show she was hiding something.

He glanced up at the word 'no' written in big, brash letters above her mirrored closet door. Nancy had made Maj the sign when she moved into the house at the beginning of the semester last year and saw how incapable Maj was of standing up for herself, especially when it came to random men who were nice to her.

"Women make the same sound crying as they do coming," her advisor mumbled, smoothing a hand over her bedspread.

Maj's eyes flew open in disbelief that he'd actually uttered what she thought he said. Not wanting to let on that she'd heard him, Maj didn't breathe a sound.

As he jotted yet another notation, she mouthed the word 'no,' sad that the pressure of that tiny word still felt so foreign against the tip of her tongue.

"What's that you say?" His voice came in a quick accusing tone.

"What? Oh, oh... nothing," she stuttered, surprised she'd said the word aloud and then wondered why not speak up.

Eyeing Maj suspiciously, her advisor frowned and looked behind her. Another bold mark on his papers.

When he rifled through papers strewn across her desk, Maj did speak.

"I'm going to be late," she repeated daringly, motioning to the door to usher him out.

Ignoring her, he gave a little nod to his letter on Academic Advisory stationary pinned to her bulletin board. Then he picked up a green folder from her desk and jabbed her carefully researched and typed report at her.

"I assume this is a term paper?" he said.

"Yes, for anatomy," Maj said awkwardly, her hand still outstretched.

"I'll want to check it over first before meeting with your teacher to discuss your progress," he said, putting down the report and leafing through several pages on his clipboard.

His words hit squarely on the back of her neck.

"Check it over?" she repeated numbly, and snapped her arm to her side.

Her advisor didn't look at her, which was good because Maj didn't think she could look back at him evenly. Didn't matter anyway since her words showed no affect on him.

He whirled around, clutching her green folder.

Confused, she reached out to snatch it back, as he hurried from the room. Missing her chance, she tripped down the stairs behind him.

"You're taking my paper?" she cried.

Without answering, he left the house. Maj slammed

shut the door, turned the deadbolt, and then leaned up against the door, fighting back her rapidly building nausea.

Outside, her advisor revved his Corvette, giving Maj the distinct impression that he was not only showing off but that he also seemed to draw power from the power of his car. She'd take him down with her GTO easy, she sneered to herself. Then she shook her head for having such a ridiculous thought in the middle of what was feeling more and more like a threatening situation.

*   *   *   *   *   *

Rather than drive to the United Automobile Union Hall Fremont as she'd planned, Maj visited the Academic Advisory Center on campus to formally request a change in advisors.

"I'll have to research your case, dearie," the woman at the counter said sweetly. Visibly scattered, she haphazardly checked first in one file drawer in a wall of file cabinets and then another.

"But if you've never heard of him, and he's not on your roster—" Maj started.

"Happens all the time, especially to me," the counter woman sighed. "This new fangled record keeping system . . . You look like a nice girl. I'm sure everything will work out just fine."

"Is there someone else I can speak to?"

The woman tilted her head with a pointed look.

"Someone who knows the recor—" Maj followed quickly.

The woman wrote Maj's name on a tablet of paper.

"Maj. Is that right?" the woman confirmed.

Maj nodded.

"We're hiring all the time," the woman said. "The records just haven't been updated. I'll send you a letter with my findings later today."

"So you'll look into it?" stressed Maj.

"That's what I said, dearie," the woman repeated, sounding tired. Then she closed the frosted glass partition and disappeared.

*   *   *   *   *   *

Come Saturday morning, Maj still hadn't heard from the advisory office. Lying in bed, she spun in a panic of loneliness with no idea how to separate herself from her academic advisor. Until she was assigned another advisor, he was in control of her academic probation. A sense of dread crept around her neck, squeezing tighter every day.

Gasping for air, Maj jumped out of bed, dressed and packed for her final weekend volunteering at Napa State Hospital. If she'd simply let go of her dream of graduating, her advisor would be a problem in the past. Sticking around was prolonging what she knew she'd eventually have to do—drop out of school. Maj knew that. But before she left, she wanted to prove to the director of the speech and learning clinic at school that the non-verbal little boy in the juvenile autistic ward at Napa State Hospital Maj had been working with had made measurable progress.

Maj's long-term plan was to continue until the end of the semester in May, and then gracefully say goodbye to school, and devote herself to Daddy. Seeing first-hand the financial statements from Daddy's accountant and how much Daddy's medical needs and running the household cost, Maj had accepted that her path was for a different sort of service than she'd first thought. Even so, she was resolved to attend classes until the end of the month.

In the parking lot in front of the speech clinic at school, Maj's program director waved to her from next to the ten-seater school bus. Raul stood in line to board, wearing the same red kerchief around his forehead he'd worn at the Fillmore. By the time Maj loaded her things and stepped onboard, all the seats in the back of the bus where Raul sat were taken.

*　*　*　*　*　*

Spring's feeble sun whispered Maj awake just as the van bumped off the main street of Napa. Drowsy, she memorized the wrought-iron lettering for Napa State Hospital to always remember the place she'd first learned to love listening and watching and helping kids.

The bus dropped all the volunteers outside the dormitories. Raul strode up to Maj, and her insecurities and fears shrank. Light filled her eyes. The smell of earth mixed with the scent of hard work and sweet after-shave lotion.

"Spring." Raul pointed to a lone green shoot in a stark flowerbed.

She grinned. "A promise."

"I'll see you later at the Canteen," he said, and left.

Clutching her notebook to her chest, Maj checked in with the staffers, her heart beating fast, apprehensive and excited to see Kenny.

The stench of urine in Ward B battered her. Disinfectant stung her eyes. A slew of children, as young as five years old and up to 12, filled the dirty green playroom with crying and screaming. No more than 25 kids were legally allowed, but there were always a lot more than that. Most of them rocked in place, perched on the backs of sofas, sitting at tables, or standing. Today, every child wore a football helmet. A new child banged his head against the wall. Plaster chipped away, leaving a dirty yellow pockmark.

Staffer Sara waved, in a wrinkled knit pullover shirt with no pockets or buttons and faded trousers that long ago had lost their crease. A stick-like contraption hung from a clip at her waist. Maj pointed to the child banging his head and lifted her hands in question.

Rushing to the child's side, Sara unclipped the stick and zapped him. The boy arched in pain. He stopped banging.

"Two new kids, both head-bangers," Sara shouted over the commotion, pointing to the helmets. "It's contagious."

Unable to speak, Maj looked back and forth between the stick and the little boy. Her body ached for him. Staffer Sara followed her gaze and lifted the stick in the air.

"A shock-stick," Sara said. "It's really just an adapted cattle prod, the latest technique in extinguishing inappropriate behavior. Two shocks for violent behavior."

"A violent solution for violent behavior?" said Maj.

Shaken, Maj left the chaos of the ward for the cracked and abandoned playground, where Kenny marched in a wide circle like every other Saturday. He jabbed a stick at a sky, the color of the cement walls. Maj leaned on the gate, a witness to Kenny's graceful performance of slow and deliberate movements, top-heavy in his bulky green parka and black football helmet. Before long, Maj forgot all about the claustrophobic pressures and dark thoughts cluttering her mind like a colony of sleeping bats.

Kenny completed one circle and started on the next one. He hadn't moved his eyes from the tip of his stick or deviated from his exact pattern but Maj wanted to believe Kenny knew she was there. Nancy pitied kids like Kenny, preferring to work with the mentally retarded. Maj admired him. He'd found a way to create an impenetrable protective wall around himself.

She stopped Kenny with both her hands on his shoulders. He kept his eyes on the stick, though now his tapping was more of a pattering. She searched his face under the football helmet for a sign. His eyes were averted, as usual. His little pink cheeks glowed. If he was content, who was she to assume she had anything better to offer?

"Does that big old helmet make your head hot?" she asked, not expecting an answer.

She did her best to tuck Kenny at her side, but it was like trying to bend a matchstick without breaking it. As they walked together, she reviewed the steps in the new approach she planned for today. Last things she wanted was to allow the crushing pressure of time running out and the fear of disappointment to interfere with their time together. Her task was to provide quantifiable and indisputable data that proved Kenny's infinitesimal progress or she'd feel a failure.

The deserted classroom crowded with empty tables and stacked chairs fit the sanctity of a therapy room Maj's professor had stressed, a quiet place where a child felt safe. In a cleared-out corner at one end of the room, a one-foot-deep tray with six inches of sand sat on a table about waist-high to Kenny. His therapy centered on a three-story wooden dollhouse filled with furniture Daddy bought for Maj's fifth birthday. She brought the house on the bus one weekend and told the staff they could use it, too. Everything was always exactly as Maj had left it the week before.

The first time she showed the dollhouse to Kenny, she gave him a company of toy soldiers that he promptly buried in a far corner, where they likely still were. Exposed in the sand were little plastic dolls, with movable arms and legs, and dressed in light summer play clothes.

Every action Kenny took with the family and toy house meant something to him. The theory was that by verbally relating his actions, Maj's words would bring meaning to him.

Kenny faced the sand with his eyes straight ahead and his hands at his side.

"I brought you a little dog." Maj spoke the simple sentence carefully and clearly, going through the steps she was learning in school, and waited to see what he did next.

Kenny had confirmed Maj's belief that a child as isolated as he was could externalize his inner self through play. The trouble was, and where Maj fell short, was how to prove the subtleties of his change. Nuances weren't measureable. Non-verbal communication, like the way he turned his shoulder and making sure she saw what he was doing in the sandbox, couldn't be proven. The straightening of his spine and tilt of his head when she spoke to him proved too delicate to transfer into hard statistical numbers. As seriously as Maj took the pressure to prove her time with him hadn't been useless or pointless or a waste of time; Kenny had given her the far greater gift. The chance to practice her speech without fear of being lashed out against or given a funny look was slowly building Maj's confidence, while also building her desperation to protect their time together.

Kenny snatched the toy Rin-Tin-Tin dog Maj offered and the little girl doll. His hand grazed hers, sending out warmth. Tempted to mark his act as deliberate social contact, Maj knew she couldn't prove it.

Kenny arranged the girl on a kitchen chair in the dollhouse and placed the dog at her feet. Maj narrated Kenny's play as precisely and accurately as she could, while jotting his actions in her notebook. She worked to keep her voice and expectations neutral.

He picked up the boy doll and buried his face in the sand. A spark shot through Maj. This was it. If he revealed why the boy was facedown, she could . . . what? Prove he was opening up? She was leaving him. But if her findings encouraged another student to continue . . .

"Kenny buries the boy doll in the sand." Maj said, leaning in nearer to him.

She held her breath, knowing how key the boy doll was by not being included in the sweet kitchen scene.

The classroom door opened. Panicked, Maj raised a hand to stop or at least silence the intruder. She kept her eyes trained on Kenny.

"Kenny turns the boy facedown," she repeated, tempted to urge him to go further and resigned that prompting was wrong.

Static filled the room. Kenny frowned.

Distracted, Maj looked up.

"Enough for eight," barked Staffer Sara into a walkie-talkie. "Send Jose. Over and out."

Sara picked up a child's chair, one in each hand, just as Kenny's face crumbled like a Swedish Pepparkaker cracker. He swept out an arm and toppled the playhouse with a crash. Twenty-two pieces of doll furniture flew across the room.

Maj immediately squatted down and wrapped her arms around Kenny, penning his arms at his side.

Sara drew her cattle prod and started toward them.

"Please, just go," Maj said, sticking out a hand to stop her. "I've got everything under contro—"

Sara pressed the button.

"No," Maj shouted, as tiny veins of lightening hit Kenny's chest. Holding him closely, Maj's body snapped as his body did.

Sara leaned in for the second shock. Shaking all over, as much from anger and pain as from fear, Maj rose to her feet.

"That's enough," Maj said, ready to ignite into action, as she stood guard over Kenny, squatted on the floor rocking. Maj's face burned with a choking feeling in her throat.

Sara tried to push past her. Maj shoved her. Sara dropped her prod, stumbled, and fell backwards.

"You're going to hear about this," Staffer Sara said, as she retrieved her prod.

*　　*　　*　　*　　*　　*

Later that night, Maj and Raul left the other volunteers in the dormitory singing folk songs to Nancy's guitar playing. They hiked up a trail to the top of a knoll behind the hospital, following the scent of fire. Darkened trees loomed in silhouette on the eastern rolling foothills. The flat middle of Napa County spread out in acres and acres of newly plowed fields.

Off to the west, a fire burned near enough its smoke irritated Maj's eyes. Raul laid his jacket on the ground. She was happy to be with him, as they sat in silence and watched the fire spread. Bats flew low over the freshly tilled soil.

Wanting to forget about the incident with Staffer Sara, Maj wondered how to ask Raul about the girl at Fillmore without sounding nosy.

Raul broke the silence. "You're a volunteer. They can't fire you."

"I'm on academic probation," said Maj. "I wasn't thinking about how much I need these credits when Kenny got shocked."

Speaking, she felt the connection between her practice with Kenny and her growing ability to express herself accurately without the usual pre-thought and rehearsal and self-consciousness. The reality that credits no longer mattered injured her heart.

"You stood up for what you believe in," said Raul. "You protected him."

"That outburst of Kenny's was a clear sign of progress," declared Maj. "Kenny communicated emotion. Frustration. Anger. Fear. Then this afternoon, he tucks his body next to mine at the Canteen. After months of rigidity, Kenny suddenly leans in. After the shock. I can't explain it. His honest-to-goodness first social initiation with me."

"You're meant for this work, Maj," said Raul. "Compassionate, encouraging, positive."

"I hate to think what's going to happen when the closures start," Maj said in the silence that followed.

Raul shrugged. "Closing Napa State Mental Hospital is just a part of Governor Reagan's larger plan." He jerked a thumb over his shoulder. "He's out to pound all state-run institutions into the ground. Except, of course, prisons. Group homes will pop up all over the state in a year, two tops."

"I dream of opening a home for autistic kids someday," Maj said.

Then she sighed and leaned back, not at all certain about her future with Kenny or with school.

A star streaked across the sky. The glow of the fire was too far away to block the ancient web of stars and the patterns they formed. Beneath the smell of smoke laid the scent of dusty books, wet dirt, and fat strawberries.

Raul's body was warm. Any explanation about Maj's connection to the man she kissed at the Fillmore sounded crazy, so she kept quiet. Still that one kiss, no matter how confusing, opened up an urge to be touched and kissed—not fast and passionless like the boys she'd been with in the past, but held closely by a man and understood without saying a word.

Maj relaxed against Raul, sensing that if anything happened, it would come through her, not at her—a first.

"What'd you think of Dolores Huerta?" Raul asked.

Maj listened with her heart before answering. "I'd never heard a woman strong like that, and in front of men, out in the open. I wish I could hear her again. I'm starting to think she was a mirage."

"You can," said Raul. "Come with me to Delano tomorrow."

"The central valley?" said Maj.

"Cesar is breaking his fast with Bobby Kennedy. Dolores will be there. Ten thousand people showed when we marched to the state capitol. With Kennedy there, who knows how many people will show. It will just be the two of us in the truck."

Maj compared the paper due on Monday with the chance of seeing Dolores Huerta again and Robert Kennedy and Cesar Chavez.

"Before you answer," Raul said, sounding weary. "You should know something. Papa came to this country through the *Bracero* Program in the late fifties. He never went back, but he also never stopped being Mexican. The girl at the Fillmore? When we were just babies, my father gave her father his promise we'd marry. It doesn't matter how many times I've told him no. He's waiting for me to live up to my family obligation, get a job, and marry her."

Disappointment and the wolf carving hung heavy on Maj.

Raul rose to his feet and offered Maj his hand. "I'm not going to marry her. I will choose my own bride."

Using his help, Maj got to her feet just as the memory rose up of her high school friends bubbling on about the gift of a bride to her husband. Sure that she only deserved creepy guys like Clay, Maj turned away.

Raul led the way down the bluff. "We're lions, you and me, running off into the desert."

"But can we ever really free ourselves from the dragon of thou shalt?" cried Maj.

Raul turned around, as if waiting for her answer. Her face felt warm as she looked into his sweet, dark eyes.

"I'd love to go with you tomorrow," Maj whispered.

DELANO

"Take a lesson." Brenda yelled from the front door for Billy to tag along and play golf with her sisters' husbands.

Billy was well aware that as a Tupperware hostess, Brenda didn't want him hanging around on party day. Since he didn't play golf and out of respect for the current dangerous, and some of the most hopeful times in their country's history calling for action not play, Billy passed.

Making that choice was easy. Choosing between driving to the East Bay to look for the man who bought the bright orange GTO, hoping to find the wolf carving, and going to Delano with the guys, Billy picked Delano. Standing up to management was the first real stand he'd ever taken in life. He liked challenging the status quo along with the Chicanos and Negros, the students and workers and women demanding cataclysmic change.

Billy rubbed his hands together, raring to see two of the greats—Cesar Chavez and Robert Frances Kennedy. Kennedy was going to win the primaries. Billy wanted to see the next president of the United States.

"I won't be home for dinner," Billy called, and raised

a hand as Webb drove up.

"Get a haircut," Brenda called.

Billy slammed shut the car door, rode with Webb to the union hall, and boarded the rental bus along with Mal and Red and other Green Caucus members. Alabama would never get on a bus full of Chicanos and Webb. Still, Billy watched for his adversary and his guys to appear, as disgruntled as ever. When the doors finally squeaked shut and they were on their way to the Central Valley, Billy pulled his cowboy hat down over his eyes.

A siren shrieked in the distance, like someone caught by surprise. The sound built to a high-pitched wail. Reverberating in Billy's head, the siren split into a thousand colored fragments. He was still high all right.

All the guys turned silent as the ambulance screamed past. The bus creaked back onto the highway, and the talking and laughing started up again, muted though, out of respect for guys trying to sleep. Someone fiddled with a transistor radio. Static lodged in Billy's head.

"Thought we lost you both there for a minute." Red pointed at Webb who sat rigid, staring straight ahead.

This wasn't the first time Webb had checked out. The darker the news turned in Vietnam, the more bewildered Webb grew. He'd joined the army out of honor and the desire to do something meaningful. At the Fillmore, he told Billy it wasn't the guilt that was killing him. It was his doubt that any of it meant anything. On the way home that night, Webb had sobbed and fought off screaming faces. Since then, Billy kept quiet about the acid he'd been dropping, not wanting to encourage Webb. Billy probably shouldn't indulge in so much acid himself, but the altered states of awareness seemed to broaden his sight and move him from the illusion of his everyday life. With his mind illuminated, an entry point to the future and other planes of imagination became clear to him. Surrendering to the high and trusting what he was being shown allowed him to flow more easily to the rhythm of life around him. Freed from the box he'd been living in his entire life, Billy wasn't ready to squeeze his way back in.

Red twisted in the seat in front of them, handing him a beer. "It's the siren. Flashback to 'Nam."

Mal leaned back in his seat and hummed one of his favorite Hawaiian love songs. Webb's eyelids fluttered. His sagging skin hardened.

"What are you staring at, man?" demanded Webb.

Relieved Webb came out of it, anymore, Billy wasn't sure what Webb would and would not do.

"Hell, we ain't looking at you," spit Red, piercing a can of beer with a church key and pushing it in Webb's hand.

"How much further?" A toothpick bobbed up and down in Mal's mouth.

"We'll be there when we get there," said Red.

Up ahead, a jacked-up pick-up truck sat cockeyed on the side of the highway, with a young Chicano changing a flat.

A girl in a peasant blouse and jeans stood off to the side of the truck. Long, yellow hair swayed on the breeze. The air turned sweet. The blonde again. All the guys got to cat-calling, pounding their feet on the floor of the bus and crowding the windows. The girl looked up. Their eyes met. Another chance and remarkable sighting.

The floor shook the night of the earthquake at the Fillmore with that girl, that moment, and the touch of her lips. He knew without knowing, he was destined to see her again. Beyond her face and those eyes, a familiar stand of trees swayed in the wind. A flash of sunlight glanced off the San Joaquin River not far from where Grandma still lived. The ditch where workers threw Ginger's body was paved over now.

*   *   *   *   *   *

Webb nodded to the front of the bus. Strolling through the middle of the material handlers, assemblers, spot-welders, painters, hog ringers, and forklift handlers came the only two women in the entire plant. Not surprised they'd joined the bus, Billy was surprised the girls headed toward them. The guys stomped and slapped the seat covers in front of them, calling attention to the girls as they passed.

Irritated, and wanting to come down off of his euphoric high in peace, Billy shifted in his seat, so his back was turned away. In the heat, his shirt stuck to the plastic seat and plastered against his back. His hat fused to his head.

Webb nudged Mal. The big guy snorted and coughed and fished the toothpick out of his mouth.

One of the girls was Janice, a recent graduate from New York University. Remi hailed from the University of California at Berkeley. Management didn't know the two girls were college graduates. Management also didn't know the two girls were Communists. Never would have hired them if they had, too afraid of what the girls would get management's factory peons to do in the name of Workers Unite, as if the men hadn't long ago figured it out for themselves long ago.

Not the types to be run off, the two girls continued down the bus aisle without falter. Why they joined the

Green Caucus was a mystery. Sure they were liberals pushing for workers' rights, job safety and all, but the girls were also downright radicals. Neither girl had pulled out a pamphlet, but Billy would bet the farm that both girls could recite every word of the Communists' Central Committee "People's Voice" and the "Red Flag."

Janice stopped where Red's outstretched legs prevented her from going further. Of the two girls, Janice was smaller and darker. She had a nice body, and long, black, curly hair. Behind the wire-rim glasses, her black eyes were always serious.

"Uglier than a junkyard dog and dumber than a post," muttered Red.

"Why that's no way to talk about yourself, Red. It doesn't become you," said Remi, the taller and lighter of the two.

"We want to talk," interrupted Janice, all business.

Billy kept his eyes hidden in the shadow of his cowboy hat, not really enjoying their insults flying back and forth.

Webb slid the Coleman beer cooler into the aisle to prevent the girls from getting any closer. Then Webb folded his arms across his chest with his fists clenched, giving his muscles the appearance of being bigger than they actually were. Webb didn't like the girls on account of them being so outspoken against the war.

In that time, Billy was able to get a cigarette lighted. He took a long drag and coughed.

"We've got ideas about the next election," growled Remi, still looking for a fight.

"A little early for that, ain't it?" Red gave a mock frown to each of the guys, like he couldn't figure such a thing.

Billy grinned. Remi frowned.

"Why so quiet, Billy?" asked Janice.

Billy shook his head, resenting the attention, and acting like he, too, couldn't fathom why he wasn't flying off at the mouth as usual. But Billy knew. Acid revealed to him sights and sounds, even smells and the texture of things that likely had been right in front of him all along. He was just too nerved up acting and reacting, judging and blaming. Getting high gave him a way to unfasten from dark thoughts about missteps at work and disappointing Brenda and the girls. Acid, like Grandma's visions only instead of seeing into the blonde's future, took Billy deep into unexplored parts of himself and showed him life differently.

Grateful for the broader understanding of himself, and his place in the world, than the limited view he had been exposed to calmed Billy and made him aware of his thoughts and behavior in ways he never could have in his ordinary life. Finding there was a different way, a way out of the box he'd been knocking against since he was born, made Billy feel like he could do anything. He didn't ever want to return to the way he once knew.

Not bothering to answer, he pulled his hat lower and closed his eyes. He came to when he heard his name mentioned.

" . . . and Billy's name goes up for President. That puts you, Red, at Vice-President." Janice widened her eyes and shrugged like lobbing a challenge at Red.

Surprised, Billy struggled to fill in what he'd missed, as the girls and Red talked back and forth about him like he wasn't there. The girls were up to something. Billy just wasn't sure what or why it involved him.

"Hell, Billy's only twenty-four years old," said Red. "We ain't much on taking a pig in a poke."

"And that means?" smirked Remi.

"He hasn't been tested," answered Red.

"He handled the Skypiece case with management," said Janice. "The guys like him."

"It's true, man. Billy can win." Webb looked like he was waiting for Billy to say something.

A bee buzzed in Red's window. It found its way out again.

"He's the only one who can win," urged Janice. "He's got the Chicano vote."

No way could he win. The girls were using him.

"The Negroes will vote for him, too," said Janice. "Won't they, Webb?"

Webb hesitated. He blinked once and cleared his throat, speaking to Billy rather than to the girls. "The Panthers know you bailed out Mavericks at City Hall, man. And you did right by Skypiece."

"One thing. Billy's got to declare before the Negroes put up somebody else," said Janice.

Red's face turned red, and his freckles disappeared. He glared at Billy like all this was his fault. Janice cocked her head, waiting for Red's answer.

Billy decided to relieve Janice of any further delay.

"You girls come into the factory thinking you're going to do something important," Billy started. "You pass out subversive material, get the guys riled up, and you do it to advance your political agenda. The workers are the ones who end up out of a job if we act out or call a strike that management ultimately breaks. Not you. You're off to fight for your next righteous cause. And by the way, Skypiece is not a case. He is a man who lost a finger because management shirked their responsibility." Billy's breathing broke.

Guys from the middle of the bus had turned around

and were listening. Billy flicked his cigarette out the window, disgusted at the girls' arrogance, their education, and their privilege and class.

Janice stood up. "We do care about workers' rights, and you, Billy, just happen to be our best bet."

She stared hard at Billy and returned to the front of the bus.

*   *   *   *   *   *

Route 99 took them smack dab through the center of Delano, where it was hot and dry enough to turn the air hazy. Trucks and cars and people crowded the streets. Mexican men in headbands and black armbands directed their bus into a parking lot filled with other buses—some from high schools, colleges, some with church names, and many, like theirs, private rentals. All of them glittered, saturated in a rainbow of light.

Still vibrating from the twist the girls threw at him, Billy gazed over the heads of hundreds of people in a town square lined with oak trees. Red United Farm Workers' flags, with the black Aztec eagle in the middle, flapped overhead. Banners with the UFW official motto, "*Viva la Causa*," and others with *HUELGA*, draped from taut wires.

Billy scanned the crowd without admitting to himself that he was hoping to spot the blonde.

Smoke billowed from barbecue pits. The smell of grilled hot dogs and hamburgers, mixed with hot tortillas, got the guys on the bus moving. Most of them were Chicano. Other than Webb, there were only a couple of blacks. Red and Billy were the only whites.

The last ones off the bus, Billy and Webb, joined slicked-back college boys in sports shirts and slacks, and men stooped and callused and lined. They all melted under the oak trees' shady canopies, where Mal left with the local UAW banner tucked under his arm and an additional donation they'd brought in the form of a generous check.

Before long, the giant banner was suspended between a basketball hoop and a tree branch. In line for vats of beans and rice, Catholic priests in white collars and black short-sleeved shirts mingled with Mexican and white men, women, and children.

Mal bullied his way to the front of the line and stumbled back with a soggy paper plate piled high with food.

Trying to imagine going without eating for nearly a month for a cause, like Cesar Chavez's spiritual fast for non-violence, suddenly Billy was famished.

His cowboy hat broke the sun, but it wasn't until Billy was sitting at a picnic table in the shade, eating meat that he started feeling better. Eating standing up, Mal spilled beans across the tabletop from a second plate of food.

Red mumbled around a hotdog in his mouth. "Hell, those girls got a lot of nerve."

"They're up to something," Billy said, dismissing Janice's proposal as ridiculous. Besides, any advancement in Billy's life now felt like being thrown straight into a roaring fire.

"I know you don't want to hear it, Red," said Webb. "Janice is right about Billy." Webb watched most of the rice he shoved onto a plastic fork roll off.

Red pushed his plate aside. "Hell, so now just because they say different, our plan don't mean shit?"

"First off, 'our' plan is news to me," said Webb. "Second, the guys pay their dues and don't see what it's getting them. Chavez is fasting because farm workers don't believe they can win without violence. Billy will fight so our guys don't have to."

Webb said all that while spooning rice and beans into a tortilla, as if concentrating on one thing helped him open up about something else.

An assembler came up and asked Red something. Rather than catch up with him later, Red turned away and responded the assembler's question, ending their discussion.

"Those girls are bulldogs," Mal said. "They grab hold of something, and they're not letting go without a fight." Mal raised his eyebrows and headed off for more food.

Billy ignored Webb staring at him from the other side of the picnic table and lighted a cigarette. Red kept talking to the assembler.

Webb spoke under his breath. "You'll win hands down, Billy."

"No way. Doesn't matter anyway, Brenda's harping on me to quit. Besides, nothing is going to work unless we're all behind it," Billy said, looking at Red's back.

"Brenda wants you to quit the Executive Board?" said Webb.

"She hates the factory."

"Even after all it's given you guys?"

"She hasn't forgotten the strike," said Billy, looking out over the hillside. "Most of us lost more money than we'll make back."

"President locally could get you noticed at the national level," urged Webb. "You could give your kids private schools and swimming pools."

Webb's mention of service at the national level caught Billy by surprise, and his mind ballooned out in all directions at once, more than he knew possible. National. Billy was only now starting to maneuver the challenge of living with one foot cemented in Brenda's conventional life and the other skating through the freedom in his mind. President and Vice-President both demanded more time at work and less at home. He'd probably get a pay raise. Brenda would like that. Still, Billy didn't believe Janice was telling the truth. He put the girl's idea out of his mind.

A bullhorn sounded, and someone from up front yelled for silence. The message was repeated until everyone settled down, and the noise died away.

"Cesar Chavez waits for us the UFW Field Office." And then the bullhorn went silent.

Everyone cheered at Chavez's name, and the crowd of people in the food line shifted. As they all moved out of the square and into the street, Billy thought about what Chavez had suffered and sacrificed for the sake of principle to have people cheer like that. Just hearing Chavez's name gave people hope, made them believe anything was possible—that size was measured beyond inches and feet, money and assets, physical strength and beauty. By one's actions.

Mal sang an upbeat Hawaiian song until they turned off the paved road and started up a dirt path. Dust kicked up by thousands of feet forced Billy to tie his handkerchief around his face like an old-time bank robber. Even so, the air was thick and hot. He had a hard time keeping his eyes from watering.

A crumbling, low rock wall meandered across green rolling hills, like a dragon in the San Francisco Chinese New Year's parade. A lizard slept on a stone, and a bird sang like falling water. Billy casually surveyed the crowd around him, noticing there weren't many blondes around.

Up ahead, an old packing shed came into view with an upholstered easy chair, like what's in someone's front room, and instead was sitting on the front porch. A microphone stood in the center. Two giant speakers, the size of those at the Fillmore, flanked either side of the building. Everything was faded to the same dusty beige.

The bullhorn sounded again. This time, the call for silence came from a ways behind them. A hush moved from the back of the crowd, swept over Billy, and continued forward.

The crowd parted for a man with a face marked by the sun, and who was half-walking and being half-carried by a priest wearing a religious collar and a man with thick sandy hair, a sports jacket and tie. Cesar Chavez. Robert Kennedy. The reverend wearing the collar was a stranger to Billy. The three men moved real slow across the trampled earth. When they passed him, Billy joined in clapping.

Wearing a parka in the hot sun was one of the results of Chavez going more than three weeks without food. Carved gullies in Chavez's face were others. Holding him up, Kennedy, in comparison, looked so vigorous that he made Chavez appear even weaker.

"Hell, Chavez sure knows how to use the pump handle," said Red.

"He had to do something. The strikers are no match for the growers. The workers grow frustrated. Things get violent . . . " Mal left his sentence hanging.

"Billy knows how to work it, too, how to make things happen. Don't you forget it," said Webb.

Following Chavez was Dolores Huerta, the woman from the Farm Worker's Benefit at the Fillmore. That night on acid, listening to her go on about the ills farm workers suffered, Billy didn't spot anyone like him, a half-breed who as a kid toiled the backbreaking work in the fields right alongside the Mexicans. Mostly, what Billy saw was a lost cause. If he ran for President and the Indian part of him was uncovered, he'd soon be just as defeated as the farm workers were.

Chavez's wife wore a long, white veil hanging down her back, like for church. She and Huerta settled Chavez with a blanket over his legs. Kennedy sat on the other side of him. Reverend stood at the microphone. Murmuring quieted. Then, the silence was complete.

"My name is Reverend Drake," said the man with the collar. "Cesar Chavez has asked me to read a letter to you."

As Reverend Drake thanked everyone, Billy thought about what it felt like to have someone believe in him like Webb did. Grandma used to tell him all the time he would be a leader of men. Webb made him think differently about himself than a loud mouth, screw-up. But now that the girls were talking about him running for President, Billy found he couldn't register the idea of leading anyone.

When Billy turned his attention back to Reverend Drake, the crowd was fired up, cheering in agreement.

"To be a man is to suffer for others," said Reverend Drake, still reading from Chavez's letter. "God help us to be men!"

Billy hollered along with the rest of the crowd, but he didn't accept the message. Sacrificing in a nonviolent struggle for justice hadn't helped the Indians. Only one way to get what you wanted, fight for it.

*   *   *   *   *   *

198 | MARTHA ALDERSON

Less than a month later, on April 4, 1968, Martin Luther King was gunned down, another non-violence failure. The factory was shut down out of respect. As Billy and Webb made their way out, an off-line inspector sauntered past Webb, singing under his breath.

"Bye bye blackbird
Blackbird, bye-bye."

"Fucking, Ku Klux Klan Nazi," screamed Webb and jumped the inspector.

Alabama's guys jumped Webb. An hour later, Billy, with the help of Red and Mal and some of the other guys, had everyone off each other. Mal and Red, with the help of the guards on their side, sent Alabama's guys out of the factory first.

While Billy waited for a sign from Mal to bring out Webb, he worried about the knife cut across Webb's face and arm. Billy offered Webb a beer, but mostly Billy was the one needing to get a grip. He felt like he was standing still, with life streaking past him, over him, beyond him. He wanted to give Webb time to get control. Webb was pissed. He was hurting, too. Billy also wanted to give himself time to slow things down long enough to make sense of what the hell was happening. Martin Luther King gunned down. Things inside the factory promised to worsen.

Webb shook off Billy and paced the room. The fishbowl office was eerily quiet, surrounded in a deep darkness, so unlike the usual light and chaos of the factory. The only sound was Webb's fist slamming into his hand, like a baseball player with a mitt.

"Maybe there's always got to be a war going on," Webb said. "Maybe ain't none of this matters anyway."

The violent moments of fist against fist struck in a slow rhythm, steady, and cruel.

"Let's wait and see what happens," Billy said, spotting Mal at the front doors. "I want a doctor to take a look at that gash on your face."

Mal motioned them forward. Webb left by himself.

When Webb didn't come back the next day, Billy shifted from worried to scared. He called Webb's apartment and found his telephone had been disconnected. Billy drove by Webb's apartment and banged on his door. All the curtains were closed and no one came.

*   *   *   *   *   *

Three weeks passed, and still Webb wasn't back.

Guys on the line grumbled and complained about their jobs, the conditions, each other, more and more of them every day. Johnson never would have signed the Civil Rights Act four years ago, except for all them people standing up and demanding it. Now the battle for equal rights had turned into a free-for-all. The Negroes were getting theirs. Farm workers' theirs. Women theirs. Goddammit, autoworkers wanted theirs, too. There weren't many pacifists in the factory.

The deadline for names to be put forward for the election arrived, and still, no Webb. All of them in the Green Caucus congregated in the conference room at the Union Hall.

Old Skypiece surprised Billy by nominating him for president.

Buzzed from mescaline he ate last night, Billy couldn't grasp that this was really happening. The faces of his girls flashed in his eyes. Webb flashed in front of him, too. This next statement would change his life forever. Billy didn't know what to do. He couldn't do both, drugs and lead the men.

Balancing his way to the podium, Billy carefully placed one foot in front of the other and looked straight ahead. He hesitated.

"I promise to do my best to get us our fair share," Billy breathed into the microphone.

More than surprised, Billy was stunned when the vote came in as nearly unanimous for him as President under the Green Caucus. Webb, though he still hadn't been heard from, was on the slate as Vice-President, Mal as Sergeant at Arms and Red the chairman of the bargaining committee.

After the meeting, Red waited until they got to the parking lot before he started in on Billy.

"You can't lead the men," accused Red. "You're always tripping."

Red said it like he was joking, but Billy knew he was serious. Red had every right to be pissed. Billy had surprised himself, accepting like that.

"I didn't know Skypiece was putting up my name," he said.

Billy said that by way of an excuse, knowing he couldn't ignore the truth of Red's words. On the way home to watch the California Presidential Primary results for Kennedy, Billy imagined Webb hurt and blamed himself. Maybe Red was right. If Billy had been straight, he could've helped Webb better.

DEATH

Maj squared her shoulders in front of her academic advisor's apartment door. Freaked out and beating herself for putting this off so late, she refused to give into fear. Having not seen or heard from her advisor since he took her report, she cleared her throat, preparing to simply explain she needed his help. Her psych teacher hadn't received her green folder with her carefully researched and typed report. She'd like it back. Simple as that.

She knocked. The sound echoed down the quiet of the corridor, and the door inched open. Making a face of regret, Maj didn't know whether to close the door—not wanting her advisor to think she'd opened it—or just leave. Without breathing, she listened for his step. Nothing. His black Corvette Stingray was parked alone, as usual, in a red zone opposite his building, so he had to be in there.

When he didn't answer on the second knock and the door opened further, Maj looked both ways and then peeked inside.

A red batik scarf draped over the lampshade cast her advisor's living room in a pink and shadowy light. The television was on without the sound and without him. Maj held her breath and heard snoring from his bedroom. She only wanted to do this one time, get the report and leave. The quicker she found her missing folder, the sooner she'd be at campaign headquarters with everyone else, in anticipation of Senator Kennedy's speech celebrating his victory in the California Primaries.

Fingers crossed, Maj rubbed her hands down her skirt, checked the hallway again, and slipped inside her advisor's apartment.

Forced to study here a couple of times under his supervision, Maj knew her way around his apartment. Trembling, she checked over her shoulder. All she needed was her report.

No sign of her folder in the pile of unopened mail and overdue notices on his kitchen table. One was from the phone company, demanding payment and threatening to disconnect his service. Maj rifled through stacks of newspapers cluttering his floor, each crinkle colliding with the creepy silence of his apartment.

At his bedroom door, her heart started pounding so hard it beat against her eardrums. She'd written her report on deviant behavior to better determine if she was in any real peril with her advisor's seemingly obsessive attachment to her. For her report, she'd interviewed professors who chuckled and excused a male's clinging and demanding behavior as harmless examples of boys being boys. Though her professors hardly thought so, Maj's research at the library confirmed what she most feared: if allowed to continue, deviant behavior never stayed unchanged. Deviant behavior always turned more deviant.

Asleep on his stomach in the middle of rumpled sheets, her advisor appeared innocent. Maj wanted to slap herself across the face. What was she thinking, being here?

Rushing to the front door, she resolved to simply rewrite the report. Asking for an extension so she could relocate the research and recalculate the statistics was a task that smelled like an old fish in the sun, but that bummer was better than being where she shouldn't be. On her way out of her counselor's apartment, Senator Kennedy's face filled the television screen. Maj took heart that everything would work out fine just like the lady in the academic advisory office had said.

"Who are you talking to?" her advisor asked from behind her.

Maj whirled around, mortified she'd been whispering to herself, something she hadn't done for years.

The glow of the television screen lighted her advisor's tall, lean body, naked except for white briefs. Suddenly frightened, Maj slung her bag over her shoulder and pulled open the door.

"No . . . no one. I was looking for my psych paper," she said quickly, her words sticking to her parched throat, hands shaking, and her heart racing. "The door was open."

"Well, don't just run off," he said calmly. "Let me get you what you came for."

The sudden change in him startled her. Relieved and untethered by fear and uncertainty, Maj felt hopeful.

"Oh, thank you," she gushed, stepping back inside.

When he didn't move to get her report, she squinted and fumbled with the doorknob.

"I'm meeting some friends at campaign headquarters," she said with her face burning.

He shook his head, as if remembering what he was doing.

"I understand. Your report is just over here," he

said, motioning for her to follow him.

Reluctant to leave the door, Maj tried for a smile, attempting to make it look real, and said thank you, without moving.

A flash came from the television. The white light awakened something in her, a reminder she pushed away, unable to remember. Men's faces filled the television screen. Like a nightmare, the view was crooked. A man lay facedown on the floor.

"He's been shot!" Maj cried.

Bobby Kennedy turned his head to his wife, kneeling in her party dress beside her husband, stroking his chest, and touching his brow. Ethel faced the camera, marred by anguish and pleading. Without tears, she thrust out her hands shoving people back.

"I have to go," said Maj, reaching for the door.

"I'm sure he's not dead," her advisor said quickly.

"Dead?" Dread settled over Maj and she closed her eyes.

"Just wait a minute, and we'll know for sure he's okay."

Then, he reached around her and snapped off the television, half-glancing at her.

"You don't want to see that," he said. "They'll take him to the hospital. I'm sure he'll be fine—"

"His brother wasn't fine," she croaked. "Martin Luther King wasn't fine." Her voice cracked. She shook her head and stumbled outside.

Her advisor snatched her wrist. She fought to shake loose. With a vice-grip on her, he pulled her back in his apartment, standing so near he had to fold his body to look into her face. He locked the door.

"Why, you're shivering," he said, his nostrils flaring. "Let me warm you up."

He slid his hands under her top. Panicking, Maj pushed him away and tripped on her long skirt.

She couldn't hear what he was saying over a nasty buzzing in her ears. He shoved her up against the door. She grunted at the force and avoided his mouth.

"No," he said sharply, yanking her hair so hard she moaned. He pulled again, yanking her head back at a sharp angle.

"No," he barked.

Staring with glassy eyes, he forced Maj's head immobile against the door. More insistent, he pushed past the elastic waistband of her skirt and down her belly. Busy piercing, stabbing, penetrating, hurting, he leered at her, like a troll egging her on to fight back. One thing she'd learned as a kid from Clay was that resisting made him more urgent and cruel.

Maj squeezed the carving at her neck. The tiny piece of wood denied her the help of allowing her to sink into a cold, numbing oblivion. Instead, it kept her watchful and alert. Sex was shrouded in darkness—furtive and agonizing. A white light flashed in her mind.

"Let me go," she mumbled, unable to open her mouth wedged between his fingers.

"You want your report?" he said.

Maj nodded, barely able to move.

"You get what you want," he said. "I get what I want."

"You're hurting me." Her words came out garbled. Blood pounded in her ears, and she squirmed to get away.

A storm giant, her advisor held her head against the door with both his hands and watched her struggle to keep her legs together as he slowly spread them apart with his knees. Chills ran loose over Maj's body. *Loki* was back.

"Say you love it," he groaned, his eyes gleaming.

Up so close, his face elongated and shrank, like in a sinister funhouse mirror.

His knees, still between her legs, pinned Maj against the door. She let go and fell into the familiar dead place she'd found as a child in defense of Clay, huddled in a tight little ball waiting for it to be over.

Her advisor raised a hand, his fingers quivering, and slapped her. She gasped and her face froze.

"Just say you love it, and I'll let you go. Go on now. Be a good girl." He nodded at her. "Say it."

Maj's breathing turned shallow. Her pulse raced under his sweaty hands, locking her head in place. Trembling, she fixed her eyes on the floor. He twisted her neck, and slapped her again.

"Oh yeah, baby. Chicks make the exact same sound when they cry as when they climax. But you're going to have to be a little louder. I can barely hear you. Have you ever come, Maj?"

He spoke fast, his voice agitated and his words a blur. His hair stuck to his neck.

In a burst of laughter, he held her arms up against the wall. Unable to catch her breath or speak, light-headed, and fully terrified, she curled forward, her ears ringing.

When he was finished, she ran for the door. Her fingers refused to work, and it took some frantic tries before she slipped from her advisor's apartment. The moon was dark and the night bright with stars. Maj ran into the middle of street as he stumbled out the front door, zipping up a pair of jeans.

*   *   *   *   *   *

Maj ran with her heart flaying in her chest, sure her advisor was right behind her and too afraid to look back. Speeding faster, she didn't know if the sound of pounding feet was coming from her or from him closing in on her. Blinded by a grey slate of nothingness, suddenly her guidance counselor twisted into Clay. Flashes and fragments taunted her.

Finally out of breath, Maj stopped running. Instead of going home to scrub herself clean over and over again, she found herself in front of Raul's two-story apartment building. Light-headed, she pushed back hair tinged with blood, and quickly crouched over so as not to faint.

Light streamed out of all the windows of Raul's apartment. Voices and the radio blared through the opened door. As much as Maj wished she could stay, she left in one direction and then turned, suddenly confused how to find her way home.

"Maj, is that you?" Raul called.

He trotted down the stairs from his apartment, wearing a felt hat with a crooked feather tucked in the band. His eyes were blurry and red.

"Come inside," Raul urged, gently leading her to the stairs.

Maj backed away from him, fumbling to pull her top around her and smooth down her long, peasant skirt, now blooded and torn. In the time she'd known him, she'd been careful to only show him her earnest and hopeful side. She hated herself for shoving her shame and humiliation between them.

He put out his hands.

"Okay. Okay," he soothed, nearly whispering.

"Everything's okay. You're safe now."

"I've got to go," she mumbled.

"I'll drive you."

Even then, she didn't appreciate how bad she looked until she peered at Raul through her eye slits, and saw how still and chalky-white he stared at her.

"Let's get you cleaned up first," he said.

Maj gazed up the long, steep stairway. Wearing an encouraging smile, Raul motioned her forward. With a deep shuddering breath, she mounted the stairs. At the top, she leaned against the smooth stone pillar separating Raul's apartment from his neighbor's. Her jaw hurt and her stomach felt brittle and raw. Her lip was bleeding. She followed with her fingertips blood caked down her chin.

"Is he going to be okay?" she whispered.

"Who did this to you?" Raul asked, stepping towards her.

Shivering and nauseated, she backed away.

"Senator Kennedy. Is he—?" she asked, unable to say the word.

Overcome with filth, Maj turned away from Raul.

"Let me help you," he said, gently leading her into his apartment. "Let's see . . . KQED reports that Kennedy was shot repeatedly. He's conscious with good color. Another station says only that the extent of his injuries is unknown."

Raul spoke calmly and his voice soothed her.

"You're shaking," he said. "Should we go to the hospital?"

Maj shook her head and immediately turned dizzy. He offered her a red bandanna like the one he often wore around his forehead.

Inside his apartment, every chair was taken around

the massive table in the front room. Paper lanterns hung from the ceiling and shone on a sleeping baby in the middle of the table next to the radio. Posters with brown fists and "Chicano Power" hung alongside black Aztec birds on a red background. A dog looked up and thumped its tail. A pregnant girl stood, rocking back and forth, her bare feet solid and apart, a modern-day version of La Virgin de Guadalupe glowing from a poster behind her. Upon seeing Maj, the girl started towards them. Raul raised a hand, stopping her. Most of the people Maj recognized from the campaign office. She stayed out of the light and averted her face.

"Hi, Maj," said Petrana.

Petrana, the girl she first saw at the Fillmore, and who was promised to Raul by their fathers, came out of Raul's bedroom. After she met Petrana, Maj told her she wouldn't see him anymore if it bothered her. By Petrana's answer, Maj knew that unlike him, Petrana wanted to marry and Maj had backed off. Since then, things had been pretty friendly between them. Now Maj wanted to reassure Petrana she was only here because she had nowhere else to go.

Also a college student, Petrana's long black hair was parted down the middle. Beads hung around her neck. Seeing Maj in the light, Petrana gasped.

Raul shook his head. That one tiny gesture of his to Petrana spoke of an intimacy between Raul and Petrana that turned Maj's legs weak. He helped her into the kitchen. She felt lost and confused.

He touched her arm. "How about some coffee?"

"I should go," she said, fumbling with her top, knowing she had to do something and unable to think what.

"You just got here," he said, sitting her in front of

someone's empty coffee cup, a thick oversized envelope, a dirty ashtray, and a poster of Robert Kennedy.

As Raul tore a napkin in two and formed a filter in the coffee percolator basket, Maj squirmed in the chair, sore and uncomfortable and unable to ease the burning between her legs.

Raul handed her a wet hand towel.

Confused, she stared at cold water dripping off her hands and looked back at him. He gentled lifted her hands, and she gingerly held the rough cool cloth to her fattened lip while he dumped three scoops of coffee beans into a grinder. The noise jarred her.

Flicking his thumbnail across a matchstick, the smell of sulfur filling the air, he lighted the gas burner. Then he grabbed a couple of mugs from the open shelves, reaching up thick plaster walls into a high ceiling, stacked with plates and glasses and bowls and cups and saucers and jars. A small three-dimensional bright green, gold, yellow, and red papier-mâché skeleton—decorated with pink blossoms—hung from the bottom shelf.

"I saw Kenny for you," Raul said, as the smell of sulfur faded to the aroma of brewing coffee.

Maj traced a finger around Kennedy's face, whispering Raul's words. Not only did she lose three units for pushing Staffer Sara, Maj had to wait and reapply next fall if she wanted to see Kenny again. Thinking the young boy might wonder why she hadn't come back made her ache and doubt she'd ever be good enough to create a future working with kids.

"He didn't even know I was there," said Raul.

She smiled at the thought of Kenny tapping his stick in a circle. Smiling reopened the cut. The sting slapped her serious.

She must have cried out because Raul was suddenly asking questions again.

"Who did this to you?"

Maj knew he meant well, but talking about what had happened was unthinkable. She turned her head away. The perky bubbles of the coffee brewing died down. He poured each of them a cup.

"Did you ever figure out how to slay Nietzsche's dragon of Thou Shalt?" he asked.

Caked blood gave way to the damp cloth as she shook her head. Sadly, she leaned back in her chair and sighed.

"You?" she asked.

Her advisor's evil snare flashed in front of her. Alert, she leaped to her feet and nearly doubled over from cramping in her stomach. To hide her pain, she limped to the sink and held onto the side of the cool enamel. She rinsed and wrung out the cloth, watching the water turn from candy-apple red to shocking pink down the drain.

"I dropped a class last semester," Raul said from behind her.

Maj's head snapped up. The reflection staring back at her in the darkened window showed true distress. She ran her fingers through her hair and slowly rearranged her clothes.

"So you could help with the oranges," she said weakly, studying her calluses from helping him with the harvest.

A quickening of understanding pulled her to the dusk of his words. She turned around.

Raul had taken off his hat to reveal a gleaming skull under a sheer crew cut, just like Daddy's after the accident. Maj dropped her head and covered her face with both hands.

"Why is this happening?" she cried, knowing nothing would ever be the same.

"Three lousy units and a change of status." He sat down at the table across from her. "I'm ordered to the Oakland Induction Center next week for a physical."

Rather than freeze up and give into the panic, suddenly Maj was speaking urgently and miserably, giving a rote accounting of whatever popped into her head, like when she'd relate Kenny's actions back to him.

"More than 200 faculty stood with nearly, what was it? 900 draft resisters? At the rally last month. Our philosophy prof was there. Maybe he can help. Or, you could ask the demonstrators out front of the center to cause an uprising that prevents you from entering and making you unable to obey the order. The police will tear gas and arrest people. You'll never get in."

That was a lot to say with a bare bulb hanging from the ceiling lighting her face. She wasn't making much sense and didn't know what else to do. Raul stretched his long tapered fingers across the tabletop. She put her hands on top of his.

"I'm not a slayer of dragons," he said. "I'm a pacifist, like Cesar Chavez. It's taken a lot of soul searching, and I'm ready to join up."

"You could go to Canada," she said quickly. "Or to your *abuela* in Mexico."

Raul winced, and Maj longed to tell him she'd go anywhere with him.

"I can't run away," he said. "I have an obligation to my country. I also have an obligation to my family."

Maj wanted to cover her ears, so she wouldn't hear

what he about to say.

"I can't go to war and possible death without my father's blessing. He won't give his blessing unless—"

"He's marrying me."

Light from the living room glowed from behind Petrana standing in the kitchen doorway. Maj slipped her hands to her lap. Rather than scoot out his chair and let Petrana sit on his lap, as she seemed to want, Raul pulled out the other chair at the table for her.

"I thought . . . " Maj started.

What? She thought he wasn't going to marry Petrana? He might marry her?

Petrana told him how sad one of their friends was about Senator Kennedy. Maj quickly lost the thread of what they were saying. When she remembered to pay attention again, Petrana was still speaking. This time was to her.

"When the sun comes up tomorrow, our families arrive. By afternoon we'll be married."

1969 - MAY

Billy shot into his house, greeted by Sadie slamming her paws against his chest and nearly knocking him over. Boxes and suitcases lined up at the front door kicked him in the gut. Dizzy and puffing hard, he pushed away Sadie and yelled for Brenda. Alternating between nosing him from behind and running ahead, Sadie led Billy to the bathroom.

Leaning against the door-jam, he caught his breath. Trying to act natural, he scratched Sadie behind the ears, and her hind leg twitched.

As soon as he was able, Billy tried for a casual approach.

"What's happening?" he said.

Brenda snatched the shampoo bottle from the shower and slapped it in a brand new toiletry bag on the sink.

"Shows how much you know about your own family, now doesn't it?" she said.

A couple of deep breaths did nothing to slow down his heart. The air was so hot and so thick Billy wiped sweat from his face, ready to split inside out. He tried not to wheeze.

"I've sacrificed too much to run for President," he said quickly, rolling the sleeves of his shirt up around his elbows. "I know that now. Me being president isn't going to change yours or your sisters' low opinion of the factory, the men, or of me."

Her sisters groaned from the kids' room, packing. He grimaced and banged the wall to back them off.

Brenda opened the medicine cabinet and closed it without removing anything. Taking hope, Billy stepped forward.

"I'm tired of doing this by myself, Billy."

"So you pick today to leave?" he said. "Just give me a little time. I'm working my tail off for us."

"You've been drinking, haven't you?"

"The board election results are coming in any minute. Sometimes a man gets himself an opportunity to make a difference. That's not something you can just turn away from."

"You have such a romantic view of yourself. Husband and father aren't good enough for Billy Wayman Wolf. Oh, no. He's got to be the leader of men."

She swaggered across the bedroom with her hands on her hips. He knew right off Brenda was imitating him. She played him with a nasty voice. "Listen to me, I know everything."

"You're the one with the romantic views," he shot back. "Wanting to be something we're not. What's wrong with being an honest working-class family?"

As soon as the words were out of his mouth, he groaned.

"We're only working-class because you want to be. Bob gave my sister a middle-class lifestyle. With a new station wagon and a few nice things. We're there, too."

Lowering her voice, Brenda added, "You're a lot smarter than Gene is, anyway."

Lost in surprise over her calling him smart, Billy forgot what he was going to say. Brenda tossed the kids' plastic Tupperware toys in an empty suitcase.

"Well you are smart, Billy," Brenda said, nodding sharply. "Why do you think I married you? But you're stuck, and it's not the world holding you back or the factory or even me. It's you. You're not afraid of being poor again. The thought of being rich scares you half to death, and so you drink yourself silly. You take drugs. Even when you're here, you're either tripping or hung over. How much fun do you think it is for the rest of us?"

"There are more important things going on out in the big wide world than Tupperware parties. I asked you not to work anyway," he said. "And I'm good for a hell of a lot more than making a living, so you can show off."

"Tupperware is the exclusive home-party sales company. Sarah says I'm a natural. She promises I'll make good money at it."

The house turned quiet, except for Billy's breathing and the drone of conversation from the kids' room. It was like they'd been talking from two separate planets that suddenly collided.

"Running for president of local is something I believe in, Bren, something I think you and the girls can be proud of me."

"Why did you make all those promise to me before we were married, anyway?" Brenda asked, picking up toys.

"Why are you breaking up our family, Brenda? You can't just leave."

She brushed past him to the suitcase. He got there first and slammed shut the lid. She stared at his hand like she had all the time in the world, and there wasn't anything else in the room to see.

"The fine car," she said. "A grand house. Even a kidney-shaped aquamarine swimming pool, no less. You in a hat. Me wearing gloves. Our kids skipping to the candy store."

Billy frowned. "What are you talking about?"

He asked her that even as an old image from his childhood materialized of a family at the candy store in Oakland. He wasn't surprised to remember that the yellow-haired girl with the wide eyes stood at center stage of the memory—her father wearing a felt hat and driving a new Cadillac, her mother wearing white gloves, and the rich lifestyle he'd imagined for them. The blonde was responsible for inspiring those early dreams of his.

"Why'd you promise all those things when you never even wanted to be a husband? Or a father either. Did you? I wouldn't mind you being gone from us all the time if I thought we were getting somewhere. But this? Your eyes are pointed in two directions at once. Can you see me, Billy? Can you hear me?"

Brenda kept her eyes trained on his hand on the suitcase, waiting for as long as it took him to move, emotionless and unbothered to make him. Confused, Billy couldn't remember the last time he'd thought about that old dream. All this time, he'd been seeing a bright new future for him, for them, for the country, the world, and with Brenda stuck in a future from an earlier life and a different generation.

Lowering his voice so her sisters would have to work to hear, Billy tried not to hiss.

"The picture I had for us back then, that's not me. Not anymore. It was all a pipe dream anyway. What do

I know about being a husband or father either? But I've been trying, Brenda. I have. Those things? The car. The pool. They're just surface things, material possessions designed to tie us down. Then, when we're all tied up trying to pay for them, the corporations steal everything that's not nailed down."

"Don't you dare bring your political garbage and your big-bad-they're-out-to-get-us into this," snarled Brenda.

"Daddy, Daddy," cried Melissa.

Billy whirled around and opened his arms to his little girl. Melissa jumped up, knocking the wind from him.

"Can we go to the beach again?" she asked, picking at his collar. She smoothed a hand against his cheek.

"Anytime you want, Sweet Pea."

"Oh, goodie," Melissa cried, jumping out of his arms and zooming out of the room. Sadie barked, and chased her.

Tears pooled in Billy's eyes.

Brenda stuffed the bathroom bag in the suitcase. That she packed so helter-skelter and unlike her usual organization made him tired. Maybe if he lay down and slept, he could figure out a way to fix this mess he was in, fix his family.

The suitcase snapped shut.

"Why are you taking away our kids," he said.

"It was your dream, Billy. You painted the words so pretty, I just followed right along beside you."

"You've never been beside me. You've always been ahead or behind. You have never been with me," he spit.

"Hi, Daddy."

Billy stopped talking suddenly and looked down. Squatting in front of Lisa, he gave her a big hug.

"Hi, baby doll."

"Where are we going, Mama?" Lisa asked.

"We're not going anywhere, baby doll," Billy said.

"To Grammy's house," Brenda said. "Pack three stuffed animals. Hurry now."

Lisa leaned her head sideways and hummed as if deciding if he looked different from that angle.

"You look like Jesus in the chapel," Lisa said.

"That's because his hair is so long," said Brenda. "Now, scat."

Lisa righted herself, smiled, and gave him a kiss on the cheek. On her way out the door, she was singing "*An Itsy Bitsy Spider.*"

With Lisa gone, Billy had nothing. His eyes blurred. An intolerable heat and crushing pressure surged through him.

"You believe I'm going to lose the election today, don't you?" he said.

"I'm quite sure you'll win. And with you as president, there's sure to be a strike. Standing still is hard enough. I'm not about to backslide, again."

"If there is a strike, I'll be home a lot more. Isn't that what you want?"

"I think 6,000 grown men having a great big temper tantrum because they can't get what they want is disgraceful."

"Isn't that what you're doing, Brenda? Walking out on me so you can get what you want? I'd say that's pretty embarrassing, myself."

"I don't intend to come back."

A sweet melody came from Lisa's room. All she did lately was sing. The more that went on between Brenda and him, the more his little girl sang. He lighted up a cigarette, knowing it was going to make him suffer, while hoping that holding onto it would prevent him from throwing something. What had he done? He'd risked everything and for what?

Billy wiped sweat off the side of his face and nose. It was about a hundred degrees in the bedroom. A chill passed down his neck. Dizzy, he held onto the doorframe.

"You're drunk." Brenda picked up her suitcase and stomped out of the room.

Her words slugged him like fists in his face. He marched right after her and plowed straight into the door jam. Damn. She knew just how to club him over the head with his worthlessness and bludgeon him with his faults.

The luggage and boxes were gone, and the front door closed like shutting him out of his own family. Seeing *The Velveteen Rabbit* left on the coffee table, he picked up the girls' favorite nighttime story and considered all the ways they made him real. With an anchor drowning his heart, he hoped his girls didn't just abandon him like the boy tossed the rabbit in the story.

The house was quiet. Brenda put down her suitcase. Sadie immediately curled up next to it, as if to be sure she wasn't left behind.

Brenda straightened her purse.

"You're the one always going on about how workers need people like you to step up," she said. "But I also remember years of complaining about how the union was invented by management to control the masses. Isn't that why you're drunk all the time? Because now you're the one screwing the guys."

Grateful she was still willing to talk, Billy tried to explain. "I'm not a politician. I use what I've got for the guys, not for my own personal gain. I'm hoping to change the way the little guy is treated."

"You aren't the little guy anymore," Brenda said pointedly.

"This is something I got to do. Be patient. Please. Give me this one."

"You know, if I thought you really could be a politician, I'd probably stick around to see what happens. But you're more pain than pleasure. More hurt than help. An agitator."

"This could take me to International," he said. "You and the kids will have everything you want."

"You wear a brand, Billy. You're a militant, a union activist. You're the first one they'll get rid of. When I met you, I never considered a life like this for myself. I couldn't believe my luck when you asked me to marry you." Brenda touched Billy's cheek with the saddest look on her face. "You and your stories and all your dreams, I didn't think I deserved any of it. Your vision of the future gave me a new vision for myself. It's all I can see."

He grabbed her hand, shivering and knowing full well he'd taken a wrong turn. It wasn't her fault what was happening. Not Ma's or the guys, either. He'd done it to himself. He was the furthest away from his future than he'd ever been.

She picked up her suitcase and opened the front door.

Somber, Red stood with a fist raised to knock.

Sadie shot out to the car.

Brenda called Sadie back. "I'm leaving her with you," she said, catching Sadie by the collar. "I know how much you hate being alone."

Billy buckled, as everything that held him up in life disappeared. Brenda transferred her suitcase from one hand to the other as Billy reached out to her.

She checked the front room and walked out the door.

"I can see this isn't a real good time," said Red, standing outside the door.

Red's car sat at the curb with the engine running. Mal and Webb waited inside. Webb had come back from Death Valley a month ago and something wasn't right with him anymore. In front of Red's car, Brenda's sister's car motor was running. From the car radio, Joni Mitchell blasted something about clouds getting in her way.

"Brenda, hold on," called Billy.

"Hell, Billy, they're ready with the results," interrupted Red.

Weakness pulled at Billy, and his knees wobbled. Brenda threw the suitcase in the trunk of her sister's car, all loaded up with bags and boxes. Lisa stuck her head out the window of the station wagon. She wasn't looking at Billy, more concerned with watching Mal. Summer and Melissa were laughing and playing in the backseat, without a clue their lives were breaking apart. Billy pushed past Red to stop Brenda before they pulled away.

AUGUST

The Marlboro Man winked from a billboard advertising cigarettes at Maj's Bay Bridge exit. The advertising man's face and posture pulled her to the much younger man she'd kissed at the Fillmore, less weathered, and even more gorgeous and mysterious than the smoking man looming over the steady stream of cars ahead of her.

The GTO zoomed onto 9th Avenue. Flashing lights and a piercing siren, a police car appeared in the rear view mirror. Guilty, Maj pulled to the curb, her heart thrashing against her chest, and she fumbled for what was left of the joint in the ashtray. She ate it, smoothed down her hair and wondered how loaded she was.

A blur of red, black, and white screamed past her. She let out a stream of breath, sick of being scared and crying all the time. Pulling back into traffic, her arms felt heavy. She was tired, tired of feeling so helpless and deficient, dirty and ashamed, worthless and alone. The sooner this photo shoot was over the sooner, she could tug the covers over her head and go back to sleep.

Up ahead on Market Street, Halloween cats hung in the windows of the old Crocker building. A catalog-shoot for next spring's bathing suit line on a drizzly October day made it difficult for her to stay closely related to the natural world, homework she remembered from her Native American history class last year. Yet another example of how the new ideas she'd learned in school conflicted with the expectations demanded of her in modeling. The two—school and modeling—had never been a good mix, and further confirmed that dropping out of college had been the right decision.

Everything she'd learned in school came from a book, written by a man, from a man's point of view. Male teachers gave every lecture she sat through. Men even dominated the entire fashion industry—women only expected to be blind, deaf, dumb, and beautiful.

As near as Maj had come to achieving her dream of graduating, Mother never even knew she'd been going to college. Without school and Kenny and Raul and the mystery man, Maj slept and she modeled. She was good at modeling and liked the positive attention she received and that she was earning money for Daddy. School, on the other hand, had always made her doubt herself, and her efforts rarely found reward. That's what she told herself anyway, hiding from the real reason. Maj was running from her academic advisor.

The GTO purred like a new car down city streets slick with fog. Except for the gash in the bumper from sideswiping a mailbox after she learned of Daddy's accident nearly two years ago, no one would suspect the car was four years old. The GTO booked, maneuvering so smoothly she could drive, light a joint, and sing along to Aretha Franklin's *Respect* all at the same time. Before long, shoulds and insecurities melted from Maj's mind.

Eric Burdon came on the radio, singing about warm San Franciscan nights. Maj's skin pulsated. The air felt electric. She slowed down to watch a mime in Union Square walk like a clown, every movement exaggerated. White-faced and blue-lipped, he braked with one knee bent to his chin, and winked at her. Maj smiled for the first time in forever.

From this vantage point, the city was not a fantasy but more of a yearning. Wannabe hippies arrived more every day, looking for a world apart from the din of hypocrisy, scandal, and the lies of the establishment. Here, they hoped to find a forgiving world. Maj recognized the futility, she on her way to help create more lies through photographs. Still, she loved the city no less for its imperfection.

Pulling into the studio lot, she parked in a far corner and appraised herself in the rear view mirror. Her eyes were puffy and her hair greasy—make-up and a stylist could fix all that. Maj liked how the outside reflected her internal feelings. She readjusted the wolf necklace.

Inside the studio, a woman at the reception desk spoke on a telephone. The tinkle of Maj's moccasins' bells reminded her to stay focused and alert.

"Excuse me," Maj said.

The receptionist glanced up, the phone still at her ear. Despite all Maj's measures to keep centered, she wasn't prepared for the stare she got. Feeling judged and misunderstood, she ducked her head and readjusted her headband.

Jimmy trotted down a hallway of doors, wearing his trademark red.

"Maj, darling," he said.

A sagging roll of fat under Jimmy's chin hadn't been there when she first met him. He pulled in his elbows like chicken wings, bony fists the pointy ends.

"You look a fright, my dear!" he said. "Did you stick

your head in a fan? Take off that horrible little thing." He flicked the wolf carving around her neck. "Hurry. Hurry. Off. Off. Off. Dag's on his way," he demanded.

Maj raised her chin in defiance. Jimmy caught her arm and turned her toward a man with a ponytail striding towards them.

"This shoot is worth more than Paris," Jimmy hissed.

Shorter than Maj by a foot, like the receptionist, Dag was still able to look down his nose at her.

"Dag, this is Maj." Jimmy crammed a cigarette into the lacquered red holder. "I have to apologize for her. She's at her absolute worst. Please tell me you think there's hope."

He lighted his cigarette, his hands trembling.

"No, Jimmy," Maj said quietly. "Don't apologize for me."

The word reverberated in Maj's mind. She hadn't said no to her advisor, not that saying no would have stopped him. Saying no could have just as easily incited him more. But, the truth was, she didn't speak up for herself. She didn't cry out for help. When did she first learn that saying *no* to someone, anyone, made her wrong and rude and a bad person?

The only trouble with Maj's new resolve to speak up was that the more verbal she became, the more visible she turned. Finally, having learned the cost of silence, Maj was ready to pay whatever the price for speaking up, speaking back, and speaking out.

She squared her shoulders and stood up straight, taking her first step toward enjoying modeling rather than simply using it as a way to make money or expecting the same sort of passion she'd felt working with kids.

Dag's eyes were serious and made her insecure of his appraisal, as he moved around her. Suspicious of him and not wanting him to see too deeply, Maj wondered who she could trust.

Jimmy scuttled alongside Dag with his cigarette smoke bobbing behind them. An agent who still treated her like a child, when what she most needed was respect. Perhaps similar to speaking up for herself, it was time she demanded his respect.

The two men reappeared in front of her.

"Great cheekbones," Jimmy said.

Jimmy had known Maj for as long as she could remember, and the only good thing he could say about her was that she had great cheekbones.

Suddenly feeling like she was being watched, Maj checked over her shoulder. Seeing no one, she shook off prickles of fear. Then, she dropped her arms like a mannequin. Rather than turn her invisible, the stance focused her beyond her distrust in the moment. She trained her eyes on a spot partway between the clear vision of solid reality and the world of make-believe. Her body relaxed. She moved from paranoid fashion dummy to inner visionary, or so her professor used to promise.

Dag tsked, his attention still on Maj's face. Then, he snapped his fingers and started down the hallway.

"Come," he commanded.

"Ever so good of you, my dear boy," said Jimmy with obvious relief in his voice. "Run along, Maj. Make these shots surpass even the last ones. Dag is the best there is. This is important."

Jimmy raised an eyebrow and squeezed her arm.

His stare pierced through her shell. Rolling her eyes, Maj nodded and followed Dag, as Jimmy's words caught up to her. Somewhere in there was a compliment. After a confused pause, she glanced back. Jimmy wagged his fingers and left.

*   *   *   *   *   *

Finally, the camera stopped blinking. Dag would take his time checking proofs. Waiting to hear if he demanded any retakes, she collapsed on a wicker table, grateful for the break.

Stiff white patent boots stuck to her sweaty calves. She hated these plastic possessions of a plastic society—the tubes of make-up, synthetic hairpieces, fake eyelashes, artificial jewelry, plastic bottles of shampoo, plastic toys, cups, glasses, plates and utensils. Everything was turning plastic and all of it derived from oil, which meant more boys sent off to fight and die.

A clock on the wall read only a minute past the last time she checked. Impatient to be dismissed for the day, Maj fashioned her outfit's matching hat into a pillow, splayed across the wicker table and closed her eyes.

Above her spoke someone with a heavy Southern accent. "Jimmy said it's your favorite."

Opening her eyes to sticky fizz, the smell of artificial lemon and lime cleared Maj's nose. Blushing self-consciously, she swung her legs off the table and sat up as the man finished pouring a can of Fresca into a jumble of ice. Immediately on the alert, Maj looked around for the stylist and dresser and make-up man. Worried, finding herself alone with the stranger, she got to her feet and reluctantly accepted the glass he offered. Then, she distanced herself by a couple of steps and sized him up.

Tall and dark with light blue eyes, he smelled of Old Spice, Daddy's aftershave. His hair was styled, not short-cropped to be completely straight and not hippie-long either. A tanned face and wide shoulders made him appear athletic. He wore a turtleneck sweater and a Nehru jacket with its customary collar and no lapels.

The cleft in the stranger's chin deepened as he sat where she had been sitting. Lines fanned out from his eyes as he regarded her with what felt like an uncomfortable amount of interest.

"Alrighty then," the stranger said, clapping his hands together. "The instant Jimmy showed me your composite I was hooked. No one else would do."

The stranger acted like Maj should know him. She didn't, and his unexpected presence irritated her. Angry that he didn't introduce or explain himself, she put the glass of Fresca beside him without drinking it.

"When you see Dag, please tell him I'm getting my things," she said curt and wary.

She left to change into her street clothes and poncho. Not bothering to wash off the make-up, she grabbed her things, eager to go home and sleep.

When Maj came out of the dressing room, the stranger was still perched on the wicker table with his legs spread and hands dangling between them.

"No Dag?" she asked.

The stranger shook his head. Maj hesitated, uncertain whether she should wait or just leave. She wiped an arm across her forehead. Flesh-colored make-up streaked the back of her hand.

"Why so tired?" the stranger asked.

She sensed he was serious, as she dug for her keys at the bottom of her purse and started for the door. If he wanted something, he'd have to explain himself. Bells pinged from the buckskin fringe on her boots with every step.

"Where do you go to school?" the stranger asked.

Maj swung around.

"I don't go to school," she snapped.

The stranger put up both hands as if fending off a blow.

Satisfied with herself, Maj resumed walking like she had charge of her life. The stranger fell in step beside her. Determined to distance herself from him, she walked faster as they crossed the white-paper stage.

At the hallway, every other ceiling light was turned off. Her breathing turned shallow.

The stranger spoke slowly, his southern drawl almost homey. "Something has your attention. You're much too serious for that to be a fellow. Am I right?"

"I was going to Berkeley," Maj said.

As soon as the words were out of her mouth, she crossed her arms and walked even faster, disgusted with herself for falling into his trap and anxious to discontinue the conversation. Without school, she felt lost, having attended classes and wrapped her life around a school schedule since she was seven years old.

"Were going?" the stranger said.

"I'll go back. Next year, no more than two," Maj said to herself.

Hearing her plan out-loud made the possibility sound reasonable and rational and attainable.

The stranger caught up with her.

"Then you're free to accept an exclusive contract," he said. "I'll pay you twice what you earn now."

Catching her breath, Maj stumbled. Flustered, she opened her mouth and then was at a loss what to say.

"You emotionally connect to the camera like no

other girl I've ever seen," he said, almost to himself. "I want you to be the next Reingor Girl."

Maj turned and stared at him. "Car dealerships and department stores," she said.

"My grandfather started the dealerships. I opened the clothing stores."

"Would I have to walk in fashion shows?"

"We can work out details later. What do you say?"

Walking toward the back door, Maj considered his offer. One job. Money enough for Daddy. Was he serious? And, if he were?

"What does Jimmy say?" she asked.

"I haven't talked to Jimmy about this."

Again, Maj stopped walking, surprised Mr. Reingor had spoken to her before consulting Jimmy. Just as quickly and to cover her surprise, she moved forward.

"Thanks a lot for the Fresca, Mr. Reingor. Please tell Dag I waited as long as I could. I'm happy to come back for retakes if he needs me."

She pushed against the outside door. The door was locked. Her muscles tightened.

"I almost regret having to say this but the proofs are flawless. If they weren't, I'd be sure to see you again."

Loki crouched in his tone, causing Maj to wonder yet again if she gave off some sort of scent only nasty men could smell. Since her guidance counselor's assault, she'd kept to herself and in the shadows.

Mr. Reingor took a set of keys from his pocket and unlocked the door.

Exasperated, Maj stepped outside. The sky drizzled on a line of little witches and princesses, cats and ballerinas, pirates and hobos skipping single file across the street toward a group of Black Panthers marching on the sidewalk wearing black ties, slacks, leather jackets, and berets.

"If you'd told me proofs were in earlier, I'd already be home," Maj complained.

"I did just tell you now," he said, looking surprised.

*   *   *   *   *   *

A week later, a scrub jay squawked from the maple tree outside Maj's bedroom window. She rolled her head across the pillow until the sun's feeble light hit her face through a break in the branches. An intoxicating scent tugged open her eyes. Long-stemmed red roses, posing on her nightstand, turned her throat rusty. She groaned and pulled the sheets over her head.

Yet another twisted method of intimidation, this time with roses no less, proved her academic advisor had discovered Nancy's boyfriend Kevin lied. Kevin had informed Maj's advisor that she'd moved out with no forwarding address and for him to leave them alone at the house. No more excuses. It was time she moved home. All her things were packed. She'd resisted, terrified he'd follow her to Great Oaks. As much as she dreaded the thought, backing him off was ultimately her responsibility.

She tossed the roses out the window, pulled her stash from the drawer of her bedside table, and lowered the needle on the LP. A breeze sent crimson gold sunlight through the crystal vase that broke the light into a rainbow of colors dancing across her bedroom walls. She rolled a joint, singing along to Jimi Hendrix looking for a way out of here.

Maj held the smoke in her lungs as long as she could, guilty for how much pot she was smoking. Like a screen, getting high softened a harsh world, wiped out her negative feelings, and silenced the unrelenting criticism she flung at herself. Lately though—rather than bring peace and tranquility—the more she smoked, the more paranoid her thoughts grew.

Seeing the time, she pulled on the first clothes she found slung across the chair and grabbed her bag. She'd have to hurry if she wanted to call the UAW local office and still be on time for today's shoot. With a full work schedule, rather than wait any longer to have enough time to drive to Fremont to ask about her mystery man, Maj decided calling was best. Humming with excitement for what she might learn about her mystery man, she vaulted down the stairs two at a time.

In the kitchen, the blender whirled. Haas handed Meagan a peeled banana for their morning smoothie. Maj's mouth dry with anticipation, she rooted in her bag for the local union office's telephone number she'd gotten from the operator.

Meagan shouted over the noise of the blender. "Your roses. Did you see Maj's roses, Haas? A vase of the longest stemmed red roses."

"Yeah," Haas said. "I answered the door. Remember?"

"How much do you think long-stemmed roses cost?" Meagan asked.

"What? Are you writing a book on roses?" Haas' voice sounded sore.

Hurt that Meagan would make light of anything that had to do with her advisor, nevertheless, Maj was grateful for Meagan and Haas both—Nancy and Kevin, too—for standing beside her at her darkest and most helpless time. Her roommates and their boyfriends blocked the door to her advisor and stuck to their story that Maj was modeling in New York. Somehow, he'd gotten wise to their scheme. Maj's heart turned weak at the thought of facing him.

She picked up the telephone. It had no dial tone.

"Who is Gerald Reingor?" asked Meagan.

"Gerald Reingor?" Maj repeated, confused.

"I read the card," said Meagan.

A man's voice with a familiar southern drawl boomed in her ear.

"Yes, Gerald Reingor here. Is this Maj?"

Maj took a step backwards, nearly dropping the telephone. Behind her, Meagan sang to the melody of the children's song, *sitting in a tree, K-I-S-S-I-N-G*. Maj blushed and motioned Meagan to be quiet.

"I apologize for my thoughtlessness. Gerald Reingor here."

"Is there a problem?" Maj asked.

"Only if you find my need to see you again a problem."

Maj sighed and pressed her fingers against her temple to stop the throbbing. The difference between the guys she'd known and Mr. Reingor was that he was willing to pay a lot of money to get in bed with her. Even if his job offer were real, her acceptance wouldn't make her any more of a tramp than she already was.

"I'm calling to inquire whether you are free for dinner tonight."

"I'm sorry—"

"Not tonight? Alrighty then, tomorrow night. Strictly business, you understand. By then you'll have had a chance to consider my proposition. You at least owe me that. Actually, you don't owe me anything. It would be decent of you to hear me out. I promise to get you home early. I'll send a car for you at 6:30. How does that sound?"

"I won't—"

"Of course, I'll pick you up myself. 6:30 sharp tomorrow night. Right. I'll see you then."

The telephone clicked dead, with Maj's hand tangled in the cord. A man had walked on the moon, and still she couldn't say no. She left a message for Jimmy to call Mr. Reingor with her refusal. Then she dialed the UAW office in Fremont. The telephone rang on the other end without anyone picking up.

DECEMBER

Billy waited in a gravel parking lot beside the tiny Diablo post office hung with Christmas lights. Drumming his fingertips on the steering wheel, he wondered what exactly he expected to accomplish. Odds for getting directions to the Hawthorne residence were fixed against him. Ruffling Sadie's fur, he was grateful for her company.

When the postal clerk arrived for work, Billy left Sadie in the car.

He greeted the clerk as she unlocked the door. Inside, a miniature Christmas tree sat on the counter circled with holly and red berries. The clerk was slow to remove the cardboard block in front of her enclosure, and bought Billy time. Nervous about how to word his request, he tried and rejected several different approaches in his mind.

Finally ready for him, the clerk's hostile stare momentarily threw him. He tried for a sincere smile.

Rather than softening her demeanor, the clerk folded her arms and frowned.

"I need your help," Billy started.

The clerk didn't answer. Behind her, rows of cubbyholes were filled with letters standing on a slant. Feeling a bit tilted himself, he suddenly grasped that his long hair was either disgusting or frightening the clerk. Either way, he didn't belong here.

"Let me get to the point," he said quickly as she turned to leave. "I'm looking for the residence of a Mister Robert Hawthorne."

The clerk's face closed up.

Billy quickly unfolded the paper and spread it open in front of her, thinking the factory lady's fancy penmanship might help somehow.

"He bought an orange GTO several years back and—" Billy started.

"I can't help you," the clerk said, replaced the cardboard, and disappeared into the back room.

*   *   *   *   *   *

At the end of the year, Billy waited until everyone left before he came out of hiding at the old Manteca graveyard, right up next to the railroad tracks. The bouquet he placed on the freshly turned mound of dirt covering Grandma's coffin looked big compared to the others. Weighted down by her sudden death, and not getting a chance to see her before she died, Billy said goodbye now.

"You'd be proud of me, Grandma. I haven't had a drink in three months, two weeks and four days. I'm real sorry I never got you that big house like I promised."

Ashamed of failing her, Billy hunched his shoulders as he rifled through recent memory for any little accomplishment he could share about himself and came up with ten million ways he'd screwed up his life. He hadn't seen his girls since Brenda moved them out of state, while the emptiness inside of him kept growing bigger. At work, more and more of the guys were acting out about the shitty conditions and their shitty pay, and Billy was less and less able to accomplish much on anyone's behalf. He couldn't seem to do anything right.

"I lost the carving, but you probably already know that, don't you? I'm real hopeful I'll get it back soon. I haven't been able to get the exact directions, but driving around the neighborhood, I'd say the wolf is living high on the hog and running with jetsetters."

"Where's your coat, Billy?" The hand Ma put on Billy's shoulder was cold enough to send a chill though his shirt.

Startled, he lowered his shoulder. Ma's hand slipped away, and Billy immediately regretted losing her touch, craving affection since Brenda left. He flicked his cigarette. A January wind snatched the smoke. Red embers from the cigarette dulled to ashy gray.

"The service was real nice," Ma said. "Everyone was asking about you."

"I don't much like funerals."

The wind whipped Ma's cotton dress around her calves and lifted yellow leaves littering the gravesite. Grandma would like that there was a tree nearby with leaves blowing. His throat tightened.

"I knew you was coming," Ma continued. "I told Ray he could say hey himself when you bring me back to your Aunt Ida's."

The white fur collar of Ma's black sweater was already smeared with suede-colored makeup. A gold cross hung at her neck, and she wore a plastic pin of Santa with Rudolph the Red-Nosed Reindeer.

He was twenty-five, a quarter century, which made her forty-two. That meant Grandma was only fifty-eight when she died.

A train roared past the cemetery. Cattle cars brought the stench of manure and death. The train whistle faded in the distance. Billy shook out a cigarette from the pack and pinched his lips around it.

"Hear about the Indians on Alcatraz?" Ma asked. "Now that takes some imagination. 75 Indians taking over the island as their own."

"Feds will have them rounded up and hauled out before you know it," Billy said, offering Ma a cigarette. "Brenda left me. Took the girls with her."

"You don't seem particularly surprised she's gone," Ma said, holding the cigarette to her lips for a light.

Billy lighted his first. What with the wind, it took a couple of tries and getting real close before he could get Ma's going, too. Just as soon as their divorce was final, Brenda was marrying her boyfriend and moving the girls to Arizona. Billy never figured Brenda to leave her mother and sisters. Showed how little he knew the woman, even after seven years of marriage. Time he took responsibility for his life.

Ma took a drag off her cigarette and fiddled with bangs coiled like springs across her forehead.

Even after nearly eight months of not taking psychedelics, Billy's mind seemed unwilling to turn right side in. All his flaws stared at him and exposed the untruths in his life, like Brenda leaving was somehow Ma's fault. His entire life Billy had blamed Ma whenever anything went wrong. Anymore, he couldn't hide behind blaming others for anything. Brenda leaving wasn't her fault, wasn't anyone's fault but his own. A great weight pressing down on his shoulders became two giant wasps' nests buzzing with resentment and the destructive fire of his anger.

"You're right, Ma," he agreed.

"D'she give you fair warning?"

"Oh, so now it's all my fault?"

"You're awful high-spirited, Billy Wayman. You get that from me."

Ma offered Billy a flask from her purse. His mouth watered, imagining the feel of the cold metal against his lips. He tasted the high and shook his head no. The swig she took, he swore burned down his throat, too. She wrapped an arm across her belly and rested her elbow with the cigarette real close to her face, making the distance to reach for a puff barely an inch.

"You sure do resemble your grandma with your hair long like that."

"You mean like an Indian?"

"Yeah. Like an Indian."

Billy looked at her more closely. "Are you crying?"

"Feeling a mite lonely without her."

He flicked his cigarette to the ground and crammed both hands in his pockets.

"Brenda warned me she'd walk out if I ran for president."

"Is that why you ran? So she'd leave you?"

"I don't know why I even try talking to you."

"That's a horrible thing to say to your own mother."

"You're right. I didn't come here to fight. Fighting never got me anywhere."

"Pray for forgiveness, son. God will take you and leave everyone else to deal with the devil. These are the last days. You know that, don't you, son?"

Billy shook his head, his mind fixated on the flask in her pocketbook.

"Well it's true. You're saved if you know it in your heart. We had us some pretty good times together, you and me. D'you ever think of them days? Or you so goddamned poisoned against me, bad is all you got now?"

"I wasn't the one doing the poisoning, Ma. You took care of that all by yourself."

Billy said that, but in truth he wouldn't have traded growing up with Grandma for anything and, in the end, living with Ma hadn't turned out so bad either.

Before Billy could apologize, Ma chimed in. "You ain't so perfect yourself, Billy Wayman. Until you forgive me, boy, you ain't never going to forgive yourself."

With no reason to argue the truth, Billy didn't say anything to that. The wind sent leaves flying across the tight-fisted dirt.

"You think it's your God-given right to deserve something from me?" Ma continued. "Well it ain't. I birthed you all right. Who's to say I owe you anything more than that?"

"A little love might've been nice."

"You can't say I ain't loved you your whole life now, Billy. Besides, the Bible don't say nothing about any one of us having something coming, except what we're able to cobble together for ourselves. Now that I think of it, I do believe the Fifth Commandment says something about loving your mother."

"Why'd you have all of us?" he asked. "You certainly didn't want to raise kids."

"People have babies for lots of reasons besides being a parent. Never having nothing wears a body down. I wanted excitement and fun. You know about excitement and fun, don't you, son? Having a little fun and making babies go together. Least in my day they did."

Another train whizzed by. Grandma was never going

to get any rest.

"It's your life," Ma continued. "Just don't let all that pain and bitterness make you into someone you're not."

"What the hell does that mean?"

"Always the smart-aleck. You got that from me—and your loud mouth and stubbornness and bull-headedness, too. Quick to temper."

Billy stopped listening. Damn. What he wouldn't give for Ma's flask.

"You and me, son? We did all right. I'm sorry I'm a disappointment to you. And I'm real sorry about Brenda and the girls. I know they miss their daddy, and for that I'm truly sorry. Let me ask you something, Billy. Seeing as we was talking about what a mother owes her son, I wonder what exactly does a father owe his kids?"

Ma moved out of the wind, and Billy grabbed the chance to fight back, nearly desperate to prove he wasn't a complete loser. Then perhaps he'd accept it himself because he was beginning to believe that all his hard work and dreams were worth no more than a puff of smoke.

"We've given more money to the farm workers than any other organization. We were the first to speak out against the war. The teamsters got in bed with Nixon after he let Hoffa off. Not us. I'm standing firm, making the world a better place for my kids. I want them to be proud of me. Someday, I hope they learn we changed things at the factory for the workers like they haven't been changed before. It's going to take everything I got. Someday my kids are going to know the good that came of my work."

When Ma stayed quiet, Billy looked over his shoulder. She was halfway through the cemetery on her way to the dirt parking lot. Of course. Ma always had to have the last word.

1970 - JANUARY

Maj walked through the mission cemetery of the historic Nuestra Senora de la Soledad, or, as Raul translated in English, Our Most Sorrowful Lady of Solitude. She slipped into the back pew of the chapel, shaking her head at how aptly the name captured her feelings lately. Soothed in the quiet, Maj was comforted that at least she didn't look as miserable as the nearly life-sized statue of the most sorrowful lady propped in the altar alcove. Or, so Maj hoped.

The chapel smelled musty, reminding her of old people and incense and spent wax. Though the chapel was small, Raul and Petrana's vows didn't reach Maj in the back. Raul spoke softly, and the veil covering Petrana's face muffled her voice.

Rather than marry as Petrana had predicted last year, Raul went missing, hiding out in Mexico until his grandmother convinced him to return. Since then, he'd been working toward conscientious objector status based on his religious opposition to killing. Joan Baez's husband recently went to jail for resisting the draft. Hoping to avoid the war *and* jail, Raul planned to propose to the draft board that he serve a two-year volunteer job at a halfway house in Berkeley for men recently released from Napa State Mental Hospital. His hope was that the board would approve such work as service to his country.

Leaving before the ceremony ended, Maj wondered if Raul considered marrying Petrana giving up. Stopping at a gas station to have the GTO filled with gas, Maj suddenly was struck how she was no different. The day she gave up school was the day she'd willingly given into fear and accepted doing things the way they'd always been done.

Now without school, Maj was free for the much higher paying assignments in New York and Paris. Travel was not something she wanted or was looking forward to.

*   *   *   *   *   *

On a whim at the gas station, Maj checked the map. El Camino Real would take her straight from Soledad to Fremont. Time she tracked down her mystery man and finally discovered who he was in her life.

An hour and a half later, she pulled into the weedy parking lot of the UAW Union Hall, turned off the engine of the GTO, and then didn't get out of the car. Questioning her logic, Maj reached to restart the engine and come back another day when she was better prepared.

Breathless, she opened the door instead, knowing that surrendering to fate and stepping into the great unknown had nothing to do with logic or rational sense. Second-guessing herself, she swung her leg back in the car and slammed shut the door. She smoothed her hands down her pant leg. Twenty minutes later she got out.

"Hi," said the woman at the front desk pleasantly. "May I help you?"

Well aware how out of place she was, Maj quickly outlined seeing the UAW banner at the Fillmore for the Farm Workers Benefit. The woman nodded.

Pushing back a stray curl that escaped her upswept wedding-appropriate, friend of the groom hairstyle, Maj started with the easy ones first. She described the man who'd reminded her of Olle-the-Loyal.

Drawing a curious stare, the woman blushed.

"Malakaton," the woman said, fiddling with a silver clasp holding together the sweater thrown over her shoulders.

Raising her eyebrows, Maj grinned at the woman's obvious feelings for the man. Their connection fed her confidence, and she described Tjovik-the-Wise who the woman identified as Webb.

Now that Maj was so near what she'd dreamt of, she held back tears threatening to fall. Swallowing hard to clear the lump in her throat, she began, hopeful.

"There . . . there . . . was a third man," she stuttered, at a loss how to describe his glow, his spark, his touch.

The woman looked toward the solid double doors leading into the union hall.

"Is he here?" Maj asked in a rush.

"Who wants to know?" the receptionist interrupted, narrowing her eyes and twisting her mouth, as if suddenly suspicious of Maj's motives and protective of the man.

"He's someone special to me," Maj murmured, hoping to appeal to the woman's softer side and unable to come up with anything else.

"That's confidential information," the woman

snapped, each word sharp and heavy. She pointed to the door. "I'll have to ask you to leave."

Disappointed and unable to think of anything else to say, Maj waited in her car for him walk outside. By the woman's reaction, at least she knew her mystery man was real and not just some longing of hers for an imaginary prince. While she waited, she surveyed the lot wondering which car was his. She imagined herself physically storming through the double doors. As much as she could actually see herself formally stopping time long enough for answers from him this time, she waited for more than an hour without taking action. Finally, letting the sob that had been waiting to escape, Maj gave up and cried all the way to Great Oaks.

*   *   *   *   *   *

From the musty smell of the chapel to the dusty smell of the union building, later that same day, Maj lost herself in the stale and stuffy smell of old family antiques, heirlooms, jewelry, and first edition novels. As she inventoried one room after another at Great Oaks, an idea began forming in her mind. Nodding to herself, she chuckled, excited about the possibilities.

With the curtains swept back, the dark and forgotten ballroom on the second story of the east wing transformed into a glowing, honeycombed expanse of light. Sitting on the floor, Maj glanced up at the high-beamed ceilings, sure she heard the echo of a string quartet, quiet laughter, the ping of crystal glasses, and murmurings, as the swish of ladies' gowns swept across the floor. Rock stars of their day, symphonies still permeating the room joined and contrasted with the music of her world.

Returning to her work, Maj added a silver looking glass, part of a set, to her list. Steps sounded on the stairs that were immediately recognizable as Mother's. At the sharp staccato her heels made crossing the hardwood floor, Maj braced herself for a tirade.

"Not that," Mother cried, lunging for the mirror.

"Sorry, Mother," Maj started gently. "We agreed—"

"If your father were better, he would not approve."

"Yes, he would," Maj answered, not backing down.

Having roamed the house as a kid, when Maj moved back, she'd flung open the closed-off spaces. Well aware of the value of the antiques shut away for generations, every piece been left as Jenny Watson had originally arranged them. The amount of money they would bring at a major auction house—possibly enough so she wouldn't have to travel—motivated her.

"I don't see why—" Mother started.

"The funds will buy Daddy the best care," reminded Maj.

"Thanks to you, he has been receiving the best care. And, until you fired them, most of the doctors said whatever he hasn't recovered by year three he likely never will. We are nearly at year three."

"How can you say that?" Maj cried. "He's doing so much better."

Mother ran a hand across heavy velvet ceiling-to-floor draperies that protected the old hardwood flooring from sun damage. Satin, marble, crystal, stained glass, Shreve silver, ornate furniture, Persian rugs, gaslights, feathered fans, and Victorian gowns filled the closets—all of it valuable.

"It's time we transfer objects we don't use into the hands of people who will," said Maj.

"Don't part with anything without speaking to me

first," demanded Mother. "I'm going to the club now. Your father is with Carmen."

"Yes, Mother."

*   *   *   *   *   *

As soon as Mother's car rumbled across the bridge, Maj raced downstairs to work with Daddy. The practice she gave her father—under the supervision of his speech therapist—was a slender ribbon, tying her to her dream of someday returning to school and continuing her work with autistic children. She was relieved to no longer have to deal with her academic advisor and, for now, had just about talked herself into believing she was better off without the challenge of school and the quaking anticipation of another exam, another failure, catastrophe, wrong answer, and poor assessment.

Deliberately setting up Daddy's therapy room in her childhood bedroom, Maj pushed back the hanging beads she'd hung, to Mother's chagrin, in place of the sliding closet doors. Grabbing his file, Maj was finally desensitized to the bad feelings the room used to bring up from the past. Her old bedroom no longer made her jittery. Still, the closet held secrets and lies. Her psych classes taught that one only moved on from the past by talking about it. More words.

"I colored this graph to show your improvement," she said, flipping through Daddy's file.

When they'd started together, therapy consisted of helping him overcome his shame of not being able to speak and encouraging him just to try.

Daddy paused for a moment. Maj could almost see him picking through his mind for understanding, and coming up blank.

"Improvement?" he asked.

Maj explained the best she could, using the colored graph to show him what she meant and to reinforce her words.

Nodding his head, Daddy studied the steadily rising line she pointed to.

Dressed in tennis whites, long pants in deference to the season, and with a white, V-neck fisherman's sweater draped over his shoulders, no one would even suspect Daddy's old money fortune had evaporated. During the week, he still arose at six o'clock every morning and dressed like a businessman for work. On weekends, he wore tennis attire, although as far as she knew, he hadn't picked up a racket since the accident. Maj hadn't told Daddy about all the political goings-on and assumed no one else had either. Words and images were clearer to him, though his world was still relatively small.

His palms in her hands were warm, and his fingers thick and blunt with both thumbs bowed out. The clean scent of his Old Spice reminded her of Mr. Reingor, whom she hadn't heard from since his flirtatious offer. Maj wished she could speak to Daddy or at least know what he'd have said when he was well. Back then they never discussed money. Even after a few late-night crash courses in finance, Maj still stumbled through profit and loss statements.

Now, his hands weighed less than air, lighter than the last time she'd tested. She'd only kept on the couple of doctors who still held out hope for Daddy's sense of smell to return and reawaken his ability to taste. She refused to hear that time for him to begin eating on his own again was running out.

The setting sun flamed red through the window over

his head. Dusk, the time between light and dark, made Maj uneasy.

Carmen, soft-footed and smelling of lavender, stood in the doorway. "Excuse me, *por favor*, *Senor* Hawthorne. *Mi hija.*"

"*Hola, mi abuela,*" said Maj.

"Your mother asks you outside."

Maj gave Daddy a quick look. He shrugged.

"Mother is home?" Maj asked.

"*Si.*"

At the French doors to the back garden, Carmen stepped aside. The grounds were awash in light.

Maj raised her eyebrows, impatient for Carmen to give her a sign about what was going on.

"Is someone here?" Maj asked.

Carmen nodded.

"*Como estas?*" asked Maj.

"*Bueno,*" said Carmen, answering in code that, in her opinion, their guest was okay, not great, just okay.

Carmen helped Daddy with his sweater. As the door shut behind them, Maj immediately turned suspicious about what Mother was up to. Her feet sank in the thick lawn, and the nearer they came to the lilac-heavy gazebo, the slower Maj slogged through the evening dew.

Sitting at the wrought-iron table in a long blue chiffon dress, Mother spoke gaily to a stranger. Seeing who it was, Maj stepped backwards, distrusting the picture before her. Mr. Reingor wore a navy-blue, double-breasted suit, much like the suits hanging in Daddy's closet. Mother threw her head back in laughter. Her face shone.

Mr. Reingor spotted Maj and Daddy, and rose to his feet. Mother's head snapped, and her expression turned hard. The dragon awakened.

Struggling to cool her face from the jolt of finding Mr. Reingor here, Maj steeled herself for the worst and kept her eyes on the glimmering princess lights. Daddy patted her hand.

Mr. Reingor said something to Mother. Her facial expression switched from evil to pleased like a traffic signal. Carmen carried across the lawn a tray with the scent of Baltic herring and red onions.

Aloof and curt, Maj introduced Daddy to Mr. Reingor. They shook hands.

"Nice to meet you," said Daddy.

Maj restrained herself from yelping for joy. Daddy had practiced that statement more times than he ever practiced his tennis swing. Mr. Reingor wouldn't even suppose the accident unless the first thing out of Mother's mouth was all about her brave struggle.

Daddy's cheeks glowed. He was thin, too thin really, but fit. His success gave Maj confidence.

"I must apologize, Maj," said Mr. Reingor. "I had no idea your mother didn't know. I mentioned your schooling situation. I didn't know. I'm so sorry for both of you."

Mr. Reingor glanced back and forth between mother and daughter, irked, and shaking his head. Just as irked, Maj glared at him and refused to face Mother. Her heart already at a breaking point turned erratic.

"Sit down." Mother pointed to the wrought iron chair next to her.

Mr. Reingor sat in the seat on the other side. When he noticed Maj didn't sit down, he stood up again.

Maj turned to Mother, finally freed from the terror of having to tell her the truth and the shame about keeping what had been such an important part of her life separate and secret. Mother would have bullied Maj into doing things her way. That's what Maj had always told herself. She was coming to understand that the real reason she hadn't told Mother was because deceit was easier than standing up for herself.

When Mother said nothing, Maj felt like she was floating. The lies were gone. Liberated, she could fly.

She helped Carmen lay out a *smorgasbord* of pickled herring and *crispbread* and *limpa*; soft and hard, yellow and orange cheeses; deviled eggs with caviar; olives; open-faced sandwiches of cucumber and shrimp; pickles; and a bowl of mixed nuts. The aroma of her childhood had been missing for so long, Maj had nearly forgotten MorMor's favorites.

Arranged amongst the foodstuff sat four small glasses and a bottle of Aquavit encased in ice. Green bottles of beer next to tall glasses were ready to chase down the potato-tasting Swedish vodka, an extravagant celebration.

With her head down arranging the display, Carmen zapped Maj a smile. Carmen's warmth calmed Maj. Carmen had made Ramon quit the garden and get hired-on at the nursery in town when she'd learned about Maj paying the bills. Thanks to a promised high-paying assignment Jimmy had set up for her in Milan, Ramon was coming back at the first of the month.

"If what Mister Reingor says is true, seems to me it would have been far easier if you'd just told me," said Mother.

"Gerald," Mr. Reingor murmured to Mother. "Please, call me Gerald."

Mr. Reingor turned an earnest face to Maj and, as if afraid of what he saw there, just as quickly switched his full attention back to Mother. That he didn't even give the pretense of including Daddy, Maj knew that Mother had told him about the accident. His omission told the kind of man Mr. Reingor was.

Carmen gave Maj's hand a squeeze and left. Daddy wandered to the far side of the table. He closed his eyes and his chest swelled. Worried about his breathing, Maj kept an eye on him, waiting to see what happened next.

"We have far greater issues to discuss than school." Mother raised an eyebrow like an exclamation mark.

Distracted, Maj watched Daddy lean in close to the plate of hard-boiled eggs. He picked up an egg and sniffed it. His nostrils flared, and his face broke into a grin. One simple breath and suddenly his sense of smell had returned.

Maj held her breath, waiting to see if Daddy could taste now, too. Feeling Mother's eyes on her, she moved so she could see Daddy and keep him out of Mother's range of vision. Mr. Reingor had no business being part of such a milestone and Maj knew to take her time with Mother.

"Perhaps both," Maj said, hoping it matched with whatever Mother had said.

Maj hadn't been paying attention, more concerned with watching Daddy bite into the egg and slowly chew. His eyes closed against tears on his face.

"Gerald has delivered a very generous contract to you." Mother smiled up at the mogul. "Your father's attorney is on his way to take a look."

"What about Jimmy?" asked Maj.

"I'm prepared to reward your agent with a very handsome settlement," said Mr. Reingor.

"You don't need an agent anymore," dismissed Mother. "Not with Gerald's offer."

Maj shook her head and sighed at the humiliation of

being bought and sold one man to next. Tempted to reject Mr. Reingor's offer outright, Maj first had to shape the energy she'd need for the fight she'd get from Mother. Still, if she could negotiate on her terms . . .

Daddy's chewing speeded up. He pushed an entire egg into his mouth and reached for a cracker. He looked stoned, devouring pickles and nuts and everything else in front of him. His act of complete abandon was intimate. His joy made Maj happy.

"Take all the time you need," Mr. Reingor said. "I want you to approve every term."

"Yes, every term," Maj repeated, in a futile attempt to keep up her end of the conversation.

"We'll give Samuel a chance to review the contract and then we'll celebrate with dinner," said Mother. "Gerald and Samuel have both accepted our invitation to stay."

Daddy pulled a slicer across the block of cheddar. He put the piece of cheese on his tongue and rolled it around in his mouth. Mother hadn't noticed his orgy. If Mr. Reingor did, he didn't show it.

"Maj!" exclaimed Mother. "Mr. Reingor is speaking to you."

"A strict agreement guaranteeing nothing interfere with school—yes, I plan to reapply immediately," Maj said, rejoicing. "No shows. No travel. With those terms, I'll sign."

Self-conscious, Maj finished winded and flushed.

Mother looked surprised.

"Good for you. Let's have a toast." She twisted in her chair to serve Mr. Reingor. "Have you tasted Swedish Aquavit, Geral—"

Daddy stood in front of Mother with his mouth full. He smiled. Cheese mashed in his teeth drooled down his chin. Even with all he'd been through, Daddy had never lost his good manners. Maj celebrated his complete wildness even as she witnessed anger distort Mother's face.

"Robert! Stop that at this instant. What nonsense have you done to him, Maj?"

"His sense of smell has returned," Maj announced quietly.

"Robert, I said stop that! Maj, take him away. Now. Go. Get." Mother stopped herself just as she was about to blast off in a rant.

Though Maj knew she was seething, Mother daintily blotted the creases at her lips, careful not to smudge her coral sunset lipstick.

"Tell Carmen to feed him in the kitchen," Mother said calmly, back in control. "Then dress for dinner."

Maj snatched the platter of food, grabbed Daddy's hand, and tromped across the lawn, furious at Mother for humiliating Daddy in front of Mr. Reingor. Daddy leaned toward Maj and breathed a lungful of air through his nose like the afternoon he smelled marijuana on her high school friends. He smiled. Maj laughed out loud. Daddy's step was light and his face youthful.

FEBRUARY

i.

The late afternoon sun squeezed Maj outdoors. In nearly a snap of her fingers, she had a dream job and was suddenly back in school. Joyful to again be living in Berkeley, she took a break from catching up on the semester of coursework she'd missed, memorizing all the parts of the inner ear and the throat, transcribing phonetically recorded speeches from a cassette recorder, learning the science of sound transmission as it related to hearing and a child's speech and language development, analyzing the psychological and emotional influences on stuttering, outlining normal language acquisition from infancy to adolescences, studying statistical analysis, cramming for tests, and writing and rewriting papers.

She had just enough time to swing by school first before joining Raul and Petrana at their apartment, and then driving together to the Oakland Army Induction Center. Vines wrapped around the palm tree and engulfed her bicycle. Freeing the bike from the creepers proved harder than Maj expected. She hopped on, eager for exercise and the outdoors.

Keeping track of the time, she steered towards campus and fast-pedaled to the Philosophy

Department. Winter turned her cheeks cold.

When Maj had taken his class as a sophomore, Professor Hicks stood tall and skinny like Ichabod Crane. Now, hunched over his desk marking papers in red, he looked mousy and grey.

What sounded like President Nixon's inaugural address from last year replayed on the radio.

Where peace is fragile
Make it strong
Where peace is temporary
Make it permanent

"Excuse me, sir?" Intimidated and leery, Maj interrupted the professor's work.

"What is it?" he said, without looking up.

Anxious for a quick answer, so she could be off to support Raul at his final conscience objector's tribunal, Maj stepped inside the musty office. Dust motes streamed on a shaft of sunlight through a gap in the Venetian blinds. Books filling dark ceiling-to-floor shelves, a bust of Plato on a pedestal between stacks of books, and the green-shaded lamp lighting the professor's desk looked so ordinary and predictable and stuck in the past. The 1950s were long gone. The just-ended 1960s demanded moving beyond the expected and old-fashioned.

After a period of confrontation,
We are entering an era of negotiation.

Professor Hicks peered over reading glasses he usually wore perched on the top of his head for class, and were now sitting on his nose.

"I don't have all day." He held a red pen over the paper.

"I was in your Philosophy class, sir," Maj said respectfully.

He flipped his grade book open and ran a finger down the list.

"No, no," she said quickly, stepping forward to save him the effort. "A former student. Maj Hawthorne."

"Ah, yes, the mute."

She blushed.

He turned down the radio and pushed his glasses on his head. Frustrated, Maj refused to drop her eyes as he appraised her, something she'd grown accustomed to from men.

"If I remember correctly, you passed," he said, as he put back on his glasses and returned to his reading.

The light outside faded. Well aware that her impatience was making her jittery, Maj spoke calmly, having memorized the question before she got there.

"In class, you lectured about how before we can pass to the next stage of our lives, we first must slay the dragon of Thou Shalt. I looked in the library and I couldn't find where Nietzsche explains how one slays the dragon," she said and straightened her posture, having clearly stated her dilemma.

"Ah." Professor Hicks leaned back in his chair and rested his elbows on the arms. Forming a gun barrel with his fingers, he tapped them against his lips. Maj waited until it was obvious he wasn't going to say anything, and turned to go.

"As implied, to slay a dragon involves great risks," he said finally. "Not everyone is up to it, young lady."

Unlike Raul, Maj was ready to fight for independence from the shoulds and coulds and have-tos sucking magic from life and turning her into a robot.

"If one were so inclined, how would one go about it?"

"Slay the dragon?"

"The expectations of others." Her voice trailed off.

"Well, let me see. First you have to locate the dragon." He aimed at her the gun barrel his fingers formed and flung them in the air. "Then, you have to face it." He shot her again.

"And?" She leaned forward, impatient to learn the lesson.

As the weight against her heart had lifted, the less inhibited Maj felt. No longer reserved and shy, words marched and bullied their way out her mouth and into the sky. Over time, rather than tumble out, speaking was becoming a graceful practice of spaciousness and light. Slowly, Maj was coming to understand the part communication played in the need to be heard and what it meant to be human.

"There are as many ways to slay the dragon of Thou Shalt as there are people, Miss Hawthorne. That's a question only you can answer."

Frustrated by his lack of help, she turned to leave.

"Miss Hawthorne?" Professor Hicks called, posing his glasses halfway between his head and his nose. "Before you face the dragon, you'd better have your sword and shield at the ready."

ii.

Billy's head filled with the sweet smoky smell of leather in downtown Berkeley. Brown roof shingles covered the inside walls of the shoe store, crowded from ceiling to floor with shoeboxes and psychedelic posters. Colored lights turned on and off a scrawny leftover Christmas tree.

A salesgirl carried a stack of boxes from the back room.

Red stuck out a hand to the girl, his red hair frizzy and long like a stoner.

"Name's Red Harper. Perhaps you've heard of me."

The salesgirl's eyes grew wide, like she believed him worthy of fame.

"Why, no," she said. "I'm pleased to meet you. Did I happen to mention these boots are genuine alligator?"

Red settled back in the chair, like all of a sudden he was on a social visit. Worried he'd forgotten to shut the closet door in his new apartment, Billy gave Red a head-jerk. It was time to leave. Last thing Billy wanted was to come home to the other half of his boots gnawed and shredded. Sadie hated being left alone.

Someone shouted from outside. Scrutinizing the people swarming and demonstrating for change, Billy spotted bare feet everywhere. By the look of their clothes and the spring in their step, he knew they weren't barefooted because they couldn't afford to buy themselves a pair of shoes. The pilgrimage from the Midwest, and further points east, to Northern California brought people intent on becoming flower children and wearing second-hand clothes and ripped jeans. Their fantasies of the place were changing the heart and spirit of the Bay Area. No longer sleepy little towns, they faced directly into the heat of the ever-expanding war in Vietnam. Berkeley and San Francisco now were places of revolution.

Sunlight caught the window across the way and blinded Billy. Suddenly, his eyes started twitching. Disoriented at first, he prepared for one of Grandma's visions, the first he could remember in a long time. The blonde must be nearby.

Groping for the window frame, Billy fought the vision. Annoyed, he could find no reason for seeing the blonde again after all this time. She'd been a major contributor to the destruction of his family from the start. Billy didn't want her anymore in his life or in his mind.

A scent of fish and the sea saturated him. The blonde came into view, eating on a yacht. Two men told stories and made each other laugh. Another girl laughed right along with them. The blonde remained aloof from the others, watchful of how much wine the taller man was drinking.

The other man yanked the starter line on the little boat. They motored to a beach with an oily rainbow trailing in their wake. The blonde smoothed her pants, tucking and untucking her hair behind her ears.

Red slapped Billy on the shoulder. He stumbled, and the dream vanished. Blinking and rubbing his eyes, Billy was left with the strongest sensation that it was time he started accepting himself for who he was and quit with the fantastical imagination.

Trying out the boots, Red spoke under his breath and nodded toward the salesgirl with a click of his tongue. "Snappy-looking girl."

Keeping his opinion to himself that the salesgirl looked more like she'd been dragged through a knothole, Billy kept his eyes on the look-out outdoors. Despite his indifference towards the blonde, he found himself wondering where she was.

A guy wearing a hat and white bell-bottoms, with no shirt, wound through the crowd talking to himself. He was puffing on a joint in public and in broad daylight, with a cop walking towards him on the sidewalk.

Red strutted in front of a standing mirror, trying out the look and the fit of his boots.

Billy heard another shout. The joint-smoker was in

handcuffs.

"Get a load of this," he said, directing Red's attention outside.

Red whistled low. "What the hell's going on?"

"A cop's in there," said Billy. "He's got that guy with the hat and long hair handcuffed."

"They've all got long hair," said Red.

The salesgirl joined them at the window. A crowd held back the cop from leading away the hippie.

"Wow! Dig all the beautiful freaks!" the salesgirl exclaimed.

"If you plan on buying those boots," Billy said, "I suggest you pay the girl, so we can get out of here while we still can."

Billy wandered outside.

iii.

A flash of white light floated through a gap in the trees, as Maj sped down Telegraph Avenue with the wind in her face. Campus buildings and student housing turned into restaurants and storefronts. Worried about the time, having spent far too much of it with so little results, she sped towards Raul's apartment to drive with them to the Army Induction Center. Maj admired Raul's decision—all wars would end without any soldiers—and had been helping him with the steps and procedures to register for conscientious objector status. Finally, last month, his request was conditionally approved. This afternoon, he'd finally learn if his volunteer job at a halfway house in Berkeley qualified as service to his country.

Going over paperwork side-by-side with Raul and Petrana, Maj wondered if she'd ever find love. As much as she'd always dreamed of being with her mystery man, she appreciated how rare her chances of ever being at the same place at the same time and both of them ready for each other. And, what if she'd been wrong all along and unlimited chances weren't a promise?

A car swerved in front of her, and she turned hard on her handlebars. With parked cars taking up the side of the road and traffic building, Maj rode on the sidewalk instead. Nearing downtown, she approached a circle of chanting Hare Krishna dancers, gawking tourists in white tennis shoes and wrinkled clothes from the fifties, and a guy playing the polka on a tuba.

Wondering why so many people were congregated smack in her path and frustrated she couldn't get through, Maj hopped off and pushed her bicycle. The murmur of street musicians and the smell of incense competing with scents from a nearby Chinese restaurant—all sensory details missing from a photo tableau. Passing through a cloud of the bluegrass scent of marijuana, she inhaled deeply.

"Good vibrations." A guy muttered the words as a foregone conclusion, not simply a desire.

The crowd thickened around Maj. Jostled, she knocked into a woman panhandling for change from a tourist.

"Sorry," Maj apologized.

"Nothing to be sorry about, darlin'. You didn't do anything wrong."

A guy wore a sign across his chest that read, "Take a hippie to lunch." Pushed and elbowed and shoved, Maj's frustration turned to apprehension. Hemmed in on all sides, she heard a shout. She gripped the handlebars of her bike for balance. Afraid she'd be separated from it, she tried moving to the street. The crowd had already spilled out, stopping traffic.

iv.

Billy spotted the blonde in the tide of humanity, pulling toward the cop and hippie. At the sight of her, without warning, a smile spread across his face. He shook his head curious about the hold she had on him.

Like a high-pitch whistle only dogs hear, hundreds of hippies crossed between Billy and the blonde. Guys strutted in bright shirts and giant Afros, girls in skimpy paisley tops, and mangy-looking white guys with scruffy beards and long hair.

The blonde's eyes widened and her head disappeared as if sucked under water. Fighting against his stubborn belief that she was the root of all his problems, Billy stepped forward. A car slowed in front of the shop. Within seconds, the car was surrounded. The driver got out and disappeared in the same mob as the girl.

A Beatles' song played in the background of the shoe store. He'd found the girl with sunlight in her eyes. As always, she'd gone.

Billy turned away from the street and wiped sweat from his forehead.

v.

A shift of energy spread through the business district. A light flickered from the window of a shoe store across the street. Knocked from behind, Maj stumbled, feeling eyes on her. As if pre-determined long ago, her mystery man stared at her from the giant window. The sense of inevitability he'd be there made breathing difficult. A shiver spread across her shoulders.

Maj held his gaze as if floating above the mass of

people. The look in his eye was one of recognition and something that looked a lot like longing. Hemmed in by the people, Maj craned her neck. The wolf carving caressing her skin made her blood flow faster. A light and hopeful sensation ran from the top of her head to the tips of her toes. This was it. The time. The place. Now, the question became, were they both ready this time?

Two real flesh and blood people ending up at the exact same place, at the exact same time, was accidental, twice infatuation, three times chance. Five times was fate. Maj forgot where she was and what she meant to be doing, intent only on slowing down her intersection with him long enough to talk to him this time. She smiled, unable to take her eyes from his, even as she found herself pinned in and sucked along with people surging forward.

Resisting the tide, Maj waded in the opposite direction toward the man who, unlike her teachers and Mother and just about everyone else she knew, made her feel full of promise. No longer lost and insecure, she didn't find it odd she was unafraid. Her future stood right in front of her. All she had to do was to hurl herself forward. Armed with her voice and her words, Maj stepped out in good faith.

vi.

Billy found the blonde again and kept his eyes glued to her as she urged her way against a human tide with her bike and a look of utter faith he'd help her. And still, he held himself back. He didn't go to her.

"It's going to be impossible to get out of here," Billy said, turning away and having lost the thread of conversation with Red.

"I vote we wait it out," said Red. "By the looks of it, things could get real messy. I don't want to get caught in the crossfire. Hell, this is the pair for me, all right."

The brass ring at the ankle of the black square-toed boots glowed as the salesgirl took Red's money.

Restless and edgy and ready to tear out his skin, Billy lost sight of the girl again. When he finally caught a glimpse of her, using her bike as a shield, she no longer moved against the crowd toward him but rather toward the cop. Worried about her safety, though unwilling to help, he was grateful the blonde was tall enough that he could track her deliberate movement into the heat.

A guy in a purple vest worked his way to the cop on one side of the sidewalk with the blonde on the other.

He cupped his hands around his mouth. "Overthrow the pig."

The crowd heaved forward. The blonde shouted something indistinguishable. Her face turned red and she stood her ground. Billy would never forget that face or the fire in her eyes as the crowd forced her and the cop and hippie backwards.

Unable to stand being cooped up, Billy started towards her. People blocked his way. He quickly found he couldn't get anywhere without pushing a lot of people around. The way things looked that wasn't the best idea. Red followed him outside.

Cornered, the cop stepped up on a ledge against a display window and hauled the handcuffed guy beside him. Purple Vest moved his lips, his words lost in the din of the mob. The cop shot out a hand. Purple Vest shoved him against the store window. The reflection of the girl in the window quivered, like in a light show. Billy stood taller for a better view.

"Back away," shouted the cop. "I'm taking off the

cuffs."

Purple Vest lunged for the cop's gun.

Billy widened his eyes and glanced at Red, shocked at seeing an honest-to-goodness gun involved.

"Berkeley cops started carrying at the beginning of the year," said Red, slinging his arm around the salesgirl's waist.

The blonde stepped forward. Two guys appeared, blocking her path. Relieved to see Mal and Webb, Billy watched Mal snatch Purple Vest from behind and haul him off the cop. Webb protected Mal's back, facing the mob, dressed in his old Marine fatigues and ready to fight.

A guy in front of Webb started spewing wrath and spat at him. Webb punched aside the guy's face, so most of the spit landed on the sidewalk.

"How many babies you kill?" the guy screamed.

Webb pushed him down the sidewalk. The guy stumbled. Before he could sling more, Webb pushed him again and then again, until the guy left yelling attacks at him.

Standing beside Mal, Webb folded his arms and scanned the mob. A fierce scowl on his face dared someone to say something.

In that time, the hippie had stuck out both arms and the cop stuck the key in the handcuffs. A shout went up from the crowd. People pointed for those who hadn't spotted the action. The cop's face was candy apple red. His eyes were hard as concrete.

The crowd turned quiet and even from where Billy stood, he heard the click of the lock.

Everyone cheered.

"That was so bitchin'," said the salesgirl.

"What's the world coming to?" Billy asked.

He searched for the blonde as a siren sounded. The hippie took off in the opposite direction. People started moving away. The guy with the car in the middle of the street got in and drove off.

Billy saw the blonde just as she was hopping on her bike. Pedaling toward the shoe store, when she was side-by-side the squad car and blinking red lights, she flashed a peace sign. Then, with Billy standing right there in front of her, she rode straight past him and winked. He opened his mouth to stop her when his brain registered what she wore around her neck.

"Hey!" Billy shouted, running after her. "Hey, you. Stop. Stop, I say!"

The blonde vanished down the street, leaving Billy standing out of breath and alone on the sidewalk. The carving. The GTO. The girl. Billy nodded his head, thirsty for a shot of whiskey and wondering why the blonde having the carving should surprise him so much.

SEPTEMBER

Word came down that International was hitting General Motors with a nationwide strike. As ready for a strike as Billy genuinely was, the union's decision surprised him. In May, Walter Reuther died in a suspicious airplane accident. Since then, the union had been moving to the right. A general strike did not qualify as a particularly conservative move, quite the opposite, though striking now was probably as good a time as any. The GNP grew with American auto factories running full tilt and market increases mostly steady. A strike would unite the rank and file, blacks and whites and Chicanos alike. If they stood together as a united front for better wages and improved working conditions, they'd win.

Skypiece told him what he thought of the union's decision. "The UAW sat down against GM in the thirties. Changed American labor history forever. Sure the corporation has the profits to pay a rate increase, but those fat cats aren't giving up their growth to guys like us. You saw the National Guard at the Democratic Primaries. What Reagan did to those kids at People's Park last spring? Heck, look at what happened to the kids at Kent State. And then, there are the Indians on Alcatraz. They ain't seen nothing yet. Management isn't going to take a strike from us lying down. If they have to, they'll involve the government."

"Government can't act against us," Billy snorted.

"They got wiretapping now," Skypiece said.

"That's for organized crime."

"Don't be surprised."

Later that week, Red drove Webb and Mal and Billy in his green Impala to the strike ratification meeting at the Union Hall in the pouring rain. From the road separating the Hall and the assembly plant, the size difference between the two buildings was glaring, like Lisa standing beside Mal. Afternoon fog and rain and mist cut off the tail end of the factory, a giant freighter bearing down on a measly raft.

The Hall's parking lot was already full of cars. Even with the nasty weather they were having, guys had hung out here after work, drinking beer in their cars and smoking pot and waiting for them.

"Slow down, Red," Billy said, drawing his pea jacket closer around him and trying to contain his hyped up buzzing energy. "Don't want to fire up the boys by coming in like Grant taking Richmond."

The vote today was mostly for show, but having all the factions in one room together—everyone suspicious of everyone else and armed with knives and guns—made him edgy. They were all waiting for something to happen. Nothing you could put into words, but the guys were wound up tight enough to blow. Billy planned on being real careful and stick to talking about better wages and improved working conditions. Whichever way the meeting went today— peaceful or erupting into a nasty fight—would define the mood and tone of the real deal, the strike.

Billy tightened the band around his hair as Red

drove through the front lot real slow, like out for a Sunday cruise. Careful to avoid mud puddles, Ray swerved to miss a flooded patch. Guys honked and flashed their headlights, momentarily lifting the gloom. With a random peace sign thrown in here and there, everyone was acting friendly enough.

Red told Billy his long hair was freaking out a lot of the guys.

"You got half an hour," Red finished, peering at Billy in the rear view mirror.

Webb grinned over his shoulder from the front seat, wearing his military fatigues. His eyes were real glassy, and with his Afro grown out at least six inches, no one from the old neighborhood would recognize him. The day after Martin Luther King was murdered, Webb had said it was time to choose sides. He stayed with the caucus because, though he believed the war the Panthers waged was just, he was tired of fighting. No one else understood why Webb wore his special forces' fatigues. Billy knew Webb was proud of the service he gave his country and stood in solidary with his brothers still on the battlefield. Webb didn't want anyone taking that from him. His current obsession with Jimi Hendrix, who he considered his soul brother on account of their similarities—Indian grandmothers and service in the military—worried Billy. Hendrix skated along the edge of a hypodermic needle.

"You ready for what's coming, Webb?" Billy asked, shaking out a cigarette.

"Let me put it this way, brother," answered Webb. "There's a lot more to life than factory politics."

Bob Dylan came on the radio. Webb turned the song up full blast. Red parked the car and turned off the engine, wrapping them in the drumming rain.

"Set yourself free, man," said Webb. "The time's they are a-changing."

"That so?" said Billy.

"Yeah, man," said Webb. "That so."

Inside the Hall, Webb and the others unlocked the front doors and greeted the guys, everyone loud and shaking off the dreariness and the rain. Down the corridor in the opposite direction, past the bathrooms, Billy entered the meeting hall alone. Quiet and dark, the place felt like being in church. Windows sat up high. Outside, the rain continued.

Billy snapped on the lights. Chairs enough for an ordinary meeting were out, not nearly enough for everyone that would be crammed in here today. Many would have to stand, which could cause territorial misunderstandings, who stood next to whom. He slung his drenched pea jacket on the chair back, as guys entered by special-interest groups.

The Panthers wore black berets, blue shirts, and black leather jackets. The Brown Berets—or Mexican Mafia—the hillbillies, the communists, the Hell's Angels, everyone had a buck knife folded in the sheath at their waist. Couldn't see the guns, but they were out there, slipped into shoulder straps, under shirts, and calf belts hidden in cowboy boots.

They'd all witnessed Black Panther Party Chairman Bobby Seale on television at the Chicago convention, yelling at demonstrators to defend themselves by any means necessary. Most of the demonstrators were white middle-class guys with no thought of a weapon, so it didn't account for much. Guys in here were working men and fighting men. Attacked from inside or out, it was going to be up to Billy to prevent an outright war.

After Mal—as sergeant at arms—brought the

meeting to order, Red read the long list of demands management had rejected. On the stage with the rest of the Executive Board, Billy breathed real slow and deliberate in air that was thick and sticky. With everyone soaked and the furnace turned up high, steam filled the room, making it smell like one giant sweat lodge. Billy's chest tightened. He wheezed, panicked, and caught a breath.

Red was standing in front of him. Billy's turn now became a single-minded focus of bringing the guys together as one. Leading these men into a nationwide strike was his purpose and Grandma's prophecy that he'd been waiting and preparing for his entire life.

Guys clapped when Billy rose. Beaming, he thrust out his chest, moved aside the podium and wheeled out a schoolroom blackboard from the side of the stage. Chalk rolled off the ledge. Billy bent to pick it up, and his breathing turned shallow.

Taking a wide stance, his hands clasped behind his back, Billy looked out over the crowd of faces. By now, a blue cloud of cigarette smoke hung over the room with something big and armed and vicious just beneath the mumbling, coughing, and scrapping. Most of the heavies holding the highest seniority sat stoic up front. They were hard as iron drug dealers, pimps, Bickers, and the La Familia—who had all earned their jobs and weren't about to let anyone or anything threaten their positions in the final-repair and final-paint inspections, material and handling departments, and as forklift drivers. Even the so-called cush jobs weren't really so cushy, and they still didn't get paid enough or receive adequate benefits.

The longer Billy took, the quieter the room got.

"Gentlemen, we are working men," he started. "We

show up on time every day, walk five miles from the parking lot to inside, work an eight to ten hour-shift, and overtime when we can get it. Doing mostly manual labor, for every two hours on, we get a 12-minute break. We stop the line for 42 minutes for lunch. Why 42 minutes exactly? Because six minutes is a tenth of an hour and that's how they calculate our lives—by the hour."

Without a power tool or oilcan, a punch tool or car part in hand, most of the guys fidgeted and looked awkward glancing over their shoulders, well aware of where everyone was and what they were doing and not doing. In the factory, guards and supervisors and factory officials prowled the catwalks. Here, union members were on their own, stuck together like overcrowded sardines in a rusted tin can.

"And you do this, why?" Billy asked, raising his voice and pulling their attention away from each other to listen to him. "So you can buy new houses and cars, refrigerators and dryers. And that makes each of you men who are keeping this country's economy rolling. Each one of you is responsible for the rich getting richer. As long as we working men are well compensated and respected, we're happy. Discontent, we wage a revolution."

Guys erupted out of their seats and onto their feet. Their speed and intensity surprised Billy, as they whistled and clapped and shouted. His breathing was clear, and while he had everyone's attention, he drew a circle that covered most of the blackboard to make his point.

"This much goes for raw materials." He shouted over the chaos and marked out pie slices all the way around as he identified each section he'd researched. As the guys quieted and sat down, Billy lowered his voice.

"This much for overhead and rent. This big slice is for executive salaries. And this much for us—labor. We're here today, gentlemen, because we are not entirely satisfied with the way this pie is divided."

Billy went on to describe management executives with big college degrees playing golf together and their three martini lunches while the guys sweated, busting their humps inside the factory, and management's mistaken belief that they held all the power.

"They ain't worried about us," Billy continued. "Can't be. Too worried about how to improve profits in the next quarter, so they can grab bigger bonuses and pay their shareholders bigger dividends. But all that greed has made them forget about us. We're the oil in the engine of this boom economy. We walk until we get our share. We walk. Now."

Grinning, Billy looked out over the men shouting and clapping each other on the back. His blood pumped like theirs. As he waited for the excitement to die down, he suddenly noticed how glassy the guys' eyes were, the set of their jaws, and the snarls across their lips. A shiver hit between his shoulder blades. Worried now he should have chosen his words more carefully and written down a plan, Billy upbraided himself for speaking from his gut as usual. The country was coming apart at the seams, and the last thing he wanted was the same thing happening to the guys. He got the strongest sensation he better pull everyone back and quick. Their churned up and barely bottled energy was about to detonate.

Billy put out his hands, calling for calm.

Instead of dying down, their clapping grew, and Billy realized too late that he'd already lost them. Two guys in the back broke into a fight.

Billy's heart pounded. Rather than unite the men around the shared cause of better wages and improved working conditions, he united them against management, identified the opposition, and set the battle lines. All of the men unhesitatingly and boldly crossed over into enemy territory. Their boot stomping shook the stage.

Riled up himself, the voice in his head screamed to slow down, put it back, and shut up. Trouble was there was no bringing them back now.

With his heart hammering, Billy knew something bad was going to happen.

The vote went through.

*   *   *   *   *   *

After the hall cleared, most of the guys stayed outside, milling around the parking lot. The rain had stopped, and bits of night sky showed through black storm clouds. The temperature had plunged. Standing in front with Webb, Billy thrust his fists into his pockets, buried his chin in his pea jacket, and lifted his shoulders, trying to get the collar to cover his ears.

The spot at the roof corner of the Hall cast a dim light on the parking lot turned swamp. Across the road, the factory that never closed looked eerily empty tonight. All the lights were on with security guards smoking cigarettes and their eyes trained toward the union hall and the men..

With everyone staring right back and swearing and drinking, they egged each other on about how bad they'd been done by management and spitting how it was their turn now. More and more anxious about the consequences of the power going to his head, Billy had to get the guys to go home.

"I need your help," he said, suddenly aware of heat pouring from Webb. "We got to keep a lid on the guys."

Webb smashed out his cigarette and stretched, like he had something stuck between his shoulder blades. The bulb over their heads flickered and popped. The porch fell into shadows.

Webb stepped off the landing and strolled toward the darkened road. Drawn along with him, Billy started to ask for his help again when Webb started talking like he was in a trance.

"All that talk of yours makes me feel mean," Webb said. "I been trying to make it go away. I don't like feeling mean."

Webb was talking but his attention was obviously somewhere else.

"I know, man," said Billy quickly. "It's all my fault. You know me and my big mouth. Thought I'd learned to control myself. It ain't easy, is it, Webb? Controlling our natures."

A group of about twenty guys fell in line behind Webb. Billy followed, too, tripping in a ditch and scrambling back to level ground.

"Don't it make you mad, Billy?" asked Webb. "All them things you were saying?"

"Sure it makes me mad," Billy said hastily, his voice calm and steady.

Not knowing what else to do, Billy kept talking. He was afraid for Webb.

"That's why we're striking and not doing something crazy we'll regret later."

"I got blood on my hands, Billy. Blood on my

hands."

Webb reached the road with a crowd of about thirty Panthers making it hard for Billy to hear. He pushed his way forward and grabbed Webb by the arm. When his friend's muscle turned rigid as steel, Billy felt suddenly thrust into a deep, lonely pit where nothing made sense anymore. He clenched his teeth to prevent them from clattering and dropped his hand. Webb's gaunt ravaged face and flat rumpled hair scared him.

Billy shook his head to clear it. "You're a good and decent man, Webb. Come on. Let's go back."

"All those words of yours got me riled up inside. I'm sick of getting screwed. I can't just let it be anymore."

Tears streamed down Webb's cheeks. Swallowing hard, Billy leaned forward and spoke softly.

"That's right," Billy said. "And now we have us a chance to do something about it. We're young, and we're on strike. It's a brave thing we're doing, Webb. A powerful thing. Come back inside. Let's talk about this."

"No more talking," Webb said in an eerie and disconnected voice.

A shout came from inside the factory's chain-link fence.

"We changed things, brother," said Webb.

Suddenly Webb grabbed Billy by the shoulders and for the first time in years, Webb looked Billy straight in the eye.

"Everything we've done has been for the good." Webb gave him a sad smile and started forward.

"Let's keep going together," Billy said, trying to keep Webb there. "Let's focus on wages and conditions, and change the way things are done on a fundamental level. I was wrong. Everything doesn't always have to be someone against someone else. One group against another. War. We don't have to be against management. Simply being for what we want is enough. Standing up for our rights is enough. We don't have to go up against anyone. Hold out for our due and we'll get what we want."

Billy held Webb back from an oncoming car, but it was like a zombie took his old friend's place. Billy stepped away, afraid of the man he'd known all his life.

Webb and his wave of men disappeared into the dark. They reappeared in the light at the factory entrance, pushed through the security guards at the gates, and spread out across the parking lot. Keeping Webb's Afro in his sights, Billy stayed fixed where he was.

Webb swerved left, like he changed his mind after all. Billy let out his breath in relief. Instead of coming back, Webb ended up at the garbage area. Men's shouts fired across the road, no words, only sounds.

Billy addressed the men crowding around him. "Remember guys, we're trying for non-violence here. Cesar Chavez. Martin Luther King."

Workers, fired up to speak their truths and offer their lives, weren't listening as they brushed past Billy. More and more of the guys he'd known and worked with and represented followed Webb's gang across the darkened street and into the factory parking lot.

A blast of light flashed. An explosion hit. One of the garbage trucks burst into flames. A roar went up from the workers. Red and white and blue flames curled in and out of billowing black smoke.

Lurching backwards, Billy shouted, "Call the fire department!"

His words were lost in the blast of another garbage

truck blowing, and then another. The sky lighted up, and the faces of the men glowed. Mean faces, frenzied, and ready for a fight, a mob of them.

When fire trucks arrived, a few men surrounding the garbage trucks refused to let the firefighters near enough to fight the fires. Immediately, more men joined the line of defense, operating as a unit with absolutely no prompting, automatically following the leadership and internal organization on the line at work.

A painter ran across the road to catch up with the others just as a car barreled straight towards him.

"Get back! Get back!" Billy shouted, running and waving his arms, hoping to alert the poor stiff in the wrong place at the wrong time.

The road was dark. Car tires screeched. Billy flinched as the painter's body thunked against the hood of the car.

"Call an ambulance!" Billy shouted.

He ran into the road, his ears echoing with the sound of two tons slamming against what he estimated could be no more than one hundred and fifty pounds. The guy was ghastly white in the wash of headlights coming their way. Billy dragged him off the road.

Winded in the ditch, Billy doubled-over with his hands on his knees and his teeth clattering with cold, wondering what the hell was happening. He rubbed his hands across his eyes. With a violent shudder, he wiped and rubbed faster and harder, smearing blood over his face from the guy slumped on the ground. The guy's eyes fixed on nothing; he was barely breathed and hemorrhaging badly.

"Hang in there, buddy," Billy whispered. "You're going be okay."

Slumping back to let the emergency medical

attendants take over, Billy reeled backwards as a mob surrounding the attendants. Guys lined up on one side of the ambulance, and together flipped it on its side. Frozen in place by the violence, Billy yelled at them to stop when they turned on the attendants. They started pummeling.

Nearly losing his balance, Billy stumbled through madness, keeping low in the weeds and mud. Intent on dragging the painter to safety until he could find him some help, suddenly Billy stopped—sweating heavily and convulsing with chills. He lost it, vomiting the horror of what he'd seen happening—worker attacking worker.

Shaking and drenched in sweat, he kept trying to line up the assault, the fires, and the physical damage to fit a different picture that made some sort of sense to him because all that shit out there made absolutely no sense at all.

Finding a dry spot under a bush, Billy settled the painter.

"I'll be back with help. Hang in there just a little bit longer, buddy," Billy said, miserable that he couldn't remember the poor guy's name.

Still shaking his brain for the missing name, he turned to go, and stepped into a pothole. His jaw crushed together at the unexpected drop. Billy found himself doing the splits, one leg lock-kneed straight in a freezing, rain-filled hole, and the other leg stretched out along the ground at an odd angle.

Unable to catch his breath, the shock of ice water numbed his submerged foot up to his knee. Groaning in pain, he shook his head to clear the brain-freeze he was having. The movement widened the splits and caused his foot to slip further in the rain-soaked earth.

Sweating, he hunched forward. Catching himself straight-armed in weeds smashed with mud and filth, he flinched as a flash of pain shot up his spine.

He searched the area for help. In the cockeyed, lurid headlights of the ambulance, a riot raged near enough that Billy heard what he imagined were crushed bones and bashed heads, along with very real war-cries and screams.

Breathing hard and sopping-wet, he dragged an arm across his forehead. A smearing of mud and blood and sweat and rain gushed into his eyes as he pulled himself to his hands and knees. He tasted blood and spit. Somewhere behind him, he heard a twig snap. Out of the pit-black edges around him, Billy thought he spotted someone in the dark.

"Hey, I could use some help here," he called, twisting his upper body.

Everything went black.

ON THE BRINK OF THE WORLD

i.

The local news coverage of the factory riot stunned Billy.

"I don't remember cameras," he said, with his brain fuzzy, watching himself on television.

Pulling guys back. Blood smeared across his face. Yelling for calm in the middle of flames and violence and death. Billy kept waiting for the fog to lift and the nightmare to vanish. Wasn't going to happen.

The report ended with a news flash that Jimi Hendrix had died.

"I'm going to look for Webb," said Billy.

"People who don't want to be found generally aren't," said Red, but he and Mal went with Billy to the strike line.

None of the guys remembered seeing Webb. Hobbling on crutches with a big white bandage wrapped around the twenty-five stitches in his head, Billy asked at their old neighborhood. An uncle of Webb's said he'd been hurting himself something awful and there was a cloudiness in his eyes.

Billy kept looking, and when he found himself dizzy and needing a break now and then, he slowed down for some deep breathing. The doctor had warned him to keep his leg elevated and his head still, and he'd be fine. What wasn't so fine was that the deep gash and concussion came from the hand of one of his guys. Billy had a pretty good idea who it was.

Three days later, the landlady of a Haight flophouse found Webb OD'd. When Jimi Hendrix kissed the sky with his exotic spellbinding music, he must've known others would take seriously his invitation to hell. Webb's hope had turned to rage and ultimately to despair.

Haunted by the words in Hendrix's song, maybe Billy couldn't help his friend go the distance because Webb was just too wounded, too beaten, too numb. Billy resolved to continue working in his name for better working conditions and higher wages.

Every day, they posted strikers out front of GM from six in the morning to nine at night. The longer they were out, the more cocaine and heroin started showing up. The Fillmore had closed its doors in the spring, marking the official end of the Flower Children. Hard drugs had finished it off long before that, as played out in the violence at the Altamont Festival that ended in deaths of all kinds. Guys were coming back to the factory from Vietnam pretty screwed up. Unlike pot and psychedelics, cocaine and heroin cost money. The longer the strike went on, the harder it was to keep the guys focused on the long-term gains, when all they really wanted was to chase the almighty dollar and get high.

A week before Thanksgiving, and without warning, the fight ended. International settled the nationwide strike that Billy truly believed would bring about positive change so quickly that the rank and file got not nearly enough.

Deceived and angry that he hadn't figured out the political motives before he went and caused so much damage, Billy fought back.

"Billy, I'm warning you," advised Red. "International won't tolerate this kind of dissention."

"Eighteen-year-olds deserve better than slapping on tires knee-deep in oil and grime and factory chemicals. Fifty-five-year-olds driving forklifts and smoking cigarettes deserve better, too."

Billy convinced the guys to stay out longer.

International got wind, and damned if five reps from Solidarity House didn't breeze in from Detroit.

"You're out," said the head guy to Billy.

Billy was locked out of the union hall on his 26th birthday.

Out-of-town reps, each one using a river of words—all of which were dried up and empty—explained things to the men. The workers followed their instructions. The plant started up without Billy.

From that one additional week Billy had convinced them to take, they got 100% of doctor and hospital bills, no dental, medical expenses for having babies—100 percent. In the end, a dollar an hour raise, for a grand total of 75 dollars a week with some overtime, just didn't cut it.

Billy complained to the International reps.

"Six thousand families. How many years do you think it's going to take them to make back the money they lost during the strike? If I'd known you were going to just cave like that I'd have fought against going out in the first place."

"They let you grow your hair long like that out here, huh?" commented the main negotiator, a polished slick guy with hair gel and shiny fingernails and a name Billy couldn't seem to remember, even after asking a bunch of times.

"You look just like Charlie Manson, don't he, boys." Making notes in a big binder, the guy shuddered along with the rest of the men in his alliance.

Because of the likes of Manson and his cult of brutal killers wearing long hair, now everyone viewed anyone with long hair as a potential murderer. The convicted serial killer had long hair, but he wasn't a hippie. He was a five-foot-two conman, a mental midget, and sadistic maniac. Being lumped together with the likes of him shook Billy. He finally faced up to how deep the fear of long hair hippies ran in people.

ii.

Thirty-two miles north of Fremont at Great Oaks, Maj was distracted and not much in the mood for work.

"You're working to heal yourself with the same intensity I remember as a child," she said to Daddy, gathering up the test materials she needed to administer to him.

Like trying to have two conversations at once, Maj spoke to Daddy and, at the same time, kept chiding herself for her cowardice. If she'd presented her idea to Mother months ago, as she should have, they'd be moving forward on her plan to convert the east wing of Great Oaks by now. Time she faced the fight she was getting herself into. Resolved, Maj turned to Daddy.

"I'm sorry for taking what you did for us for granted. I won't ever again," she promised.

Her hands full, she motioned with her chin for him to sit, so they could get started. Instead, he squeezed her by the shoulders, his reaction confusing her.

"I did," Daddy said.

"Yes, I know you did," said Maj.

Daddy squeezed harder. Maj squirmed to get away, sliding the testing materials across the desk before they spilled on the floor.

"I did. I did. I did," he repeated.

Maj rested a hand over his, calming him as the needle in his mind skipped.

"You did," she agreed again, feeling his hands relax on her arm. "You created all of this for us. You're learning to speak again. More than just want to, you're making it happen."

Daddy shook his head yes and then no and sighed. Usually Maj was able to figure out what he was trying to say. Now she was bewildered. Not wanting to agitate him or herself any further, she peeled back his grip on her shoulder.

"How about a spin in the Caddie?" she asked.

Daddy dropped his hands, grinning with guilty pleasure. Happy for a break, Maj replaced the test in the closet, arranging their things in such a way that the next time she could easily determine if Mother had moved anything. After telling Mother Maj had been accepted to graduate school, she often found Daddy's file moved or left open. Knowing that Mother was curious, and rummaging through Maj's things, gave her an odd sense of comfort and hope that Mother would agree to her plan.

iii.

Locked out and put on ice, Billy slid into darkness. Having lost his work, his family, and Webb, he felt a child again, lost and confused.

"Come on. Get up. Let's go support the Indians on Alcatraz," said Mal, yanking Billy to his feet.

"Helping them helps us, too," urged Red.

Worried about winning the next union election, last thing anyone wanted was to end up back on the line.

Billy glimpsed out a darkened window of his apartment not at all ready to be alone, and sick to death of talking.

"The workers are struggling," he said, absently petting Sadie. "Last thing they want is to see their hard-earned money go to Indians."

"You'd be surprised, Billy," said Mal. "When a man gives something to someone else it means he's got enough for himself. Gives a man dignity. And besides, everyone predicted the Indians would fail. Instead, they continue to control the island. Wouldn't hurt capitalizing on their success."

"It's no success," scoffed Billy. "Their spokesman even deserted the cause."

"More reason to go," countered Mal.

"Count me out." Billy grabbed his jacket and went outside, Sadie right on his heels.

"Hell, Billy—"

"I'm on ice, remember? Consider me a liability because I'm sure as hell not an asset," Billy shouted and opened the car door for Sadie.

Together, they headed toward the highway for a drive in the country.

iv.

On their way to the five-car garage, Maj and Daddy stopped to admire Daddy's rose garden. Now that Ramon was back, he helped, but most of the pruning and grooming of the neglected roses, Daddy did himself. A sea of color sent out an aroma of love and longing. He pushed back his favorite felt hat and dragged Maj to smell the red Abraham Lincoln. The pride on his face proved to Maj anything was possible.

At the garage, Daddy pinched the crease of his slacks and cranked down his window, as she maneuvered his prized Cadillac onto the drive. Around the far side of the house, they upset two mourning doves to flutter away.

Gravel crunched under the car tires as they slipped through the old oaks, past the vast lawns and winding creek, and into a shifting pattern of sunlight and shade. Maj pictured Kenny, and children like him, living on the grounds. Not running and jumping, they'd more likely be rocking and pacing and twirling, resisting wading into the creek, stiff on horseback, eating Carmen's fragrant foods, and sleeping to the sound of crickets and frogs.

The master oak tree that tucked the butterfly house under its protective arms reached out to caress Maj. She eased the car onto the wooden bridge. Boards creaked beneath them. Totem poles on either side of the bridge reminded her of the days when she was a captured Indian princess, and only the totem animals knew.

They drove into the late afternoon, wind tangling her hair. Daddy grinned. Maj grinned back. She'd always had more fun with him than with anyone else. Since his accident, she'd grown comfortable in their veil of shared silence. He opened up stillness to her beneath the chaos of her ordinary life, fending off judgments and slights, criticisms and misunderstandings.

Daddy hummed a wordless tune. "I did what I did. My life. Not yours."

Maj felt in her body, more than knew in her mind, how much time and effort he put into that simple declaration. Modeling wasn't her life. Maj was grateful he knew that. Still, she didn't have enough money to just quit, not yet anyway. Her investments needed time to grow, not only for her parents, for the school she had planned, too.

v.

Exiting the highway with Sadie half out the window, her tongue hanging and ears plastered against her head, Billy turned east on a hunt for the GTO and his wolf carving.

Passing newer homes built more recently, he veered south in search of the older estates. Poppies and lupine blanketed hillsides in sprawling patches of orange and blue. Red-winged blackbirds whistled from cattails swaying in the wind. The air smelled musty, of last year's fallen oak leaves and acorns.

Billy drove up and down on the off-chance he'd spot the GTO in the driveway of one the estates. He often found himself doubled back on the same roads. Up ahead, a grove of towering eucalyptus trees crowned with buzzard nests became his compass. Grandma used to tuck buzzard feathers in her hair to clean away the past when she danced on the brink of the world.

Slowing down, Billy came upon an old sprawling home with thick clay roof tiles and faded blue shutters spread out like a hacienda, with plenty of oak tree-studded land all the way around.

He took his time studying the house. Not seeing any sign of the GTO or the girl, he moved to the next house. Trouble was, old growth trees hid the houses set back from the road by long stately driveways, some behind wrought-iron gates. Billy didn't have a clue if he was in the right place, if the car was still in service, and if the girl still lived there. Too many ifs for his liking, but he had nothing better to do, and Sadie looked the happiest he'd seen her since his girls left.

Church bells chimed in the distance, as cowboys herded rust-colored cattle silhouetted against the setting sun.

vi.

On the way home, Maj watched a slow moving car approach from the opposite direction. In front of Clay's parents' estate, the car nearly stopped. Maj was surprised both because the road was usually deserted and because she knew the house was closed. Clay's parents were traveling in Europe, and Clay was flying back and forth over the Mexican border, smuggling in kilos of weed.

Maj passed the car, wondering if she should offer her help, but the driver's head was turned and she doubted he even knew they were there—more intent on rubbing his eyes and searching for something.

A dog in the passenger seat suddenly leaped into the driver's lap and lunged, taking up the entire window with the biggest grin.

Maj laughed and pointed. Daddy joined in. The dog's joy was irresistible.

Back home, Maj waved to Ramon who'd turned on the spotlight at the outside corner of the garage. As Ramon tended to a tower of broken tree branches, he looked more hunched over than she remembered, years stacked against bending and reaching.

Maj gave Daddy a hug, something she learned in encounter groups for her psychology classes. He hugged her back, his warmth so unlike Mother's ironing-board body.

The drive settled Maj. She was ready to go into the

fire for her dream and face Mother.

THE FIRE

Mother darted around the side of the garage, looking stricken.

"Maj. Richard. Where have you been?" Mother said, accusingly.

"What's wrong?" asked Maj quickly.

She hadn't heard panic in Mother's voice like that since Daddy's accident. Now Daddy pulled Mother near, looking down at her, dashing and sincere. She sagged against him, the first show of need Maj had seen from Mother, perhaps ever.

Mother pulled away. "I'm fine. Just fine."

Daddy grasped Mother to him again. Rather than watch Mother turn rigid and push Daddy away, Maj watched Ramon dump a wheelbarrow of leaves on the teepee of branches he'd arranged for a fire. The wide brim of Ramon's straw hat hid his eyes. Now, Maj told herself. Now was the perfect time to introduce her idea for Great Oaks to Mother.

"I don't want you getting a chill, Richard," said Mother. "Go inside and put on a sweater."

"Daddy is quite capable of knowing what's best for him," said Maj.

Hearing her own words, Maj wondered why she'd never spoken them for herself. Just as quickly, she chastised herself. Now was not the time to irritate Mother. She needed her blessing if her plan was going to work.

"It's . . . okay, kiddo," said Daddy.

He gazed down at Mother, his eyes soft. Mother and Maj watched him leave around the garage, giving Maj the chance to introduce her idea.

"I want to talk to you abou—" she started.

"Clay is dead," Mother said as if in a daze. "His mother telephoned from Cairo. He let go of a tree rope over a shallow spot in the Delta and broke his neck. Died instantly." Mother's held-back words gushed out in a rush.

Maj nodded her head even as her hands, as if separate from her, squeezed into fists, fingernails cutting into her flesh. Trees blocking the garage kept most of her face in shadows, as a roar built up from inside of her. She stomped her foot, angry Clay had died and robbed her of the chance to shift the burden of shame and guilt and betrayal to him. Now she'd never be free all the guys she'd slept with and hadn't loved, guys who disrespected her because Clay had taught her to disrespect herself. Just as quickly, Maj turned numb and wanted to run.

"I was so fond of that boy." Mother spoke with an intimacy that shook Maj into a state of alert.

With her ears ringing, perhaps she had misunderstood. Maj spun around and tried to read Mother's face, but couldn't. In a constrictive trance, Maj's breathing turned fast and hoarse.

"Are you going to tell Daddy?" she asked.

"It would break his heart," said Mother.

Ready to accuse Mother of lying, Maj stepped back and shook her head at the truth. Daddy would mourn

Clay's death and miss him. She hated Daddy for that. Mostly, she hated Clay. Once upon a time, she'd also loved him like a brother.

In the distance, Ramon knotted braided strips of Mother's old paint rags and then dipped the rope in a pail of turpentine.

"Daddy is improving," said Maj.

"Is that all you can say?" said Mother. "Really, Maj. Clay is dead. He was your best friend."

Uncoiling the patchwork cord several steps from the wood, Ramon buried the other end deep in the three-foot teepee of kindling and branches and leaves.

"There's not much I can do about Clay," Maj said. "I can do something about Daddy."

Ramon lighted the fuse.

"The funeral is planned for Friday." Mother's voice rose above the whirling fury, as flames from the fire shot into the darkening sky.

Fixated by the power and majesty of the sparks and the heat and the smoke, Maj grew somber. Fire burned away the old and the dead and the past. The finality of what was. The end.

"If you asked him, Gerald will take you," said Mother, fiddling with the loopy bow collar of her blouse.

"Oh," Maj said, laughing bitterly. "All this time I thought it was you and Mr. Reingor."

Mother stared at her funny.

"Sorry, Mother," Maj said, shaking her head and laughing it off. "I want to talk to you about converting Great Oaks into a home for autistic kids."

Winded and astonished, Maj heard the words actually coming out in one clear sentence. Mother opened her mouth and closed it. Taking advantage of

Mother's uncharacteristic speechlessness, Maj positioned herself so they both were looking in the direction of the house.

"I have it all figured out," she said, excitedly. "I'll take the east wing. You'll never even know we're there."

She pointed to the far corner of the house.

"See how the kitchen blocks off the rest of the house? You and Daddy will have the entire main house and west wing. We'll live separately, though at first we'll share the kitchen until I can have another one built."

As Maj waited for some response from Mother, excitement built as high and burned as bright as the flames of the fire. The smell of smoke teased out memories of MorMor's blazes, and singing at the turning of the seasons and warmed her.

"I have no idea what you're talking about," said Mother, giving her a harsh stare.

"I'm sorry," said Maj. "I shouldn't have just thrown it at you all at once."

"You really should stop wasting your time at that psychobabble school," Mother said, her voice sharp, and marched toward the house.

"What do you mean?" Maj cried, running to catch up. "We're talking about kids who need a home. Daddy will love them."

"I worry about you when you're there," Mother said. "Berkeley is coming apart at the seams. Things are only going to get worse."

"Worse?" Maj put out a hand to stop Mother from going inside until she explained herself. "We're talking about a school," Maj said. "Giving children a safe place to thrive."

Mother lowered her voice. "Clay was on LSD when

he let go of that rope," she said in an undertone, her voice wavering. "He was such a special boy. Full of talents and dreams."

Maj snorted. "What about all the boys dying in Vietnam?" she snapped, unable to stop herself. "What about their dreams? They're all dead. And it's because of people like us. People who take more than we need."

Maj was suddenly tired and ready to be alone as the definition of psychedelic floated into her mind. She'd learned from her Greek homework that psychedelic meant to reveal: soul made visible. Without words to explain, Maj understood that by the way he died, Clay's soul revealed itself in the end.

"I have to go to work," Maj said. "We'll talk about the school later. Oh, and the director of the speech clinic says to save April fourth."

"Your birthday," breathed Mother.

"I think I'm being honored for something. I want Daddy there."

"That's impossible."

"I've already told him. He wants to come. He's delighted really."

Mother went inside without saying good-bye.

*   *   *   *   *   *

The next morning, before going to the Reingor studio, Maj stopped off at the university police. With no sign of her academic adviser since moving back, she'd cautiously allowed herself to relax. Harder, she found, was pushing away the terror of how he'd hurt her. Knowing aberrant behavior turned more deviant over time, she worried who he was hurting now.

When she walked into the office, neither officer on

duty looked up from reading the newspaper.

Tongue-tied and humiliated, Maj used vague innuendoes about a friend of hers who'd been hurt by her academic advisor. As she attempted to allude to what happened, one officer lowered his paper and, slowly looking Maj up and down, nearly sneered like she got what she deserved.

Hating him, she turned self-conscious in her Indian print sleeveless top and shorts. She wished she'd dressed more formally.

"Seeing as how the encounter occurred off campus, and all," he said, going back to his reading. "Your friend needs to file a report about the incident with the Berkeley police."

"He's a university advisor," Maj cried, cringing at the desperation in her voice and hating the feeling of being overpowered and scorned.

"Downtown. Can't miss it," he said, dismissing her.

＊　＊　＊　＊　＊　＊

In her dressing room after work, and with a scrubbed face, Maj pulled her hair into a ponytail. Mr. Reingor came in to discuss the month's sales figures for his department stores. Even after more than a year, still Maj felt awkward calling him Gerald. Tonight, his presence added to the pressure she felt against her chest, like a giant thumb pinning her down. He made her uncomfortable, but he didn't scare her. Clay had taught her fear. Now, he was gone. And still, the thumb pressed.

Nodding in front of the mirror, Maj retied the carving at her neck. She only half-listened as Mr. Reingor thanked her for her part as the Reingor Girl.

Finding his conversation confused, as usual, instead she replayed her conversation with Mother this morning.

She still believed Mother was sweet on Mr. Reingor, but Maj wasn't so sure about him anymore. Lately, his body postures and hand gestures, inflections and tone often conveyed a deeper meaning. He liked telling her what to do, leaving her to wonder what happened to negotiation, compromise, and true communication. Rather than a circle of connection, his words created distance and, more and more often, uncertainty. He narrated his thoughts and feelings to her. Maj often didn't understand what he meant.

"Is it old?" he asked.

Puzzled, she looked up. Mr. Reingor pointed to her carving.

"I'm not sure how old," she said. "I found it a long ti—"

"May I see it?"

Instinctively, she covered the carving with her hand. "I don't usually take it off," she said, her pulse racing.

"I'll give it back." He reached out a hand with a little nod.

She hesitated but could find no rational reason to deny his request. Pleased he was interested, she untied the rawhide cord.

"It looks very old," he said.

She leaned in nearer to show him. "I think it's—"

"It really doesn't belong around your neck," he said.

"Excuse me?"

"It's awfully crude."

Maj's face colored as Mr. Reingor handed the carving back to her. As much as she wanted to put it on her neck, she slipped the wolf in her pocket instead.

*   *   *   *   *   *

Exhausted from work, Maj found herself alone in the house she shared with her roommates. Hope blew in the opened window, as twilight shadows skipped across a card stock envelope on the kitchen table. Addressed to Maj, the invitation was from Petrana. Raul would not be in attendance at his baby's christening. Due to a foul up somewhere along the chain of command, he'd been denied conscientious objector status and shipped off. He went missing in action two days after he arrived in Vietnam.

Maj collapsed at the table. Over the sink, the window opened to the maple tree she also saw from her bedroom window. One limb, in infancy, had grown down instead of up. It formed a bench across the ground before finally righting itself like a beckoning finger. The air sighed and leaves shuddered. MorMor would caution Maj to watch for the little ones—the elves and the fairies. Maj put her head in her hands. Kenny and Raul and his baby made fairies and elves silly and frivolous.

A shout came from outside. Slung at her like a fist, Maj instantly recognized the voice. She gagged. Slipping to the floor and keeping out of the light of the setting sun, she crawled to the edge of the window. Her advisor cruised past her house in his black Corvette. He flicked his lighted cigarette in a shower of sparks.

Revving the engine, he shouted the same nasty abuse, as if all these months of thinking he'd moved on, and she was safe, were merely part of his plan to torment her. The Corvette's horsepower sparked his voice, inflated his grand view of himself, and bloated his delusions of power over her—just like Clay's privilege had done for him. Deafened by the ringing in her ears, Maj missed some of what he said, but the vengeance in his voice left no question of his meaning. The louder the car engine screamed, the nastier his abuse grew.

Sick of herself, Maj covered her ears, wishing he'd drive full-speed into a brick wall, and well aware that only she had the power to end this.

She lay on the cool kitchen tile, her cheek against the slick surface, wondering if she'd be sad to die. As she vacillated between yes and no, she fell asleep. When she awoke, she knew what she had to do. She just hoped when the time came she really could.

ALCATRAZ

i.

Lost in fog, Billy and Sadie waited to board a boat called the Clearwater, in honor of the Credence Clearwater Revival Band for the fifteen thousand dollars they donated to the Indians from a benefit rock concert. Joining Billy, Mal, and Red were the captain and six other guys, all of whom were obviously Indians what with their long, dark hair parted down the middle and the color of their skin.

Everyone held their breath as Mal boarded, worried he'd capsize their boat. Even with the UAW banner tucked under his arm, Mal made it just fine. Sadie leapt onboard behind Mal. From the Hawaiian tune he hummed, Mal was in pretty good spirits.

Recently chosen as the UAW goodwill ambassador to China, in less than a month Mal was leaving on a ninety-day tour of Chairman Mao's Cultural Revolution, at a time when no one was allowed in Red China. Choosing Mal made sense, somewhere in the middle between the Chicanos and the Blacks and whites.

Red spoke to the captain. "We're from the UAW East Bay Executive board."

"Heard you were coming. Welcome aboard."

Everyone introduced each other as they handed

down boxes of foodstuff, clothes, and blankets they'd brought to support those on the island. One guy slurred his words, obviously drunk.

Billy picked up a box of his girls' outgrown clothing, left behind at the house, and spotted someone marching down the pier, back-lit in the foggy morning light. Billy raised a happy hand. Webb made it in time after all.

The shadow materialized into Janice and Remi with their latest convert in tow.

Webb was dead.

"What are they doing here?" Billy demanded of Red.

"Hell, it can't hurt to hear them out."

"You know about this, Mal?" asked Billy.

Avoiding him, Mal held up the UAW banner he insisted they bring along for publicity.

"Anyone want to help me with this?" Mal asked.

A guy named Threefingers, a self-described *Anishinabe* with all of his fingers and a knit cap pulled down over his ears, followed Mal to the front of the boat.

Billy started to board. Remi shouted for him to wait up.

"Hell, Billy, I'm telling you," said Red. "Arm up with the girls, we win hands down."

Then, the girls were upon them.

Janice motioned to Paul, a new assembler—young and rebellious and an easy mark—slouching next to her with a scowl on his face.

"You remember Paul, don't you, Billy?" Janice asked.

"Sure," Billy answered. "Hey, Paul."

Paul nodded and yawned, like early morning wasn't his thing. Red helped the women into the cabin, without giving them any of the usual shit he used to always go on about. With all the other women who'd been hired since the Civil Rights Act, Janice and Remi weren't such an oddity in the factory anymore.

ii.

Sailing across the San Francisco Bay to Angel Island, Maj sat on one side of Gerald's yacht, still confused about which side was port and which was starboard. As the wind tugged the main sail, Maj slipped under a taut wire stretched in front of her. Nervous and excited, she held tight to the cable and tentatively leaned out over the water. A chill seeped into her bones, and she wondered if she was coming down with something. Her contract as the Reingor Girl was up next month. Gerald had brought her on the boat to convince her to stay. She came to tell him she was done.

Perched over the edge of the boat, she became more liquid than form. Wind whistled with the sea. The cables cut into the fleshy part of the palms of her hands.

In spots beyond the Golden Gate Bridge, the afternoon fog burned off where blue sky and water merged. Cold, brilliant sunshine glinted off a line of sea lions bobbing toward the city, like a string of shiny, black pearls. The skyline shimmered in blue shadows and white spines, as seagulls soared in the wake of the little boat trailing the yacht. The sea was frog green.

Gerald's voice rose from behind Maj and carried above the wind and the seals, as he joked at the wheel with his friend Charles and Charles's girlfriend, Clarisa. Gerald waved. Maj lifted a hand and quickly re-gripped the wire. When no one was watching, she leaned back. The boat sliced through the water and created a smooth swath. Sea spray wet her face. Salt formed on her lips.

With the ends of her hair trailing in the bay and the words to *Aquarius* playing in her head, Maj longed to live in harmony and understanding like in the song. For her own true liberation, first she had to act according to her own beliefs, most of which she found more and more stood in direct conflict with both Mother's and Gerald's expectations. Today she'd tell Gerald. Next, came Mother.

iii.

On deck of the Clearwater with Sadie, Billy watched as fog drifted over the top half of the Bay Bridge. The expanse was clear from San Francisco to the tip of the long, flat landmass of Treasure Island. From Treasure Island to Oakland, with the span locked in fog, sleek lines turned boxy and chunky.

Ma's first and only house hid high in the Oakland hills. The only time she'd ever seemed truly happy was the year or two they'd lived in that house. Grandma even came for a visit, the only time she came to the Bay Area other than for his wedding. Then Ray went and lost his license for drunk driving, and the bank foreclosed on them.

The bay was choppy, and puke-green caps sprayed Billy. Tugging up the collar of his pea jacket, he hunkered down. Still his cheeks froze, and his ears turned numb.

Yellowdrum, the drunk of the group, leaned over the side railing. "We ain't Indians, you know?"

Hearing him speak, Sadie's tail thumped the deck.

"We've been here a whole lot longer than America, so we're not Native Americans neither." Yellowdrum lost it right in the bay.

Scratching Sadie behind the ears, Billy shook his head, ready to condemn Yellowdrum as a typical stereotype. Then Billy remembered visiting Willie Wolf with Grandma in San Quentin. Now Billy was on his way to another prison.

Janice poked her head out from the cabin below. "Come talk to us."

With the boat rocking so much, Billy didn't particularly care to go below. Hoping for warmth, he might as well get this talk over. At the bottom step, he peered into the cabin for a place to sit. The kid wedged in a booth between Janice and Remi gave him a look Billy wanted to flip off. The kid called himself a Communist. Likely didn't even know what that was.

Red faced them in the bench on the opposite side of the table. Mal stood with his legs spread apart and his arms braced against either wall. Sadie settled between the big man's legs as Billy slid in next to Red.

"Coffee?" asked Janice.

"Sure," Billy said.

Janice nudged Remi who got to her feet and banged around at the tiny kitchen counter.

"It's never too early to talk about the next election," said Janice.

"Let's make things easy and negotiate right up front," Billy said.

Even as he spoke the words, Billy knew he wasn't a negotiator. Brenda was right. The essence of politics was negotiation and compromise. Billy had learned that the hard way. You gave things away, sometimes everything else, to gain one thing. If that didn't work, inflict pressure from the outside. Dissident factions he could unite, or so he once believed. Negotiation and compromise, not his thing.

"Nobody gives a shit about the guys." Billy leaned forward. "Do you give a shit about the guys, Paul?"

"We're being asked to produce an inferior product in unsafe conditions with unfair pay," Paul recited. "There's no possibility for exportation or market increase. Consumers sure as hell aren't going to continue buying shitty cars and trucks. Management is making it so we'll eventually work ourselves out of a job."

Hearing words from his strike speech, Billy leaned back. During the strike, the destructive conflict burned the fight out of Billy and out of the men. The war was over. Now came reconstruction. The establishment of a new order was needed in order to work successfully together. Not something he exceled in—getting along.

His job with the Union, and the factory, too, Billy knew was over. Panic flared at the thought. His family was gone. Next he'd lose the guys at the factory, too. Let others take over. He'd done his part. Time off for good behavior. Time to face himself.

Billy warmed his hands on the coffee cup. Maybe that was his true destiny. To live alone.

"Times have changed," said Janice. "A revolution is underway. The younger guys want in."

"You're wrong," Billy said. "The revolution is over. And who the hell are you to tell me what to do anyway? Red and Mal and me? We're the only real deals here. We work to feed our families."

Paul rose up and leaned across the table. Red reached out a hand to back off the kid.

"I'm sure we can work something out." Red spoke easily.

Hating him, Billy looked at the kid and saw himself.

"You've moved to the right. The strike made you

cynical," said Janice. "You need to step up, Billy. You have to show the guys you're still one of them."

"I'm done putting the guys on any more high balls."

"We don't need him," said the kid.

"Hell, I ain't doing this without Billy." Red rose to his feet.

Mal moved forward. Billy motioned Mal back and pulled Red down beside him. Their loyalty jarred his senses.

He'd lived his entire life on the turbulent surface of things, fueling and fighting the same misunderstandings, petty jealousies, and quarrels that hung in the cabin. Having lost everything, including his own fear and ambition, Billy still had something left to lose. He had his girls to consider. They may not be around, but the little girls were still his.

"The kid's right," Billy said. "You're a lot better off without me. The guys, too. You need Paul now. Not me."

iv.

Striped spinnakers leaned into the wind. White caps stood out against dark depths. The salty world of fish and rocks and big animals lay safely hidden below.

Alcatraz appeared upside down on Maj's left. She ducked under the wire and sneezed. Between studying, being unable to sleep, and worrying out the details of her plan to finally back off her advisor, her body ached all over. She didn't have time to be sick.

Studying the island, she smoothed her hair into a ponytail and squeezed out the water.

A tall narrow building next to a beige two-story, and even the land itself, looked wet and cold and dismal. A flock of water birds circled the dock where a few people huddled. Rocks climbed out of the sea, where an old stone retaining wall hugged the earth. An arched cement banister ran along the far side of the island, where tall grasses and Yucca trees surrounded a water tower with *Indian Land* printed in bold black letters.

To the left beyond the tower, fog faded from the Golden Gate Bridge. To the right stood Sausalito, with its forest of ship masts. Angel Island appeared to be floating on a cloud. Alcatraz, the prison, stood bleak and dark and stark in the surrounding beauty.

"Nixon called out the National Guard." Gerald held out his hands to Maj. "It's high time we storm the place and arrest the whole mess of them," he said, gloomily.

Feeling chilled, Maj let him help her to her feet. "I wish we could stop. I'd love to see what's happening."

"When the Indians are gone," he said. "We'll make a day of it."

Maj and Gerald faced each other at the back of the boat, well out of reach of the boom. Maj opened her mouth, and then shook her head and sighed. Going along with what he wanted had always seemed easier than speaking up for herself. She was done with taking the easy way out.

"I don't think so," she answered simply.

"Why you're trembling," he said. "You look absolutely wretched. What have you done to yourself?"

"I'm tired."

"You're sick."

Brushing off her windbreaker and low-slung cotton bell-bottom pants, Maj didn't disagree. Things worked more smoothly when they went according to Gerald's ideas.

"If this talk weren't so important to me, I wouldn't have given up study time for a boat ride," she said.

"Not now," Gerald said quickly. "We'll talk after a light dinner. I promise."

"On our way back, right after dinner," Maj clarified, reminding him of his promise to get her back before dark.

Having been unsuccessful at arranging a meeting with him at the studio or even at his office, when Gerald suggested this outing, Maj had seized the opportunity. She felt an obligation for all he'd done for her to tell him in person she's wasn't signing another contract. Trouble was that even with the most superficial details, he only listened to her when she was agreeing with him. The times she'd brought up the future, he ignored her communication.

"There, there," he said, patting her on the shoulder. "Go below. Take a nap. Go on now."

v.

Outside, a bitter wind gusted. The sun had risen above the fog, but gave off no warmth. During the talk with the girls, for once in his life, Billy hadn't blurted out whatever words popped in his head. He'd kept back certain words and pushed away others.

Out of the mist, a desolate-looking water tower appeared. Bile rose in his throat. Big black letters covered the top of the tower.

"Peace and Freedom
Welcome
Home of the Free
Indian Land"

A lump formed in his throat, and his chest swelled. Surprised as hell by his reaction, Billy took his first deep breath in years.

As the Clearwater approached the island, monster

waves slammed against the rocks. A lone man huddled on a rocky crag with a tipi towering behind him. Beyond, stood a mess of government-issued prison buildings, sterile, and as razor sharp as the factory.

Threefingers leaned up against the railing next to Billy at the bow of the boat.

"We have lookouts stationed on all sides of the island day and night." Threefingers pointed to the man at the tipi.

Billy nodded, appreciating the pride the guy had in what they'd put together on Alcatraz.

The boat came around the island, where men stood on a flat cement dock, atop piers and posts out over the water. Behind them emerged a four-story beige building with elongated red letters.

"You are now on Indian land."

Looming over the building stood a burned-out lighthouse and a structure with no roof. Smudges like blackened flames on walls outside the windows showed the direction the wind had blown during a fire. The stark reminder of what the island was, first and foremost, and always had been—a prison—turned his stomach queasy.

As the Clearwater slowed, everyone clustered on deck. Monster waves crashed against gigantic landing posts. Billy spread his legs and clutched the boat railing.

"How do we get from here to there?" Janice pointed up the six to ten feet to the dock landing.

An upsurge of water pitched the Clearwater five feet higher and dropped them into a ten-foot trough.

"The Feds confiscated all the landings." Threefingers shouted over the wind.

Even in the aquatic roller coaster, they were able to tie the boat to the pier. Wind froze Billy's face, and mist and fog seeped into his bones. From above, a couple of guys swung out a makeshift-landing platform that the wind tossed like a toy. Using a series of pulleys, the landing lowered, inch-by-inch. All of them in the boat reached up in unison to keep the landing platform from smashing into them.

When it was his turn, Billy jumped from the boat to the platform with Sadie right beside him. He grabbed her collar and clutched the rebar pole.

Threefingers gestured to him and shouted. "Stay dead center."

Mal scrambled on. The landing platform teetered. Janice screamed. Sadie started to slide.

"Hell, straddle the middle, Mal," shouted Red.

Mal grabbed Billy's arm, his grip like a vise. The platform leveled.

Threefingers closed a little gate behind Mal, giving the big man something to grab hold of besides Billy, just as the wind flicked them forward. Billy clutched the railing and squatted low beside Sadie. Below them, Paul looked green, which pleased Billy no end.

On the island, a woman with a headband pulled over her forehead, rode a bicycle through a puddle of water. The peace sign she flashed reminded Billy of the blonde, and added to the gloom of the island.

When all of them were standing on solid ground, Billy asked Threefingers what it was like living in a place built for punishment, the end of the line.

"No worse than living on the reservation," answered Threefingers. "Come on. Everyone's waiting at Cell Block 10."

Queasiness sloshed in Billy's gut, but it wasn't seasickness. The cracked cement and falling plaster, a little girl with no shoes, and a boy without a coat were all reminders of the kind of poverty he'd lived with as a kid. His hands broke into a sweat, even in the damp and fog.

Threefingers started up the hill with Mal and Red, and Sadie racing ahead. Billy lagged behind. Mal's attention turned to the sound of kids' laughter. Out of shape, the big man puffed hard on the uphill walk.

"Urban kids usually have had little or no tribal contact," explained Threefingers. "We put them in art classes and a crafts' training center, where they learn skills normally passed from one generation to the next. Beadwork, leatherwork, woodcarving, costume decoration, dance, like that."

The further they hiked, the harder it was for Billy to put one foot in front of the other. The vibes of the place were thick. Every step, ghosts or something passed through him. They could have been convicts. To him, they felt tribal.

"Hippies wear headbands and want to be Indians," continued Threefingers. "Most of us don't even know what that means, being Indian. The children know the occupation of this island, the fact that we defy the entire United States government, is for them, for the future of all tribes. Being here together is like coming home."

Red cupped his hands and blew to keep warm.

"Is that why we don't see more people?" asked Mal. "Because of the cold?"

"Everyone's preparing for tonight's *pauwau*, or as white people pronounce it, a pow wow" said Threefingers. "You'll see more people as the day picks up. This is the only place Indians of all tribes can come together. Making a trip to Alcatraz is a pilgrimage. After the first month or so, most of us moved out of the cells, too drafty and cold, and into the main block. Not much further now."

Hearing they weren't going to the actual prison block, the weight of a full-sized Mac truck lifted from Billy chest. Sadie rushed a yellow mutt, running up to them with its ears plastered against its head. Threefingers introduced Many Moons. The two dogs took off up the hill.

"We have a live turkey, two ducks, several rabbits, chickens, and a couple of friendly dogs. What tribe are you?" asked Threefingers.

Billy shrugged at the looks of surprise Red and Mal shot him. Secretly, he was pleased Threefingers picked it out in him.

"Your friends don't know," Threefingers said, nodding his head. "I'm not surprised. We get good at hiding it. I can always tell. You get real quiet when you first arrive here. You think it's the prison, but it's being on Indian land."

"*Bode'wadmi ndaw.* My mother's side," said Billy.

"No shit?" Mal had a real hurt look on his face.

"People of the place of the fire," said Threefingers. "*Bozho.*"

"*Iwgwien,*" Billy replied, as way of thanking Threefingers for his welcome. Billy hoped he said it right.

"Your people and my people are two of the traditional alliance of three known as the Council of Three Fires," said Threefingers.

Mal shook his head, like he couldn't register that Billy was part Indian and never told him.

"Your people from Oklahoma?" asked Threefingers.

Billy nodded and changed the subject, pointing to a craggy point where kids were fishing. Beyond them, white caps dotted the bay like ice caps.

"What kind of fish?" he asked.

"Red snapper, bay perch, smelt," Threefingers answered. "They're snagging dinner for tonight's celebration."

"I thought a pow wow was something the white man made up," said Red.

"Some of the old chiefs say the children need a *pauwau*. 'He who has revelations.' I think we all do," explained Threefingers. "Most of us who first arrived here were college students and very idealistic. The people coming now are older. Some of them are pretty screwed up, scarred from Vietnam, cynical and with serious addiction problems. The elders want to share what they can."

Threefingers stopped in front of the long low building. "Here we are. Hungry?"

He escorted them into a makeshift kitchen where three giant industrial pots bubbled with something that made Billy's mouth water. His stomach turned weak. Groups of people laughed and talked. Janice waved from where she and Remi and Paul were headed to sit down.

Instead of the joining the others, Billy sat across from Threefingers, next to an old woman who made room for him at her table. Being around so many Indians was rubbing off on him. The lost and lonely pit he carried around since Brenda left with the girls and had likely suffered all his life didn't ache quite so bad.

vi.

After an early dinner of grilled halibut filets, salad, French bread—with Gerald and his friends drinking two bottles of white wine—Maj was bummed when

Charles yanked the starter line on the little boat. Rather than sail back now as promised, Gerald motored them to Angel Island.

Impatient to stake out her future, Maj wanted this to be over.

Beyond a small cove, an old deserted military building sat on a flat knoll. Behind it, rose a hill and deserted officers' housing.

At the beach, Maj and Clarissa disembarked while Gerald and Charles dragged the little boat onshore. Maj spotted a pure white sand dollar on the beach, mermaid money washed up out of the deep from one of MorMor's fairy tales.

Gerald came up next to her. She slipped the shell in her pocket.

"Alrighty, then," Gerald said, studying his watch. "Sunset at 5:30. We motor back no later than 6:00."

Charles and his girlfriend left to walk along the beach.

"We were supposed to sail back after dinner. What happened?" asked Maj.

Without answering, and carrying a brown paper bag, Gerald started up a narrow foot trail.

"I'd rather we talk here," she said, motioning to the picnic table in the shade of a eucalyptus tree.

Suddenly, the thought of her modeling career truly coming to an end filled Maj with burning excitement. Gerald was the reason she'd come so far toward her dream, and not only because of the scheduling, and how he always worked around conflicts. When Gerald began telephoning Mother every morning, Mother stopped pestering Maj. Telling Gerald no today was practice next for telling Mother.

Gerald kept hiking as if she hadn't spoken. She

peered up the trail, worried about what he had in mind. If she stayed where she was, he would have to come back. Instead, he moved steadily higher until he vanished into a grove of eucalyptus trees.

All sign of Charles and Clarissa disappeared, and suddenly Maj was alone and marooned on a deserted island.

Reluctantly, she followed Gerald.

She caught up to him leaning against a eucalyptus tree. The Golden Gate Bridge shone in the distance as if perched on his shoulder. He offered her a tiny spoonful of what she recognized as cocaine.

"This will make you all better," he promised.

Maj shook her head no, and watched him suck the spoonful of white powder up his nose.

"I prefer we talk on the beach," she said again.

Refilling the spoon, he pushed it toward her. "Trust me," he said.

Rather than fight him about it, she took a sharp inhale. Instantaneously, she felt pulled up taller and buoyed with confidence. A breeze carried the calming medicinal scent of eucalyptus.

He kept to the dirt trail to the top of the hill. In front of a deserted three-story military building, he wagged his finger for her to follow him inside. Her jaw tightened.

Inside the abandoned building, Gerald handed Maj the bag he'd been carrying and explained that the bottom steps of the indoor stairway had been removed.

"Part of the park's efforts to disable all the old military buildings on what is now a defunct post."

Maj passed a hand over her forehead as she glimpsed the bottle of champagne in the bag. She sneezed and lost her breath. To Gerald, champagne meant victory and success.

He dragged a tree stump beneath an empty window frame. Using the windowsill as support, he scrambled up to what was now the bottom step. He leaned down, took the bottle of champagne first, and then gave Maj a hand-up.

At the top floor, she forgot all about Gerald and all about feeling sick, as she skipped from one empty window frame to the next. Around and around, the world she'd grown up in flashed through the openings.

vii.

After eating, Billy presented Threefingers with a check from the UAW and they all smoked pot together. Threefingers left and returned with an old man. Chief White Cloud wore beaded buckskin moccasins laced to the knees and fringed around the top, buckskin pants, and no shirt. The chief welcomed them and thanked them for coming.

"*Bozho nikan. Ahaw nciwe'nmoyan ewabmlman. Iwgwien 'ebyayen ms'ote,*" said the chief.

Billy was surprised to hear the old man speaking Grandma's language. He returned the greeting.

"*Bozho nikan.*"

The chief offered a tour of the cellblock and the old, underground Army prison where military POW and deserters were housed during the Civil War.

Janice bowed out. "We'd love to stay, but it's getting late. We have work to get back to."

Paul looked relieved. No beer or alcohol was allowed on the island. Red and Mal wouldn't stay any longer than they had to either.

Outside, Sadie and Many Moons greeted them with tails wagging. Billy offered the bacon he'd stashed in his coat pocket. Each dog pulled back their mouth in giant clown smiles.

Everyone said their goodbyes and took off for the docking area. When Billy didn't follow, Sadie barked. Mal turned around.

"Go on ahead," said Billy. "I'm sticking around."

Mal looked like he wanted to say something, and then decided against it.

Billy took a deep breath with no wheezing or coughing.

Threefingers went with the others down the hill to the boat landing. Chief White Cloud led Billy in the opposite direction.

"You feel it, don't you?"

Billy asked what the chief was talking about, but he knew.

"Reconnecting with your grandmother," said the chief. "Knowing you come from a people. The feeling you belong for no other reason than part of you is Indian."

Not bothering to ask how he knew about Grandma, Billy admitted he felt it. And, for the first time, he truly did.

"I have to stick around to prepare for tonight. Many Moons will take you and your friend to join others on the beach. Later, you'll be given a new name, new responsibilities and privileges, decided by the medicine men's visions and sense of your destiny."

"Doesn't it make you mad?" asked Billy. "Living under a government that destroyed your way of life?"

Sadie trotted back to them and sat at Billy feet. Many Moons waited to guide them to the beach.

"We are, each tribe, a sovereign nation," said the chief. "And we are still standing. Ancient wisdom holds that when all tribes come together as one people, peace will return to the earth. Young people demand we fight back using the white man's way with guns and bullets and annihilation. The festival tonight is to remind them there's another way."

Billy nodded, willing to hope there truly could be another way beyond fighting and killing us against them, and them against us.

"You don't reek of the white man's poison," said the chief.

"Nearly a year now."

"After tonight, it will be forever."

Chief White Cloud turned to go. Many Moons barked. The chief snapped his fingers and turned back.

"You were once given the name Running Wolf. I heard it on the wind."

Billy peered into the chief's eyes, half expecting to see Longtree's brother. There was about a fifty-year age difference and no resemblance.

"What else do you know about me?" Billy asked.

The chief's face crinkled into a knowing smile. "You've learned the hard way to control your mouth. That's good. Now it's time to listen and stay alert. A reward waits to reveal itself to you."

Billy trailed Sadie and Many Moons, with the chief's words bouncing in his head. A cement path and banister ran along the water, and in places crumbled away, revealing an arched support structure of stone.

Making their way around the island, Billy came to more than one place where the path had fallen into waves lapping against the rocks. Many Moons showed him where to jump. Drums and rattles and laughter sounded from beyond the next bend.

Out here, where there wasn't a sign of the prison, he

let the wind buffet him. Billy no longer felt like he had no home, was a complete unknown, or a rolling stone.

The wind picked up and became the only sound he heard. He pulled up the collar of his pea jacket over his ears. The sun had come out and, though he couldn't feel its heat, light rippled off the water.

In the distance, the outline of a sailboat reminded Billy of the dream vision Brenda used to go on about. The yellow-haired girl and her parents and grandmother at the candy store, a new Cadillac, shiny shoes, a full stomach—his inspiration for wealth and security and everything he'd failed to achieve. Still, off on his own, with the bay and the gulls and dogs for company, Billy felt strangely at peace.

Rubbing two coins together deep in his pocket made him eager to reclaim Grandma's carving. His eyes watered. He untied the rawhide band from his ponytail and tied it across his forehead.

viii.

Spinning from one window frame to the next in the deserted military building, Maj spun to a stop. A gigantic bonfire blazed at the very tip of Alcatraz. A group of people circled a giant drum. As sparks flew, people on the beach danced one way around the fire and then back the way they had come. The solid and rhythmic beat spread a fire of certainty in her mind.

"Gerald, I—"

"When school is over," he interrupted. "I'll see to it that you never put yourself though this kind of torment again. It kills me to see you work so hard."

"I love the work I do with children," she said, annoyed he never let her finish a sentence and, if he did, immediately lost interest.

Rather than comment, Gerald moved behind her. Now that it was clear he wasn't going to make this easy for her—not that she expected him to—she was uncomfortable not being able to read his reaction. She was also relieved at not having him study her face as she went on speaking.

"I've been offered a position at a school for autistic kids in San Francisco," she said, tucking her hair behind her ears. "I move to the city next month."

She spoke quickly, keeping quiet about her plans for converting the east wing of Great Oaks into a home and school for autistic kids—Gerald didn't need to know that.

A champagne pop came from behind her, just as a giant flame licked the sky, stoking history and lighting her ideas with success. A little way off from the drummers and dancers on the beach, a man faced the wind. He was too far away to make out his features, but Maj felt as if she recognized him. A dog sat on either side of the man.

Suddenly, in that moment, Maj knew she was absolutely where she ought to be. Seeing the man and his dogs felt like a fitting build-up to the end of this season of her life. She wanted someone like that, someone who stood on an island to make a difference.

She turned and faced her boss just as the tip of his tongue reached for a spot of white wine sauce in the crease of his lips. He pushed a flute of champagne toward her.

Embarrassed, she put up a hand and shook her head no.

"Here's to a toast that school is soon a thing of the past," he said, nudging the glass at her until she took it.

"Well, no, actually the thing of the past is me

modeling for you," Maj said, after a confused silence, a hand playing with the carving at her neck, drawing comfort from the wolf.

"In the meantime, this is so you won't be mad at me anymore." He withdrew a long rectangular velvet box from his jacket.

"Mad?"

"I offended you about your necklace," he said. "I wanted the gold setting engraved, which is why it took me so long to make up for my insensitivity about your carving. Open it."

Maj hesitated. With his tongue tucked in his lower lip, Gerald carefully lifted the lid himself. Moonlight flickered off a delicate gold linked chain with a solitary empire-cut diamond as big as a pea.

Maj gasped and looked away. Gerald lifted the necklace out of the box.

"It's as old or older than your carving," he said. "I know how much you loved your carving, and still you gave it up for me. This is my show of appreciation."

Maj's eyes cleared as if a veil had been dropped. Mortified at her own stupidity, she felt her face turn fire hot. Furious for revealing an emotional reaction, she snatched away her hand he'd grabbed. Rather than romantically, as was now apparent, Gerald and Mother were linked in their mutual dismissal of Maj's feelings, disinterest in her passions, and confidence that she'd do what she was told.

Maj unzipped her windbreaker and pulled out the wolf from under her turtleneck with cold, stiff fingers. "I do wear the carving," she said, her voice distant and unemotional.

"Forget about that. Marry me."

Stunned, Maj shook her head. Weary from her own

idiocy, she was aware that the cocaine didn't last very long, at least not the part that freed her words.

Gerald took her face in both his hands. Maj's legs turned rubbery. The moment represented the kind of romance that made her ache with envy, and every inch of her long for true love.

"Say you'll marry me."

Frowning, she backed up, as the fire on Alcatraz grew larger. The drums beat louder.

"I'm grateful for all you've done for me," Maj started, avoiding eye contact with Gerald. "I never could have returned to school so quickly if not for you. The decisions you've made on my behalf have benefited me greatly."

He cut in front of her view. "I'll go right on making the right decisions for you. If you insist on working, you can move into the penthouse in San Francisco—"

"I don't want you to make my decisions."

"Don't say no to me," he said in a warning tone. "I've waited a long time for you."

Aware of a change in him, Maj edged toward the stairs. "I think you are—"

Gerald shot out an arm, snatched her by the wrist, and held her there. Maj turned rigid.

"I don't want you to think," he said. "You're not any good at it. I'll do the thinking for both of us. Marry me, and consider me your full-time job."

With his jaw a sharp and ready guillotine's blade, his words cut her rapid-fire fast. He acted as if he was still wired, though she wasn't anymore at all.

"No." The little two-letter word left Maj's lips and rebounded against her ears. She stood a bit taller.

"No," she said again and twisted from his grasp.

He took a swig of champagne and smashed the

bottle against the concrete wall

Maj ran down the stairs, jumping at the end to the bottom floor. Gerald followed her.

"Does your mother know about your plans?" he pressed.

"She will. And, I'll tell her myself this time. It's time I learn how to talk to my own mother."

"You always make a mess of things with her," he said in an ugly voice. "You know you will again."

Maj felt a growl rise up in her throat.

"You're quite good at throwing my weaknesses at me, aren't you?" she said, so mad, she trembled. "It's time I take care of myself. And Gerald, when my contract is up in June, I'm done. I'm not a girl anymore. I'm finished with being the Reingor Girl."

"Now, just you wait a minute," Gerald said, practically shouting. "I have a great deal of money invested in you."

"And I thought you wanted me to be your wife," Maj said, quietly.

THE EXPLOSION

Unable to sleep, Maj dressed well before dawn on the morning of the award ceremony. Before driving out to Great Oaks to pick up Daddy, and she hoped Mother too, first she had a stop to make.

Having laid out the night before what she planned to wear, now she took her time dressing all in black. Stuffing her long blonde hair under a black knit cap, she surveyed herself in the mirror. Worried when she saw how her pale face shone like a white light against the dark, she considered smudging black lines across her cheeks. Charged up and ready to go, she decided against it

A darkened Shattuck Avenue was devoid of students with morning classes and the usual throngs of city commuters. Distracted as she went through the steps for the ten billionth time—unknowns gnawing holes in her plan and with gaping caverns of anxiety dripping in her stomach—Maj didn't see them at first.

Something zipped out of the corner of her eye. Startled, she shook her head.

"Get a grip," she chastised herself, and shivered.

A figure shot in front of the GTO. Maj slammed on her brakes. Whatever it was—human, part-human, beast—was clothed in dull trappings. One, or possibly even three, long, frayed, and paper-thin overcoats covered a bulky sweater and balloon-like pants—the outer skin of an onion hiding many layers within. As Maj strained her eyes to determine what she was seeing, something bumped the rear of her car.

Confused, she looked both ways. Had a wrong turn landed her in this dark haunted world? She slowed at a blinking yellow light and locked her car door. Something stirred to her left. Twisting her head, before she could fix her eyes on what exactly she was seeing, movement tracked in the opposite direction.

Faces wrapped in mufflers and shawls, they limped and sprinted, dashed and galloped, slunk and scooted— as silent as the night—like a shadow species, back and forth across the wide lanes. All shapes and sizes of people with full pockets and heavy bags. Grocery store shopping carts swollen with bits of food and paper and curious shapes of lost treasures. Unimaginable things.

Here, in the dark among the invisible, breathing became easier for Maj. Whispers and shadows, betrayals and broken hearts, these vagabonds understood as she did the power of silence and the urge to move ever away from the center—out from what was, far from judgment and ridicule, while steadily expanding toward change, toward what could be.

*　*　*　*　*　*

Maj's academic advisor lived on the opposite end of campus. Maj was well aware that as things stood now, whether he quit stalking her for a month or for five years, she wouldn't ever completely be free of him.

The relief at seeing his black Stingray parked alone in

the red zone, opposite his apartment building, caused her foot to slip from the gas. The car nearly stalled. Flanking the far side of the walkway and framing his car, stood a giant shipping container.

Buoyed by the first step going according to her plan, Maj turned the GTO around for a fast get-away and parked. The street was empty. All the other tenant cars were parked orderly and by the rules in carports under the building.

Her advisor's wing was dark, except for one solitary light burning in the front window of the third floor apartment, two doors down from his. Someone was up and moving on the other side of sheer curtains.

Maj quietly opened her car door and left it ajar, so as not to disturb the quiet. Not worried about her advisor waking this early, not his style, still she didn't like that someone else was up. A wren heralded the brightening in the eastern foothills.

As Maj opened the trunk of her car, a thick, low-hanging cloud of turpentine and paint crept over the side of the car as if alive, a panther stalking its prey. Reeling at the smell, she jerked on an old pair of Daddy's gardening gloves. Quickly she snatched up the short rope she'd braided with strips of Mother's painting rags.

Leaves fell around Maj as she marched steadily towards the Corvette, her nose numb from the stench of fresh solvent. Her advisor defined himself and drew power from the one material possession that seemed to mean anything to him. Destroy the car. Maj destroyed him.

Her heart trembled, rattling her with worry that she'd over-doused the rags. Ready to ditch her plan, instead she repeated over and over again.

My goal is to be safe. I deserve to be loved. I deserve to be safe.

She carefully switched hands and untwisted the gas cap to her advisor's car.

I am safe. I am safe. I am safe.

The wren fell silent.

"Step away from the car!" His command hit hard against the spring morning.

Maj whirled around as her advisor fist-punched the window screen. The screen gave way, nearly plunging him three stories to the ground. The curtain dropped in the window two doors away.

"I've reported your threats," Maj shouted. "Hurt me and the police have a pattern of abuse. I am here to demonstrate I mean what I say. Keep away from me. And I better never hear about you hurting anyone else. Ever."

She hadn't actually made an official report yet concerned it would point a finger at her for the destruction about to happen. Still, her threat buoyed her confidence.

She stuck the rags in the gas tank, leaving a short tail hanging out.

He screamed at her to stop.

Her hands shook as she slid back the top of the matchbox. Sparking a match against the flint, she broke the matchstick in two. The lighted end snuffed itself out on the ground.

She fumbled for another, steeling her shoulders, sure he was right behind her. The matchstick blazed, burned her fingertips, and she dropped it. Still burning, she picked up the match. Using both hands to steady herself, she held it under the fuse. Shielding her face from the open gas tank, she blew on the tail.

The fire caught.

Maj ran.

Nothing happened.

Sure her advisor had gotten to the fuse in time and was on his way to punish her, she ran faster. Just as she reached the GTO, the explosion hit. The smell of smoke, unlike Ramon's garden fires at Great Oaks, stank of gasoline and oil, cruelty, and pain. Beneath the stench was the smell of something Maj decided tasted an awfully lot like freedom.

She sped away, her advisor's grief bellowing against the roar of the fire.

*   *   *   *   *   *

Maj turned onto the wooden bridge to Great Oaks with all the windows down, and a maddeningly flapping heart. Airing her pain had given her a full-bodied release of excitement, dread, exhilaration, and relief. Left with a feeling that was deliberate and exacting and, at the same time, unexpectedly open-hearted, she sang along to Neil Young's *Ohio* on the radio.

Stopping behind Gerald's Lamborghini, Maj left the engine idling and radio blasting. The musty scent of her favorite oak tree floated dream whispers from the days she hid from Clay in the tree's sheltering arms. She touched the carving at her neck.

Gerald reached through the window and switched off the car. Silence breathed her name.

Mother motioned like a crossing-guard from the portico. "No more daydreaming, Maj. Come inside."

The same words Maj had heard as a child, calling her home, softened her heart and reminded her of who she was today.

Gerald opened the door and offered his hand. Maj

emerged without his help.

"Mother invited you," she said, her voice hoarse from screaming at her counselor.

"What's that smell?' Gerald said, leaning in and sniffing at her. "Why do you smell of gasoline?"

Maj shook her head and walked toward the house where Mother stood framed in the big picture window overlooking the driveway. Her hair was parted down the middle with bangs and flipped up on the ends. She wore a coachman style V-necked dress with white piping and little white buttons running double-breasted down the front—Reingor's woman's line down to the white, fine-net stockings.

Inside, the Kingston Trio sang from the stereo about some folks being good and some being bad, and others just doing the best they could.

"I'll see if Daddy's ready," Maj said by way of a greeting to Mother.

Lines of irritation shattered the skin between Mother's eyes.

"Nurse Patricia is giving him a bite to eat," Mother said carefully. "Then she's helping him shower and shave. I've asked Carmen to prepare a light lunch for Gerald and the two of us on the veranda. Nurse Patricia will have your father dressed and ready for the award ceremony. I promise."

That Mother would go to such trouble to eliminate any chance of her leaving softened Maj even more. She followed her outside.

"You know how proud I am of you," continued Mother. "To receive an award for the work you've done with children is a great honor but—" Mother smoothed the front of her skirt.

"I'm not so sure it's an award."

"Well, I am."

Mother's confidence surprised Maj.

"What's this I hear about you teaching in the city?" Mother asked when they reached the veranda.

Maj glanced at Gerald, her neck rigid.

"Your mother asked a direct question. I couldn't lie," he said.

Viewed through her imaginary world, Gerald was the same troll that had haunted Maj's entire life with the same horrid leer she knew meant ruin. His hands twisted, gleeful, and ready to shape her differently.

"When you and Gerald are married, you'll volunteer with the Junior League," said Mother sitting down. "You'll reach so many more people that way."

So, Gerald had told Mother about Maj's school plans and remained silent about her refusal of marriage. Mother gushed about the wedding at the country club and whom to invite. Gerald agreed with everything she said.

"I'm not marrying Gerald," Maj.

Mother and Gerald went said on with their wedding plans as if she hadn't spoken.

Carmen smiled and quietly served a luncheon of chicken salad and corn tortillas.

"Gracias, mi abuela," said Maj.

"De nada, mi hija."

Talking to Gerald, Mother looked like a peacock, stuck in a prideful display around a wedding that would never be. Growing up, Maj had wanted to be a good girl, and do as she should, more than she trusted her own instincts. Now that she knew the cost of speaking up, speaking out, and speaking back in life, she was willing to pay the price of freedom.

Mother dabbed her lips and folded the cloth napkin

on her lap.

"Grace Cathedral is just the spot," said Mother. "Have I told you, Gerald? Maj sang in the church choir at Grace when she was a child."

"I'm not getting married," said Maj.

A sheen of sweat crept across her forehead and clung to her upper lip. With her throat burning, Maj went on.

"Teaching in the city prepares me for the school I told you about starting here. When our plans are complet—"

Maj stopped as Gerald whispered something in Mother's ear. He smiled, as if enjoying Maj's discomfort. Maj took her eyes off of him and turned toward the long bruising journey she knew she and Mother had to make together.

First, Mother instructed both of them to wait right where they were and she disappeared inside.

"I'm not getting married," Maj called after her retreating figure.

*   *   *   *   *   *

Gerald pulled his chair up against Maj's. She pushed away from the table and shot him a pointed look.

"I want you to leave," she said, her voice barely a whisper. She cleared her throat and spoke louder. "Go. Now." Her pitch soared an octave too high, betraying her attempt to remain unemotional. "I'll give your good-byes to Mother."

"Before you get mad, just do me a favor," said Gerald.

"No." Maj's face turned hot. Rather than duck and hide, she stared right back at him. "No," she said again, and along with the little word, she grew fierce and real.

Even with Mother and Carmen about to return, Gerald withdrew a vial of cocaine. Giving him a look of disgust, Maj told him to put it away. She looked out over the creek and the hillside beyond, fingering the wolf carving at her neck.

She still wore the necklace, though she no longer clung to the wolf as her totem, as if an old and tiny piece of wood could connect her to a man meant only for her. A man who would see her heart and love her for who she was on the inside. The stronger she felt herself becoming over these past few months, the less she worried about who loved her and for what.

Mother emerged from the house carrying a tiny wedding cake complete with a bride and a groom atop a second tier. She placed the cake on the table, clasped her hands together, and sighed. Carmen followed with a silver ice bucket and bottle of champagne.

As much as Maj craved snatching the cocaine from Gerald and snorting enough to express her feelings aloud, she knew if ever there was a time to speak up on her own behalf this was it.

"I'm not marrying Gerald." Maj's voice sounded tinny and small.

"I don't like your tone, young lady," said Mother, glaring at her.

With his tongue tucked in his lower lip, Gerald twisted the champagne cork. The cork broke away from his hand and sailed across the veranda as champagne bubbled over the side.

Maj plucked the tiny bride and groom off the cake top and tossed the plastic couple on the table, her hand shaking slightly.

"I don't love Gerald," she said.

Gerald's complexion turned a few shades greyer. In that moment Maj saw him as an old man—keeping track of social connections, brunching with Mother on Sundays, bragging about his latest acquisitions, gossiping about so-called friends in a schedule that revolved around appointments to have his hair styled, nails buffed, new suits cut to order, keeping up with regular doctor visits. The same thing every day, never very happy, always striving, looking for more, always dull, predictable, and petty.

"Marriage of convenience was for your generation," Maj said, calmer as the tight tangle of emotions unraveled. "Lots of people my age want to make a difference for others. We want our actions and words to align with the truths we believe in."

Mother drank down the entire flute of champagne. Maj hurried to comfort her.

"I've had Samuel set up a trust fund for you and Daddy. I wouldn't be where I am now if you hadn't pushed me, Mother. Left to my own devices, I would have hidden away from the world. You threw me under the lights. In spite of myself, I flourished. I made a lot of money. I made a lot of mistakes. Along the way, I found something I love doing. Something I'd do for free. I never felt that way about modeling."

Mother started drifting away. Her mouth thinned and her eyes glazing over, impatient to be done suffering whatever nonsense Maj was going on about. Hopelessly, Maj looked around her for an answer about how to communicate with her own mother.

"Now I'm ready push you, Mother," Maj said urgently. "Model for me what a woman looks and acts like who believes in herself. Then I'll know you believe in me, too."

Maj looked over Mother's shoulder and grinned. Mother and Gerald turned.

Standing in the archway dressed in a three-piece suit, Daddy looked just like he always had, powerful and handsome and brave.

"Ready. . . kiddo?"

Maj went to him and took his arm.

"I'm ready," she said.

PART FIVE

BEYOND

1971 - BILLY

An hour before the sun comes up and reflects off skyscrapers on the other side of the city, I cut through Golden Gate Park. Lighting the way to my favorite, all-night coffee shop is the first full moon of summer. Resenting how damned lonely the moon looks sitting in the sky by itself, I admit it. I've been spending far too much time alone lately.

"Least we've got each other, don't we?" I scratch Sadie behind the ears and Many Moons' leg twitches. "Later today, we get to see my little girls again. You'll like that, huh?" I say, as Sadie's tail gets to wagging. "They're not so little anymore. You'll love them, too, Many Moons. They'll certainly love you."

With my stomach grumbling, I pick up the pace, passing an old school bus covered with psychedelic designs parked and ticketed on Lincoln Way. I shake my head at all the cats who continue to pour into San Francisco, stick flowers in their hair, and see only their dreams of the place.

Thanks to Grandma believing in the old tattered and passed-down story about an island of perfect peace and pure happiness on the western edge of the world, this is my home. Grandma made up the part about the streets paved with gold. Even so, rocky shores and strange beasts guarding this place of freedom and acceptance for all who come and all who only dream of coming represent the ancestors' way.

The months I spent on Alcatraz—teaching kids the lessons Grandma had taught me and me undergoing countless interviews, in an effort to retrieve all the rituals, words, chants, and stories related to Grandma— brought up my Great Grandmother Martha Curly. Still alive when I first went to live with Grandma, she'd stumbled home drunk gobbling like a turkey. I used to laugh when she'd speak of a time people cast their spirit into an eagle or a hawk and soared over the land. After my time on Alcatraz, I don't laugh at the idea anymore.

As much as I needed to get lost in the old ways then, I'm glad to be back now. Anyone who has lived in poverty, thievery, drugs, alcohol, long hours, and bone-breaking work won't have it any other way. That's not to say I aim to go back to any of that. Only saying, I'm open to whatever disaster, risk, ruin, meaning, and success I'm destined for.

A twig cracks. I sense more than see a movement. Someone approaches from an adjoining trail. With my finger to my lips, I urge the dogs deeper into the darkness. Unless the person is up to no good, they'll eventually walk into the clearing.

As I wait, the glow on the east foothills turns blurry. My eyes start to twitch. Disoriented at first, I quickly recognize one of Grandma's visions coming, the first in more than a year. Knowing the blonde is nearby, I'm torn between letting go, and trying to stay in the here and now, and search for her.

I stick my hands out into empty space without resistance and grope for the dogs. This time, I let what wants to come, come.

A real peaceful full feeling falls over me just as the blonde emerges from a stand of redwoods. Her surroundings look familiar and resemble the trees around me.

She's whispering a chant. *"Soon he will be here, for he is coming. He is coming."*

She switches a pile of papers she carries to one arm and touches something at her neck hidden beneath a bulky turtleneck sweater. Instantly, I know she touches the wolf.

White flashes high in an elm tree. An owl with a heart-shaped face stares out from a tree hollow. The girl looks behind her and walks a little faster. I want to call out but know from past experience that visions don't work that way.

Suddenly, I'm in the vision with the girl, just as the owl swoops down in front of me. Many Moons barks. As I shush him, I realize I can hear myself. I walk into the light with both dogs straining against the leash.

The blonde looks startled, and then smiles at the secret we share.

The owl u-turns and circles us. Together, we stand motionless. The owl returns to the branch in the light of the full moon.

"She'll be riding a white owl." I speak the words Longtree's brother spoke more than ten years ago.

The blonde's Madonna smile grows to an all-out grin.

Sadie jumps up against her, with her ears plastered against her head. As the blonde stumbles, I give her my hand. Papers float from the pile in her arms, but she doesn't move, seemingly content to hold hands with me forever. I wait to see if she'll bring my hands to her nose, as she did as child.

Instead, she bends to scoop up her papers with Sadie and Many Moons licking her face. Laughing, she pushes them away. I squat beside her to help. Dew seeps into a building permit with pages stuck together.

My arm jostles hers. We stand at the same time.

Her face turns red. She doesn't duck her head.

"I'm not usually so clumsy."

"A tree root." I quickly point out the culprit to take attention from her.

A streetlight switches off, and a frog croaks in the long grass.

"Breakfast at Lou's Place?" she offers, running out of air at the end, as if breathless.

Smiling that she suggests my favorite all night diner, I nod. "Sure." I speak simply, not wanting to scare her off with too many words.

"My name's Maj. Maj Hawthorne."

"Billy. Billy Wayman Wolfe."

"It's nice to meet you, Billy Wayman Wolfe."

"Likewise, Maj Hawthorne."

As the sun comes up, Maj grabs hold of my hand and drags me with her. Together, we move into high spring grass toward a hole in the brush. Reaching the sidewalk, we lean into a warm westerly off the bay, as if following a plan we'd both decided on a long, long time ago.

The dawning of a brand new day.

Born in San Francisco, a fifth-generation Californian, Martha Alderson grew up in the Bay Area in the 1950s and 1960s. She now lives and writes in Santa Cruz. She has been writing fiction for more than thirty years. As the best-selling author of *The Plot Whisperer*, she takes readers and writers beyond the words into the very heart of a story, and the writing life. For more, visit: MarthaAlderson.com

"The idea for Parallel Lives came to me after I met my husband nearly 40 years ago. As we grew to know each other and fall in love — for me, at first sight — I was captivated to discover how many of the same places and events we both had been to at the same time, though separately and long before our first meeting. Intrigued by the notion of how, if we'd met at one of those earlier moments, we likely never would have fallen in love and ended up together — the timing wasn't right and neither of us were ready — I set to work researching. Having worked on this historical novel for more than twelve years, I am thrilled to share Parallel Lives with you."

Martha Alderson (2016 Santa Cruz)